I0663844

The Cautley Conundrum

A Chief Inspector Pointer Mystery

By A. E. Fielding

Originally published in 1934

The Cautley Conundrum

© 2015 Resurrected Press
www.ResurrectedPress.com

All rights reserved. No part of this book may be used or reproduced in any manner without written permission except for brief quotations for review purposes.

Published by Resurrected Press

This classic book was handcrafted by Resurrected Press. Resurrected Press is dedicated to bringing high quality classic books back to the readers who enjoy them. These are not scanned versions of the originals, but, rather, quality checked and edited books meant to be enjoyed!

Please visit ResurrectedPress.com to view our entire catalogue!

ISBN 13: 978-1-937022-92-1

Printed in the United States of America

Other Resurrected Press Books in *The Chief Inspector Pointer Mystery* Series

RESURRECTED PRESS CLASSIC MYSTERY CATALOGUE

Journeys into Mystery
Travel and Mystery in a More Elegant Time

The Edwardian Detectives
Literary Sleuths of the Edwardian Era

Gems of Mystery
Lost Jewels from a More Elegant Age

Anne Austin
One Drop of Blood
The Black Pigeon
Murder at Bridge

E. C. Bentley
Trent's Last Case: The Woman in Black

Ernest Bramah
Max Carrados Resurrected:
The Detective Stories of Max Carrados

Agatha Christie
The Secret Adversary
The Mysterious Affair at Styles

Octavus Roy Cohen
Midnight

Freeman Wills Croft
The Ponson Case
The Pit Prop Syndicate

J. S. Fletcher

The Herapath Property
The Rayner-Slade Amalgamation
The Chestermarke Instinct
The Paradise Mystery
Dead Men's Money
The Middle of Things
Ravensdene Court
Scarhaven Keep
The Orange-Yellow Diamond
The Middle Temple Murder
The Tallyrand Maxim
The Borough Treasurer
In the Mayor's Parlour
The Saftey Pin

R. Austin Freeman

The Mystery of 31 New Inn from the Dr. Thorndyke Series
John Thorndyke's Cases from the Dr. Thorndyke Series
The Red Thumb Mark from The Dr. Thorndyke Series
The Eye of Osiris from The Dr. Thorndyke Series
A Silent Witness from the Dr. John Thorndyke Series
The Cat's Eye from the Dr. John Thorndyke Series
Helen Vardon's Confession: A Dr. John Thorndyke Story
As a Thief in the Night: A Dr. John Thorndyke Story
Mr. Pottermack's Oversight: A Dr. John Thorndyke Story
Dr. Thorndyke Intervenes: A Dr. John Thorndyke Story
The Singing Bone: The Adventures of Dr. Thorndyke
The Stoneware Monkey: A Dr. John Thorndyke Story
The Great Portrait Mystery, and Other Stories: A Collection of Dr. John Thorndyke and Other Stories
The Penrose Mystery: A Dr. John Thorndyke Story

The Uttermost Farthing: A Savant's Vendetta

Arthur Griffiths
The Passenger From Calais
The Rome Express

Fergus Hume
The Mystery of a Hansom Cab
The Green Mummy
The Silent House
The Secret Passage

Edgar Jepson
The Loudwater Mystery

A. E. W. Mason
At the Villa Rose

A. A. Milne
The Red House Mystery

Baroness Emma Orczy
The Old Man in the Corner

Edgar Allan Poe
The Detective Stories of Edgar Allan Poe

Arthur J. Rees
The Hampstead Mystery
The Shrieking Pit
The Hand In The Dark
The Moon Rock
The Mystery of the Downs

Mary Roberts Rinehart
Sight Unseen and The Confession

Dorothy L. Sayers

Whose Body?

Sir William Magnay
The Hunt Ball Mystery

Mabel and Paul Thorne
The Sheridan Road Mystery

Louis Tracy
The Strange Case of Mortimer Fenley
The Albert Gate Mystery
The Bartlett Mystery
The Postmaster's Daughter
The House of Peril
The Sandling Case: What Would You Have Done?

Charles Edmonds Walk
The Paternoster Ruby

John R. Watson
The Mystery of the Downs
The Hampstead Mystery

Edgar Wallace
The Daffodil Mystery
The Crimson Circle

Carolyn Wells
Vicky Van
The Man Who Fell Through the Earth
In the Onyx Lobby
Raspberry Jam
The Clue
The Room with the Tassels
The Vanishing of Betty Varian
The Mystery Girl
The White Alley
The Curved Blades

Anybody but Anne
The Bride of a Moment
Faulkner's Folly
The Diamond Pin
The Gold Bag
The Mystery of the Sycamore
The Come Back

Raoul Whitfield
Death in a Bowl

And much more!
Visit ResurrectedPress.com
for our complete catalogue

FOREWORD

The period between the First and Second World Wars has rightly been called the "Golden Age of British Mysteries." It was during this period that Agatha Christie, Dorothy L. Sayers, and Margery Allingham first turned their pens to crime. On the male side, the era saw such writers as Anthony Berkeley, John Dickson Carr, and Freeman Wills Crofts join the ranks of writers of detective fiction. The genre was immensely popular at the time on both sides of the Atlantic, and by the end of the 1930's one out of every four novels published in Britain was a mystery.

While Agatha Christie and a few of her peers have remained popular and in print to this day, the same cannot be said of all the authors of this period. With so many mysteries published in the period, it is inevitable that many of them would become obscure or worse, forgotten, often with no justification than changing public tastes. The case of Archibald Fielding is one such, an author, who though popular enough to have a career spanning two decades and more than two dozen mysteries, has become such a cipher that his, or as seems more likely, her real identity has become as much a mystery as the books themselves.

While the identity of the author may forever remain an unsolved puzzle, there are some facts that may be inferred from the texts. It is likely that the author had an upbringing and education typical of the British upper middle class in the period before the Great War with all that implies; a familiarity with the classics, the arts, and music, a working knowledge of French and Italian, an appreciation of the finer things in life. The author has also traveled abroad, primarily in the south of France, but probably to Belgium, Spain, and Italy as well, as portions of several of the books are set in those locales.

The books attributed to Archibald Fielding, A. E. Fielding, or Archibald E. Fielding, are quintessential Golden Age British mysteries. They include all the attributes, the country houses, the tangled webs of relationships, the somewhat feckless cast of characters who seem to have nothing better to do with themselves than to murder or be murdered. Their focus is on a middle class and upper class struggling to find themselves in the new realities of the post war era while still trying to live the lifestyle of the Edwardian era. Things are never as they seem, red herrings are distributed liberally throughout the pages as are the clues that will ultimately lead to the solution of "the puzzle," for the British mysteries of this period are centered on the puzzle element which both the reader and the detective must solve before the last page.

A majority of the Fielding mysteries involve the character of Chief Inspector Pointer. Unlike the eccentric Belgian Hercule Poirot, the flamboyant Lord Peter Wimsey, or the somewhat mysterious Albert Campion, Pointer is merely a competent, sometimes clever, occasionally intuitive policeman. And unlike, as with Inspector French in the stories of Freeman Wills Croft, the emphasis is on the mystery itself, not the process of detection.

Pointer is nearly as much of a mystery as the author. Very little of his personal life is revealed in the books. He is described as being vaguely of Scottish ancestry whose father was a Coast guardsman on the Devon coast.. He is well read and educated, though his duties at Scotland Yard prevent him from enjoying those pursuits. In an early book in the series it is revealed that he spends a week or two each year climbing mountains, his only apparent recreation. His success as a detective depends on his willingness to "suspect everyone" and to not being tied to any one theory. He is fluent in French and familiar with that country. He is, at least in the first two books, unmarried, and sharing lodgings with a bookbinder named O'Connor, in much the manner of Holmes and Watson, though this character is absent in the later works.

One intriguing feature of the Pointer mysteries is that they all involve an unexpected twist at the end, wherein the mystery finally solved is not the mystery invoked at the beginning of the book. *The Cautley Conundrum* is no exception. Fielding introduces numerous red-herrings and subplots to confuse the reader while still largely playing fair with the reader.

When Fielding wrote *The Cautley Conundrum* the series was already ten years old, the book being the fifteenth novel to feature Chief Inspector Pointer. The author's style had matured and been refined over that period. Gone are the over reliance on disguises and other dramatic gimmicks that mark some of the earlier books. There is much more reliance on solid detection, the interpretation of clues, and judging the validity of the testimony of those involved. Yet, the Pointer mysteries have a certain flair that separates them from the "humdrum" school of mysteries that were starting to appear at the same time. Stylistically, they fall somewhere between the works of Christie and those of Ngaio Marsh or E. C. R. Lorac.

The Cautley Conundrum centers around the four Cautley cousins, the Major (Howard), Lionel, Jack, and Fabian. The Major is a successful businessman with an airplane works, Lionel is an explorer trying to fund his next expedition, Jack an aspiring architect, and Fabian, well Fabian is a former Indian civil servant who has turned eastern mystic. There are also two young women, Daphne and Edna, who are under the joint guardianship of the Major and Mr. Amplett, and who have been prospective fiancées of Jack and Lionel. Add a labour agitator and the attractive secretary of Mr. Amplett, and the scene is set for a volatile reaction.

The case begins with the death of the Major. At first it appears a case of his shotgun going off accidentally, but as the Major had always been very careful with firearms, foul play is soon suspected. The relations between the cousins are soon a matter of interest to the police, and when a valuable pearl necklace is found to be missing the local police are forced to call in Scotland Yard, which is where Chief Inspector Pointer enters the story.

In typical Fielding fashion, *The Cautley Conundrum* presents the reader with plenty of plot twists and red herrings. With each of the characters seeming to have something to hide, Pointer has the difficult task of sorting out the truth, though of course, in the end, he manages to solve the conundrum posed by the Cautley cousins. The real question, is can the reader do the same?

Despite their obscurity, the mysteries of Archibald Fielding, whoever he or she might have been, are well written, well crafted examples of the form, worthy of the interest of the fans of the genre. It is with pleasure, then, that Resurrected Press presents this new edition of *The Cautley Conundrum* and others in the series to its readers.

About the Cover

The cover of this book contains a re-worked portion of the original dust jacket for the first edition of the book, published in 1934.

About the Author

The identity of the author is as much a mystery as the plots of the novels. Two dozen novels were published from 1924 to 1944 as by Archibald Fielding, A. E. Fielding, or Archibald E. Fielding, yet the only clue as to the real author is a comment by the American publishers,

H.C. Kinsey Co. that A. E. Fielding was in reality a "middle-aged English woman by the name of Dorothy Feilding whose peacetime address is Sheffield Terrace, Kensington, London, and who enjoys gardening." Research on the part of John Herrington has uncovered a person by that name living at 2 Sheffield Terrace from 1932-1936. She appears to have moved to Islington in 1937 after which she disappears. To complicate things, some have attributed the authorship to Lady Dorothy Mary Evelyn Moore nee Feilding (1889-1935), however, a grandson of Lady Dorothy denied any family knowledge of such authorship. The archivist at Collins, the British publisher, reports that any records of A. Fielding were presumably lost during WWII. Birthdates have been given variously as 1884, 1889, and 1900. Unless new information comes to light, it would appear that the real authorship must remain a mystery.

Greg Fowlkes
Editor-In-Chief
Resurrected Press
www.ResurrectedPress.com

CHARACTERS

MAJOR HOWARD CAUTLEY, eldest of the Cautley cousins and owner of the famous Cautley pearls

LIONEL CAUTLEY, an explorer by taste and immediate heir to Major Cautley's wealth

JACK CAUTLEY, third of the four cousins and an architect

FABIAN CAUTLEY, recently back from India to practise Eastern religion in an English cottage

EDNA UPJOHN and DAPHNE UPJOHN, half-sisters and wards of Major Cautley and Mr. Amplett

MRS. AMPLETT, domineering wife of Mr. Amplett

MR. AMPLETT, a landscape architect

MISS SMITH, Mr. Amplett's secretary

FRANK HARBORD, a friend of Fabian Cautley's

MR. MASON, Major Cautley's solicitor

SUPERINTENDENT WANKLYN of the Woodhampton Police Station

CONSTABLE TODD, his assistant

INSPECTOR POINTER of New Scotland Yard

CHAPTER ONE

"THAT little tale you have just told of me merely shows what a long, long way I've come from those days." Fabian Cautley adjusted the loose white robe he wore, which was the reason perhaps why the villagers called him "Father Cautley," and shot his young kinsman rather a cat-like look from his narrow eyes.

"It certainly shows that your mind wasn't always attuned to the things of the spirit," Jack Cautley agreed with a grin on his freckled face. A good-natured face enough, as a rule, though at times it showed the Cautley smile—a subtle smile. Otherwise Jack looked rather slow-witted, with his placid round eyes and lightly arched eyebrows.

Fabian Cautley, dark, hawk-faced, eagle-nosed, with brilliant black eyes and a skin of almost ivory pallor, folded his arms across his chest and looked over Jack's shoulder at the clock in the church steeple. It spoke for his sight that he could tell the time from here. Edna Upjohn could not, yet she had the good eyes of twenty-two. The three of them were sitting outside the Bunch Cottage, as the Cautleys called the little house which belonged to Major Cautley, and which he intended to transform into something Tudor before selling it. It was all that had been left on his hands when he had sold his old home, Cautley Hall, a year ago, on buying a place where there was better hunting. For the time being, until leaded panes and wainscoting and inglenooks should be put in, any of the four Cautley cousins used it, though its owner was rarely there. Jack Cautley had called it home for nearly a year now. Fabian, back from the East, had only been there a month; and the fourth Cautley, Lionel, was coming down tonight, after an absence of some months at the Major's aeroplane works in the north. He was an explorer by taste, and had done very well on Katchenjunga last year, but an overstrained heart compelled him to choose more tranquil jobs. Hence the work in his cousin's big hangars.

"Yes," Jack went on, still grinning, "this chap who told me about your setting the snares said you used to enjoy killing the rabbits most of all—"

Edna made a little gesture with her cigarette. Her kind brown eyes flashed a look at Jack. But Fabian Cautley paid no heed to the younger man, or seemed not to.

"Five minutes to twelve," he murmured. "At twelve I begin my twenty-four hours' silence. I merely mention it to explain what may seem like rudeness. Peace be with you." He turned to go.

"Why the devil do you always say 'Peace be with you'?" Jack asked indignantly. "It's all right in the East, where one can reply with the stereotyped *Aleilum vesalaam*, but what the devil does one say in English?"

"I wish you both the hardest thing to get, and the best thing in this world," Fabian said solemnly and moved away, his loose white linen robe fluttering round the corner of the tiled garden path.

"Fancy having that for a kinsman!" Jack murmured under his breath. "Of course he's as mad as a hatter, but it's hard lines his madness should take such a turn."

"He was in the Indian Forests, wasn't he?" Edna asked, looking after the tall, erect figure in its outlandish rig.

Jack nodded, half opened his mouth as though to say something, then shook his head.

"As he's such a pal of yours, I won't tell you tales of him behind his back. He's left the Service, anyway, and now floats about doing fakir exercises."

"It seems funny to think of you four Cautleys, all related, all so unlike each other." Her eyes, as she talked, were studying the little garden before her. Her call was partly professional. Major Cautley wanted a herbaceous border on this side to set off the leaded casement when it should be fitted. Edna Upjohn was a gardener, just home from the biggest horticultural college in England, and devoted to her work. Even as she sat there, names such as sweet rocket, kings' spears, dame's violet, white candytuft, Himalayan blue poppies, were passing in and out of her head. She was a slender slip of a thing, brown and meager, but with something in her large eyes that hinted at a treasure in a cave.

"It's a good job we're none of us like Fabian," Jack said caustically, "and you may be sure that Lionel thinks there's as much distance between himself and me as I put between myself and that faker." He generally called Fabian that.

"I'll plant blue salvia there and back it with meadow rue," Edna told herself, seeing blooms before her mental vision which she would never see with her own eyes.

"You don't seem to care for your cousin Lionel, either," she remarked, thinking that aconitum would do magnificently for that shady corner, if only she had not such an objection to it. Suppose the gardener had a cut on his hands and were to be careless in handling it... no, she would try iris instead.

"Not care for Lionel! Why, I'm awfully fond, as well as proud, of the chap." Jack seemed genuinely surprised. "What makes you say that?"

"The way you talk of him. But then you Cautleys are rather difficult to read. Quite different inside, I sometimes think, from what you are outside."

"Even Howard?" he asked, in the tone of one who has caught the other out.

"Yes, even the Major." She laughed a little to herself. "To look at him, you'd never think he was good at figures, would you?"

"Perhaps not. But if you asked him for a loan you would," Jack said dryly. "However—go on—"

"You've just proved what I say. He looks so stupid and is anything but! Last week I was in despair over some gardening accounts, which are the most horrible things in the world. Some stuff comes in at once, some comes beforehand, some is charged for now, but will be sent later. I was half off my head trying to get things clear. It's no use asking Mr. Amplett to give me a helping hand, for he thinks me frightfully extravagant in the garden." Mr. Amplett was her employer. "Besides, he's worse at sums than I am. And just as I was adding up for the seventh time, and getting the seventh total, in walked your revered cousin, my assistant-guardian."

"And swotted out the right and only answer," Jack said without any enthusiasm whatever.

"Swotted!" She repeated the word with derision. "The Major merely glanced at the sheet and told me where I was wrong. Merely glanced! I don't wonder he left the army when his father died and that his works are doing so well!"

"Salaam to Cousin Howard," Jack said to that.

"There you go again!" Edna flung her spent match at him. "You don't really like him either, any more than you do Lionel. And not much more than you do Father Fabian."

"Don't call him that!" Jack said crossly, dropping the quantitative analysis of his family affection. "'Father', indeed! Humbug! Why not 'Son'? I think I shall call him Son Fabian in future and rile him."

"You can't rile him." Edna spoke with assurance. "He's far above minding anything of that sort. I admire him tremendously."

"I know you do. Women always fall for that sort of attitude."

"It's not an attitude," she said slowly. "He's really in earnest." She paused, then went on: "I've never before met any one, man or woman, who gave up a good position and faced poverty just to learn to know their own souls."

"Is that what he told you?" Jack asked aghast. "My word! Well, well! Selah!" These ejaculations were made in ever deepening tones of disgust. "You ask Lionel about him! Lionel has met some chaps out in India who've met my distant relative! But don't let's waste time talking of Fabian." He tried to put an arm around her.

She wriggled free on the instant.

"Not so fast, infant! I agree with my guardian, Mr. Amplett, and with my co-guardian, the Major, that you ought to marry a girl with money."

"You mean you won't have me at any price?" he asked swiftly, passionately.

She gave him one glance, half amused, half affectionate. "I daren't! It's not as though I were clever and could help you on."

"You think I haven't brains enough to get on by myself?" he demanded. She had stung him.

"Brains enough for one, but not brains enough for two," she said honestly. "You're an architect, Jack. You need a clever wife to collect the right people around your table, to get you into the right circle. To—"

"—adjust the footlights properly. Turn on the flood-spot, or whatever it is called, at the exact second that I'm looking my best!" he scoffed.

She nodded quite undisturbed. "That's what I do mean. That's what those other two mean really. They call it money. They mean the kind of woman who can pull strings, and all that. I can't."

He sat silent.

"If I had the brains," she went on, "I'd write a book on the men who married clever wives and the men who didn't, and show the difference in their success."

"And all this because I failed for my Little Go!" he said, trying for a tone of gentle raillery. "Exams are rot, Edna. You shouldn't judge by them. I know you think me a fool—"

"I don't!" she protested.

"Yes, you do! But I'll show you! You wait!" There was a little silence. Jack seemed quite his usual good-tempered self again as he sat smoking lazily, his long body—all the Cautleys were tall men—sprawling in a canvas chair.

"Daphne's coming down this afternoon," Edna said suddenly. She shot him a swift look.

"How do I take it?" he asked anxiously. "Not changed color, I hope?"

It was she who flushed, with irritation.

"You seem to see more than there is to see, in spite of always looking as though you were half asleep!" She gave what she hoped was a light laugh.

"The duplicity of the Cautleys, of which you have just spoken," he said solemnly, "always excepting the fakir, of course, who is as open as the sun."

Edna deliberately chose another cigarette. "Tomorrow's lunch is to be quite a function," she went on.

Jack made a face. "Your guardian, my dear child, has already broken the news to me. But as Lionel is to be the hero of the occasion, it won't be necessary for both of us to appear in frock coats and top hats, I hope," he added sarcastically.

"Are you afraid that Daphne would get mixed between you?" Edna asked. It was a catty speech and she repented of it instantly. For the position was this: Daphne was her half-sister, the child of her father's second wife, who, on her mother's death had been brought up entirely by her mother's mother in circumstances as different from those of Edna as though no common father united them. Daphne was left by her grandmother with outrageously extravagant tastes and very little money, for the old lady had an annuity, it seemed. She got a job as a mannequin at once, for her figure was close on perfection, and her carriage grace itself. Jack Cautley had met her at some evening affair, and the two had chosen to proclaim themselves in love with one another. Major Cautley fumed, and as Lionel was just back then, the Major entrusted to him the task of freeing Jack from an impossible position, as he called it. Lionel went down to Maidenhead to see the young vampire and promptly fell in love with her himself. Daphne let go of Jack and paraded Lionel in her chains instead. Lionel was Major Cautley's favorite cousin as well as next of kin. He was, therefore, heir presumptive, for the Major was a confirmed bachelor—one of the richest bachelors in England.

Jack had not seemed to mind in the least. "We were getting a bit fed up with each other," he said with the modern frankness when the subject of broken hearts was mentioned guardedly before him.

"You're sure you don't mind meeting her again?" Edna now said rather hurriedly. "I'm awfully fond of her, and we haven't been together, really together, for so long..."

"My dear old lady, I've met her dozens of times this last week." Jack said to that, laughing pleasantly. "It was quite a mistake on both our parts, and we're both jolly pleased it has ended as it has."

Edna glanced at her wrist watch. She had to be off Jack, too, was supposed to be due to meet a nearby parson at his church and give his suggestions as to altering the position of the pulpit. He walked with her to the gate. Just across the little lane was the fence that marked one boundary of Amplett's orchard. Edna had but to walk a few yards down the lane, mount a stile, and be on the path that would lead her to the Ampletts' drive. She paused and glanced back. Fabian Cautley in his white robe and yellow girdle seemed to be looking straight at the two. But he closed his eyes even as she looked at him, and showed only the blank, inward-turned expression which he wore when meditating. On his white robe was pinned a paper. She knew that on it was written: "Friend, excuse my not replying. I am under a Vow of Silence for the moment." Edna watched him sitting rigid on a wooden chair, his arms close to his side, each hand outspread on one knee, each thumb and

forefinger touching. Even his legs touched, as did his feet.
It was one of his attitudes when about to become lost to
the world. He had once told Edna that, though he might
seem to be looking at things about him, he saw nothing
whatever and heard no sound except the sounds of his
own thoughts. But for that she would have wondered now
whether the curious smile, a true Cautley smile, on his
rather thin, rather cruel lips was at Jack or at herself, or
at both of them.

She waved to Jack and jumped lightly off the stile. A
bend of the little path and the Cautley cottage was lost to
sight behind the "wild garden." Foxgloves and tall lilies
nodded at her in front of a screen of aconitum. The lovely
blue of the latter seemed to glow above its vivid green
leaves. What a pity that flower, leaf, stem and root were
all so poisonous. Then her thoughts left the flowers
around her and returned to the human beings.

There was going to be trouble with the Major about
Lionel's engagement. Her guardian pooh-poohed the
notion when she had mentioned it at breakfast this
morning, but then her guardian—Edna was very fond of
Mr. Amplett, but she did not put his mental powers on
the same plane as, say, his heart, or his moral qualities.
She considered that he took things and people too much
at face valuation.

Edna did not care for Lionel Cautley—the little that
she knew of him. But he might suit Daphne very well.
Daphne was clever, brilliantly so, really, and Lionel, too,
was very keen, very sharp-tongued, very swift to notice
inconsistencies. She thought him hard, and she knew
that Daphne was. Hard and ambitious. Edna was fond of
her all the same. You do not quarrel with a tiger-lily for
not having the qualities of wallflowers, for instance. You
took people, as you had to take plants, for the something
special that distinguished them, and liked them for what
they had, not for what they lacked. Daphne was a joy to
watch. She possessed that mysterious quality, charm, in
an extraordinary degree. She was not even pretty, but her

haughty, imperious face seemed to go with that splendid body of hers—no wonder Lionel had been captivated. But Edna, simple-hearted, loyal, blamed him for giving way to his feelings. It was all very well for Jack to say that there was nothing to forgive. She did not agree. She was sure, too, in her own emotional Celtic soul, that Jack, though he had now fallen in love with herself, would find it impossible to forget the trick that his cousin had played him.

As for Major Cautley's dislike of Daphne, Mrs. Amplett was on Daphne's side Edna knew, and Mrs. Amplett might yet turn the scale, for she was a very strong-minded lady. All her household realized that, Mr. Amplett most of all. It was odd, Edna thought, that Mrs. Amplett, who took no notice whatever of Edna, should have taken so great a fancy to head-strong Daphne. Was it here, again an instance of like attracting like? Not that Daphne would ever become such a bully as the elder woman was. She would rule as surely, Edna thought, but much more subtly. Daphne never cared to dominate. All she wanted was her own way. Mrs. Amplett wanted more than that. Edna thought that she only cared for things which she got by flattening people out. She herself avoided her guardian's wife whenever possible; and as Mrs. Amplett was a very busy woman, directing all the village activities, or rather driving them, whipping them on, and as Edna's gardening was really remarkably good and she herself talked but little, and usually wound up with an "I quite agree with you," she had had no trouble with the lady. But what about Major Cautley? He, too, was supposed, in spite of his apparent good-nature, to have a very firm will of his own. Would Mrs. Amplett be able to bend him? He was supposed to have taken a genuine dislike to Daphne. Lionel was to be his successor in the family estates, and probably at the works. The Major would have definite ideas for his future. Would Mrs. Amplett be able to swing Daphne into that future? It was certainly her doing that the Major was coming down to lunch and dinner at Fairlawn tomorrow, thought Edna, a lunch at which Lionel and Jack, as well as Daphne, would be present, and a dinner after which Mr. Amplett would have a heart-to-heart talk with his old friend and point out that the young couple had the backing of all their friends.

Somehow she thought that talk would not affect things much. She could not see Mr. Amplett in the role of an impassioned and successful pleader.

Father Fabian believed that things happened if you willed them to happen. He asserted that if all the people at Fairlawn concentrated on willing Major Cautley to be pleased with Lionel's choice his present attitude would melt away. Edna had been amused. Father Fabian had told her of the School which he wanted to found for Mental Growth, and for which he needed funds so badly. He was willing the money to come to him, and he assured her that, however remote such a possibility now seemed, he felt certain that by this time next year he would be able to start realizing his dreams, the dream of many a year, he called it.

Edna was amused at the idea of her trying to will of the Major into doing what he did not want to do, and preferred instead to concentrate on what flowers would go with which in the Ampletts' big gardens.

CHAPTER TWO

NONSENSE," Mrs. Amplett said firmly, "all nonsense, Edna, my dear. You mustn't waste your money on our gardens. As to your wanting to 'try out' new specimens—" she shook her head decisively. It was quite a handsome head in spite of rather sharp features, rather hooked nose, rather scoop-shaped jaw and hard blue eyes.

"We don't think you're not a clever gardener and all that," Mr. Amplett said soothingly. He was a small man, only about as tall as his wife, and with a wispy appearance, as though not even his body, were really firmly settled anywhere, as though his wife's habit of telling him what to think, say, do, had worn the shell of his spirit very thin indeed. "When all's said and done, however, what one wants in a garden are things that look nice and smell nice. My mother's garden, now, she had peonies and sweet-williams and honeysuckle."

"All in one bed?" Edna asked innocently. Her impish little face looked mutinous. She had pulled her beret off and her mop of curly hair, brown shot with gold and copper, glinted like her eyes.

"That reminds me, Percy, will you, or shall I, speak to Miss Smith about her paint?" Mrs. Amplett broke in.

"About her paint?" Amplett echoed in tones of utter bewilderment. Miss Smith was his secretary.

"She uses far too much of it." Mrs. Amplett replied at once. "I am not narrow-minded, not in the least, but when young women come to work as morning secretaries, they should dress and look like morning secretaries. Miss Smith, lately, does neither."

"It'll be rather awkward, won't it?" Amplett began unhappily. "She's only just started cataloging the library, and seems to be very good at her job. If you speak to her and she doesn't like it, we shall have to get another librarian down, and she may not be half so quick a worker."

This was true and gave Mrs. Amplett pause. "Well— perhaps in time her own good feeling, if she has any—and I presume she has—will make her look less conspicuous."

"I hadn't noticed her," Amplett murmured in a weary voice.

"Nonsense!" his wife snapped. "Why, you're always in the library these days! Where's Daphne?" she went on.

Even as she spoke a car could be heard swishing up the drive. It was a handsome new Vauxhall that Lionel had bought on the "never-never" system last month. It certainly looked opulent enough to have belonged to his rich cousin, the Major. Not too opulent for Daphne, however. As she stepped out, Edna thought again how perfectly at home in anything smart, anything costly looking, Daphne always was. Like cushions and Persian cats, the two seemed made for each other. Her dress was simplicity itself and fitted her with almost too much accuracy. Edna, who knew how much it had cost, or rather, how much the bill for it had been, wondered to see the way in which her half-sister snatched it off a rough part of the step as it caught. In her casual pull there was no hint of fear lest it tear.

Easily, pliant as a swaying bough, she came up the steps.

As has been said, she was not in the least pretty, and would have scorned the epithet, but she had a look of grace and chic. She had small, greenish-blue eyes, beneath carefully leveled eyebrows, hair that looked like gilded silver, and a complexion of pure enamel, which yet suggested firm and smooth skin behind it. She was always gay, dazzling, often witty, rarely charitable. One did not think of it in her presence, but the curious thing about Daphne was her lack of youth. Youth of the body she had, but otherwise there was something so finished, so assured, about her, that it seemed as though at least thirty years must have smoothed and hardened and welded her together. She did not look happy, but then who did nowadays? True, Edna did, but Edna had work that she loved doing, and besides, there was a grain of real wisdom in little Edna Upjohn, and that always means a cheerful disposition.

"Any one got a couple of aspirins?" Lionel asked, getting down rather stiffly. "My malaria is trying to make itself heard."

"You should take antipyrins," Mrs. Amplett said at once. "I always take antipyrins when I feel a cold coming on and so I never have one."

This sounded rather mixed, but Lionel did not wait to think it out. He shook his head.

"There's a bottle as usual in the morning-room," Edna said. "We always get it filled up especially for you and Daphne. By contract. And you know where to find it."

"Young people nowadays take too many drugs,'" Mrs. Amplett said. "I think tea is far better."

"I don't." Lionel disliked Mrs. Amplett. "When in doubt, one aspirin. When in trouble, two. That's my motto." And he made for the morning-room.

Big and broad-shouldered, Lionel Cautley had a look of great vitality and power. It was more than bodily power, Edna thought, splendid though his body was. There was personality behind those piercing eyes of his, personality and brains.

Lunch was served almost at once. Half way through it, Amplett was called away to the telephone. He came back in a few minutes.

"It was Howard telephoning," he said. "A message for you really, Lionel. It's about a necklace which his solicitor thinks must be still among your mother's effects— probably with her jewels at the bank."

"What about them?" Lionel asked briefly. "Mason— he's his solicitor you know—"

Lionel nodded impatiently. Of course he knew who Mason was.

"Mason wants to alter the insurance on them. Thinks it's too low for their present value. He had no idea they weren't with the other Cautley jewels until yesterday when he went over them with Howard."

"I'll run up to town and get them this afternoon," Lionel said carelessly. "I remember my mother borrowing them. They should have gone back last year of course. But I was away when she died. Yes, I'll see about it and let Mason have them back at once. Or, let me see—" He glanced at the clock. "No, I can hardly do it in time before he leaves his office. But he shall have them first thing in the morning."

"I'll come with you," Daphne said with one of her dazzling smiles.

"I shan't be able to drive you back here again," he warned her, but he looked delighted. "But I'll see you safely into your train after a dinner."

"Dinner! Train!" Daphne made a little grimace. "How bourgeois we are! I only want to run up to town with you."

"Howard said just now that tomorrow he would go to the Cottage first before coming on here," Amplett put in. "Perhaps it's just as well. It might be rather awkward..." he finished in his uncertain, hesitating way.

"He wants a word with Fabian probably," Lionel said. "Fabian has quite impressed Howard with his ideas—"

"What ideas?" asked Amplett.

"Obtaining what you want by wishing for it. That's why I'm going to marry you, Daphne."

"But isn't it rather awkward if two people wish for the same thing" Amplett inquired.

"Quite simple. The stronger wisher wins," Lionel assured him.

"Well," Mrs. Amplett murmured to that, "I often have been surprised myself how by saying nothing, just holding firmly to one's own point of view, people come round to it."

Daphne choked—over a pit, she explained, apologizing.

"Speaking of Fabian," Mrs. Amplett went on, "the Major will be able to walk over here with him, as well as Jack."

"With Fabian!" Lionel seemed surprised. "Is he coming to lunch?"

"Yes. He asked himself when I met him at Lady Hillinghouse's yesterday afternoon."

"It's rather awkward to know what to feed him with." Amplett turned to Lionel. "What does he generally go in for?"

"Locusts and wild honey," the other said gravely. "The wilder the better. Or a mess of red pottage—he likes that at times. And very occasionally, as a treat, some dry bread."

"Nonsense! He waded into his plum cake yesterday in just the same way that he used to do when he was a small child running round in a pinafore tied up with blue ribbons. And a very tiresome child he was too. So greedy and spiteful." Mrs. Amplett was always outspoken.

"What was I like?" Lionel promptly asked.

"You were a stand-offish little brute, my dear boy. In vain to try and coax you to be friends."

"And Jack?" asked Edna. She knew that Mrs. Amplett was a good, if cynical, judge of character.

"Jack was a misleading little chap. So pleasant and obliging—and with his tongue in his cheek half the time."

A silence fell after that little summary of the three Cautley cousins as children. Then Daphne began one of her stories which always made Mr. Amplett look as though he feared something rather awkward was coming, until, with a sweep around her of the green-blue eyes, she would finish up with the most demure of twists.

Edna had to hurry away to finish some orders which had to be got off at once. Daphne slipped in before she had done. She seemed to Edna to be in a genuine hurry. She had fancied at lunch that towards the end her half-sister had been longing to be off.

"Look here, Tweeny," Daphne began coaxingly, using an old nickname between the two, "I've lost a frightful sum at bridge—"

"Another psychic bid'?"

Daphne nodded sadly. "I'm in a most frightful hole, Tweeny," she went on, "and I wondered—could I give you a post-dated check, and could you help me out—I know you will if you can."

Edna nodded. She certainly would be glad to if she could.

"I could pay it by next week all right, but I've got to have it this afternoon. She lives near here and I must settle today."

"How much?" Edna asked. She jumped at the reply. "Three hundred pounds."

"Good Lord!" Edna gasped in horror. She had expected thirty at the outside, and probably thirteen. "But how on earth do you expect to pay three hundred pounds!"

"Borrow it, of course. That's easy—the repayment I mean. But the woman insists on having it today, and she's a member of my club—"

Which was more than Edna cared to be. It must be Arabella Hope-Winterton. She alone lived near here, was a member of Daphne's very smart and expensive London club and played for high stakes. Though three hundred!

"Well, it wouldn't be easy to me," Edna said a trifle dryly, "but as to lending you it—I can't come anywhere near it, Daphne. You know what a pig guardie is about letting me overdraw, and the Major is as bad. I might rise to a hundred in an emergency, but not three hundred. Sorry! Very." And she was.

"A hundred..." Daphne repeated dully, and something in her hopeless tone made Edna look at her in genuine uneasiness.

"Perhaps she would accept that for a first instalment, until you can settle."

"Not a chance! Not any use trying to negotiate with only that much!" Daphne was very pale. Without another word she left her half-sister, and a minute later Edna heard her and Lionel getting into the car and driving off.

Would Daphne appeal to him? Not very likely, Edna thought. She imagined that Lionel would be the last person to whom. Daphne would go in such a quandary. Even with her, Daphne was never really frank. Edna pushed away her lists for the moment. Just now she felt out of tune with her work. Daphne was in real trouble; Edna felt it. Something had frightened that elusive, outwardly so self-assured young woman. But of course if you played for stakes like that, with means like Daphne's... Edna wondered how Arabella could have expected her to pay... What would Daphne do? Somehow Edna felt uneasily that Daphne, when really pushed, might do strange things.

She buried herself in work again and spent a strenuous afternoon superintending the moving of some rhododendrons. At last she looked at her watch. An organ recital was going to be given next Sunday, and every evening of this week the organist could be heard practising. Edna longed for music just now. She put her hat on and slipped into the charming little church which "belonged" to the countryside still, just as it had "belonged" in Norman days when its first stones had been laid.

She saw no one but herself, she heard no one but the organist, until a butterfly, floating on some evening ray of sunlight, passed across her vision. It was a white butterfly, accursed to all gardeners. In spite of herself the spell was broken. She had been listening to some of the greatest music ever written, to Bach's incomparable B Minor Mass, but it held her no longer. The cabbage butterfly... the gardens at Fairlawn... some Golden Gleam nasturtiums... the cabbage butterfly loves to lay its accursed eggs on the back of nasturtium leaves above all others... She got up and made her way to the north door, the only one open. Standing a moment behind the thick curtains to be sure she had not left her handbag, she caught sight, through the slit in the curtains, of two figures just outside it. It was Daphne and a friend of Fabian's, a young man named Harbord.

He seemed to be just letting go of Daphne's beautiful hand, letting go of it very reluctantly.

"I'd do more than that for you!" she heard in a passionate half whisper. That was not surprising. Daphne had but to lift one of her much manicured little fingers to have almost any male within sight rush to obey, and, consider it a privilege, but it was the expression in Daphne's eyes that worried Edna. Daphne was engaged to Lionel Cautley, a remarkably good *parti*; then why was she looking like that at Mr. Harbord, a quite impossible young man from her point of view? A socialist of rather a communist tinge—a Hyde Park orator—

By this time Harbord had taken a path which would lead him out by a gate on the other side, while Daphne made for one that would take her to the station.

Edna still stood inside the church. She was vaguely disturbed, but at the moment her chief wonderment was where Daphne had been sitting that she, Edna, had not seen her when her eyes, following the butterfly, had roamed all over the building except for this little part where she now stood, which had been hidden from her. It was a dark, draughty corner which Daphne would certainly not have chosen. Nor could Edna quite imagine Daphne at an organ practise.

No, Harbord and she must have met by chance and stopped for a moment's chat. Daphne had spoken of only running up to town. She had had ample time to come back by any one of three or four trains.

Edna started, as on turning to drop the leather curtains behind her, she caught sight of some one seated quite close to the door, in what was usually a particularly dark corner, but which for a second was lit by a ray of the evening sun. It was Fabian Cautley. His eyes were closed, and on his pale but hawklike face was that look of deep calm that went with it so strangely. She passed on out of the churchyard without giving him a second thought. His presence at a music recital was not surprising—unlike the meeting between Harbord and Daphne. That suggestion of intimacy about them both... yet, as far as Edna knew, they had only met once before at the Cottage. True, Daphne could turn many a man's head in five seconds—but somehow their two faces, especially Daphne's—the look on it haunted Edna. If it weren't so patently absurd, she would have said that the girl was in love with the man. Edna decided that she was a better judge of flowers than of people's expressions and fell to cogitating on a new way to get peonies to bloom the first year that they were planted.

CHAPTER THREE

EDNA found Daphne at Fairlawn when she got back. "What about the bridge debt?" she asked under her breath.

"Arranged." Daphne spoke curtly. She looked tired and haggard. Something ruthless, too, showed in the set of her jaw. Edna was just going to refer to Frank Harbord when Mrs. Amplett came into the room, and Daphne turned to her with a certain air of gush very unusual in her.

"I wonder if you'll think me the most horribly rude girl living," she began with what looked like real hesitation. "I've done a most awful thing! I met Frank Harbord—you know, that friend of Fabian Cautley's who's staying down with him at the Cottage "

"A ne'er-do-well, if ever I saw one," Mrs. Amplett labeled him instantly. "You mean the Communist? The anti-war preacher."

"He's rather interesting really," Daphne said. "But the point is, I ran into him just now and we began chatting about mutual acquaintances and so on, and it seems he's always giving sleight-of-hand performances, and is really good at it. So I asked him to drop in to lunch tomorrow and amuse us with some specimens of his skill afterwards. I do hope you'll forgive my doing such a thing. I got quite carried away by his talk about what he can do. I love sleight-of-hand!"

"Quite a good idea," Mrs. Amplett murmured graciously. "Really quite a good idea. I happen to know that the Major likes them too. So do I—if they're well done. Do you think he would give one at the town hall next week at our Kindergarten Fund evening?"

Daphne said that she thought Harbord would be charmed to be of any use.

"Not at all a bad idea to have some one outside the family present at lunch," Mrs. Amplett went on. "It'll keep the talk on general subjects. And of course if the Major is amused—I hope this young man won't let us down? Unless it's good that sort of thing is too awful!"

"He spoke as if he were quite tophole," Daphne reassured her. "Perhaps Edna knows more about it from Jack. I never see Jack these days."

Daphne had not seemed to mind meeting Jack Cautley in the least, any more than he did her.

Edna said that she detested Mr. Harbord, and had no idea that he was good at anything—except talk.

So that was the simple explanation of what she had seen outside the church door. And Daphne's look had merely meant "thank you so much," though expressed in Daphne's way when saying it to a good-looking young man.

Next morning Edna had a good deal of work to get done. She was just turning-away after giving the boy who helped her his final instructions when she saw a tall, soldierly figure coming up towards the front door. All the Cautleys carried themselves well except Fabian, but the Major cocked his hat at an angle none of his cousins affected. Edna called to him and he stopped and came towards her. She liked him. He was about fifty years old, fit as any lad, tall and big—big in every way, she thought, though she had heard that he had a hard side to him. None of the Cautleys were supposed to be able to forget an injury.

"I've just come from the Cottage," he began after the usual greetings. "Jack tells me that he wants to marry you."

She looked up into his face with its sleepy eyes and heavy mouth. Jack would be his image at his age she reflected. She nodded.

"Fortunately, you've too much sense to want to marry him," he went on bluntly.

"I, too, think he needs a clever wife," she said; "a girl who would be able to help him."

"Jack's quite able to look after himself, but he isn't the kind of man your father would have chosen. However—as you're not going to marry him we needn't go into that."

"Why wouldn't my father have approved of Jack?" she asked on the instant, hotly.

"He wanted a steady-going chap for you—so he told me when you were around nine or ten. We were talking of the kind of man that made the best husband. Your father, Edna—" And Major Cautley spoke of his affection of the dead man. "That's why Amplett chose me to be your guardian," he went on, "when Vesey died."

Talking about her father they made slowly for the house. Amplett was waiting for them on the veranda. Beside him stood Jack Cautley and the slighter figure of Frank Harbord. Harbord was unusually handsome with his big, passionate dark eyes, but he had a wilful, undependable mouth. The whole expression was conceited beyond the ordinary, and he carried himself with a suggestion of arrogance, of push. He looked like a man who would set himself no bounds whatever, and suffer none to be set for him except such as he could not help. For the rest, he had studied abroad and was supposed to be an expert on housing problems. He was a builder's son. Returning home, he had joined the English Communist party and had spoken and written some brilliant diatribes on the complacency of the government, on the state of the slums in port towns, on the provisions for comfort in rural workhouses. His ideas were original and good, and he had a growing-following in the country. It was his pose of wholehearted admiration for Mahatma Gandhi which had first brought him into the Cautley circle. He and Fabian had met at some esoteric Eastern meeting about a month ago, and Fabian had asked him down to the Cottage for a week-end. That was a fortnight ago and he was still there, apparently on as good terms with both Lionel and Jack as he had always been with Fabian.

A white-clad figure now paced slowly along the drive, staff in hand. It was Fabian Cautley. He gave his usual greeting and wave of the hand.

"I came to excuse myself, Mrs. Amplett," he began at once. "I shall not be able to come to lunch after all. Some work on concentration circles which I have to do will prevent me."

Mrs. Amplett managed to convey politely that whether Fabian was lunching at Fairlawn or not was a matter of complete indifference to her and to the other guests, but Jack struck in:

"Pity, Fabian, for Harbord here is going to do some conjuring tricks. I never knew he was up in them or we might have had some shows at the Cottage. But as you used to be good at them yourself, you might like to watch."

Fabian shot a swift, rather keen glance at Harbord. "I think I'll postpone those mental exercises I had mapped out," he said promptly. "May I stay and see the show, Mrs. Amplett? My years in India gave me a taste for that sort of thing."

Mrs. Amplett begged him in her off-hand way to stop, but Fabian seemed to be waiting to hear what Harbord would say.

"Please yourself, by all means," came from that young man, "though I should have thought you would consider it a waste of time. Nothing to elevate the soul in sleight-of-hand, is there?"

"No, but it's good to watch just the same," Fabian replied gravely. "It brings home to one how little one can rely on observation. That is to say, if the tricks are well done."

Edna went on up to her own room. There she found Daphne by her dressing-table just draining the last drops from a travel flask of brandy. Edna burst out laughing at the picture before her; then she felt remorseful.

"Are you ill? I was a brute to laugh, but the silhouette was comic."

"I feel frightfully seedy." Daphne said, putting the flask down quite reluctantly. She was very pale under her thick paint, Edna saw. She hesitated. "You haven't any more of the stuff, have you?"

"That's my entire cellar-full," Edna assured her.

Daphne went out after lingering for a moment as though half minded to say something. Edna looked after her thoughtfully. Daphne was really nervous. She would not have thought that possible. Daphne must care for Lionel very much indeed to take this lunch as she evidently was doing. Yet what about that flirtatious parting with Harbord yesterday? Daphne was a puzzle, Edna thought, probably as much so to herself as to others.

When she finally went downstairs, she found her having a cocktail. Even Daphne gave an apologetic smile as their eyes met.

"I seem to be making myself into an illustration to The Rake's Progress," she said in a quick aside. Edna noticed the dilated pupils, the tenseness of the lips. Daphne was either ill or frightfully wrought up, Edna thought, but just then her attention was caught by Major Cautley and Frank Harbord, who were having a brisk interchange of opinions about pacifism. Harbord declared that there must be no more wars. Cautley held that men would deteriorate.

"Nonsense, Major. No more than they have done since dueling stopped."

"Ah, but dueling was only for something you—the dueler—held sacred. Fighting may be for something much bigger than that—something your country holds sacred."

Harbord made a grimace. "That's Jingoism—Nationalism. Its time is over. I know I'm talking to one of the world armorers, but your time, Major, is short. Believe me, it's shorter than you think!"—and Harbord's white pointed teeth glistened as he smiled.

Major Cautley smiled too. His rather slow, good-natured smile. It seemed to sting Harbord. The younger man's eyes fairly flamed, but he kept his tone to the light one that good manners demanded.

"You think those are just words—mere talk? Well, time will tell."

Fabian interrupted at this point in the slow, measured manner that he nowadays affected.

"There is a saying of Saint Augustine's to the effect that all talk is really vain, because words mean nothing in themselves, being but symbols standing to each man for entirely different realities. No man hears another; what he does is to listen to the thoughts raised in his own mind by the words which are being spoken."

"What utter nonsense, Fabian," Mrs. Amplett said. "I never can understand why Saint Augustine holds the place he does. When I say 'that cat is a tabby,' you who hear it, and I who say it, mean precisely the same thing. Every one knows perfectly what I mean and hears exactly what I say."

Even Fabian had to smile.

Lunch would have been a silent meal but for Mrs. Amplett and Daphne. Mrs. Amplett laid down the law in her usual brisk, sledge-hammer fashion, to which her husband, as always, meekly responded at the correct moments with "Quite, Malvina!"

Daphne seemed bent on conquering the Major and he seemed to enjoy her quips and sallies.

Fabian was very silent after those few words about Augustine. To Edna he seemed unusually attentive to the talk around him, for as a rule, Fabian never seemed to listen to other peoples words.

Harbord, in spite of his outburst about the future of wars seemed very friendly with the Major—almost as though he were trying to make up for the breeze of a few minutes before. But though he talked almost exclusively to him, he kept his eyes a good deal on Daphne. Edna was not watching the two, but even so she caught once an interchange of glances between them to which she had no clue, except a fear lest Daphne was getting into a thoughtless entanglement with a good-looking young man whom she, Edna, distrusted.

As for the engagement between Daphne and Lionel, as Mr. Amplett had said, it was not mentioned. They might have been a group of brothers and sisters as far as relationships went.

After lunch, chairs were drawn up in the lounge facing a table. Harbord pulled up his sleeves and started in. He did quite well. Coins appeared and were caught in mid-air, the family cat—the same tabby whom Mrs. Amplett had used to confute Saint Augustine's words— was produced, in an exceedingly disgruntled condition, from Mrs. Amplett's big knitting bag, paper streamers littered the floor; stacks of cards were cut and named cards duly produced.

"Now I have a string of pearls," Harbord went on, holding up on his forefinger what looked like solid drops of moonlight, "which I have been asked to send by Magic Airways into the pocket of their rightful owner. Miss Daphne Upjohn handed them to me, but unless you are their rightful owner"—here he turned and looked inquiringly at her—"you won't see them again."

"No, they don't belong to me," Daphne said with a little laugh; but her eyes were glittering.

Harbord pattered on about having often been approached by Scotland Yard to assist them in their search for stolen property, but as his own sympathies were usually with the thieves he had always refused. However, on this occasion, influenced by the desire to be agreeable to his hostess and her guests he had allowed his talents to be used in a conventional way which perhaps in his saner moments he might deeply regret.

He turned to Major Cautley. "My wand—Cagliostro's wand, of course—informs me that the necklace will by now have materialized, in its case, in one of your pockets. Kindly insert your right hand into your left-hand pocket—on no account use the left hand, it might shrivel away—and you will find there the necklace which I dangled in front of you a minute ago."

Smiling his easy, slow smile the Major did as requested, and drew out a handsome shagreen case. Pressing the spring he lifted out the lovely string of pearls that they had all just seen.

"The Cautley pearls!" Daphne cried, and clapped her hands. She was laughing gaily. "I told you to let me have them, Lionel, when you wanted to hand them over at the lunch table. Magic Airways is much more amusing."

"Rather awkward on occasions if anything went wrong," Amplett murmured. "I mean about the ownership—"

"Magic Airways can never go wrong," Harbord retorted, proceeding to his final trick, something clever with keys and a cigar and a glass of water.

"What about a receipt?" Lionel put in.

"Tomorrow will do for that, when Mason has weighed and counted and checked this off with his list." And the Major, shutting the case, replaced it in his pocket and began to follow Harbord's next trick.

When it was over, chairs were pushed back and Harbord was thanked for the amusing half-hour he had given every one.

"You ought to be in a bank, the Bank of England for choice," Jack said jokingly. "Think what splendid opportunities you would have there."

"Especially as I believe in redistribution of wealth," the juggler agreed, and then looking at his watch, excused the action, and explained that he had to hurry off for an appointment.

Lionel and Fabian were the next to follow his example. Though they went different ways they started off for the gate together. But Lionel hung about there hoping to get a word with Daphne. Jack decided to get his gun and accompany the Major for an afternoon's shooting. When the Major sold the estate of Cautley Hall, he had reserved to himself for a small yearly sum the right to shoot over, with a couple of friends once a week, such of the fields as remained. This was his day. It is amazing how near to London you can still get quite good rough shooting, if you do not disdain a mixed bag.

Meg, a spaniel, trained to the gun, and Lynx, a young Labrador with the best nose, second to Meg, in the county, would go too. Later on, Jack would take them back to the Cottage and the Major would settle down in a "hide" to shoot wood-pigeons, that pest of the farmers.

"Get the dogs, Jack, then," the Major said and strolled off into the conservatory where Daphne had gone. Edna had some matters to see to in the garden, and there Major Cautley joined her some minutes later. He was alone, looking his usual unruffled, not very clever self. At the same moment she heard a car dashing out of the garage at a pace that made her look after it. It was Daphne's Singer, going as though for a prize. Out through the open gate, down the road the car sped, and Edna, remembering that Daphne had promised to run her in to the post-office to inquire about some seeds that had not yet arrived, thought of calling after her half-sister, but gave it up. Nothing but the urgent sending of a telegram could account for that rush, she thought. But Daphne was not even going in the direction of the post-office, she was headed for town.

Fabian Cautley had come back as though for a word with his cousin. All through the conjuring performance Edna had thought that he looked like a man half interested and half impatient to be somewhere else.

He pulled his watch out of his pocket now and stood staring at the hands as though they were not moving fast enough. He held it to his ear and shook it. He kept passing his tongue over his lips as he did so, and suddenly Edna felt as though she wanted to get away— not to look at him. It was a quite extraordinarily strong feeling of distaste, and it puzzled her. She told herself

that she would not yield to it. She was by way of liking
Fabian Cautley and sincerely admired him.

"About that house of mine that you're always asking
me to let you have," the Major said to his cousin, "I'm
rather inclined to sell it to you. It's not every one's taste,
and you can have it cheap. The chap who had it for years,
a fellow called Barstairs, Major Barstairs, pulled it about
a bit and put all sorts of gadgets in it that no one wants.
He. had a button by his bedroom armchair which would
put coal on the fire—when it acted; half the time it piles
it on the carpet instead. I've taken the builder's advice
and put a gas fire in instead—there are gas fires in most
of the rooms, and thundering big ones too. Just about
right for you, Fabian, they would roast an ox, and you
always like heat."

"I should like Dunnottar for my school, as I've often
told you. But as you very well know, Howard, I can't
afford to buy any house. Besides, it's a chance for you to
earn merit—by helping on the Truth." Edna thought that
Fabian spoke as though not very interested in the matter,
and knowing how at other times he had talked to her
about that very house she was surprised. But he looked
like a man longing to get away.

"I'll tell you what," Major Cautley said now, "I'll let
you have it for the rest of the quarter rent free, and then
we'll talk about it again. Poor old Barstairs has paid for
nearly two months more. It's furnished, you know. He
rented it furnished. And quite comfortable—too
comfortable for you probably. What do you say?"

"I'm late," Fabian said with a certain explosive
vehemence which Edna had never heard in him before.

"What's that about the house? Oh yes, thanks very
much. I'll use it as you suggest. Till next quarter day.
Thanks so much." And he moved away as though he
would have liked to run.

"There's a woman down there who'll look after you—"
began the Major, but Fabian was striding along with
ever-lengthening steps and did not seem to hear.

The Major looked at Edna and laughed.

"Quite keen on something, isn't he?"

"I should have thought he'd be keen on getting Dunnottar," she said. "He told me only yesterday that he particularly would like it—and that he was willing you to let him have it."

The Major threw back his head and gave a hearty laugh.

"I'd like to see Fabian willing me to do anything. As a matter of fact the house is left to him in my will, but don't let him know, or he'll 'will' me to pass on to another state and let him have it at once," and still laughing at his own joke, the Major in his turn made for the gate.

CHAPTER FOUR

AMPLETT looked about him in surprise. Five o'clock was tea-time at Fairlawn, and though the cocktail hour of six might be preferred by his young guests, the custom of the house demanded that around five every one should at least cast one glance at the tea table.

Mrs. Amplett, usually the soul of punctuality, was not there. Daphne had not put in an appearance. Lionel was not back.

Mr. Amplett fidgeted about the room. "The Major, of course, won't be back till around half-past seven if the cushats are plentiful, but where are the others?"

Edna accounted for the absent ones as best she could by guesses. Amplett went on fidgeting.

"It's very awkward," he said at length, "for I need some tea."

Edna made no move to pour it out. Mrs. Amplett could be more than difficult on occasion. She watched the husband with secret amusement and a little pity. He did so want a cup, yet he did so dread vexing his wife by laying a finger on the teapot. Finally he sat down with his back to it and began to talk resolutely of something else.

"I rather hoped the Major would drop a word about the proposed engagement... it'll be rather awkward if he leaves without saying anything. And he may. Howard Cautley's a great believer in letting time do all the work. Hello, here's Jack! Now we shall get some tea!"

He opened the door himself and fairly rushed Jack to the table.

"You must have tea. No, no, I insist! Edna, give Jack a cup, and I don't mind having one myself."

Smiling broadly, Edna did as requested. Jack put his down at once.

"Thanks, awfully, but I only dropped in for a word with Howard. I thought he must be here, as I haven't heard a shot for over an hour."

"When did you leave him?"

"It was just striking half-past three. My eye was all out. I kept missing the birds by miles, or sending them over the boundaries. You can't think how vexed the two dogs were with me. Even Howard got fed up finally, and suggested my taking them home and leaving him to deal with the wood-pigeons. What time is it now?"

"Half-past five." Amplett spoke with deep gloom as he took his first drink of tea. "Bit light for pigeons?" He spoke interrogatively.

Jack nodded. "Bit. But Howard wanted to mend the 'hide' from inside—make the seat more comfortable, or something—"

Mrs. Amplett came in as they were still talking. "I expected you at the committee meeting, Percy," she said sternly to her husband.

Amplett looked unhappy. "It's very awkward, but—well—I think I must have gone to sleep over the paper, my dear," he murmured. "I fully intended to go, of course."

"I could have done with a nap too," Mrs. Amplett was crushing, "but when I know a thing is my duty I do it. No, don't ring for fresh tea. It's Gibbons' afternoon out. I will take what is left."

Edna hurriedly did the best she could for her, and Jack plied her with plates of sandwiches. Then the two escaped. At the door Jack turned.

"Coming, sir?" he asked cheerily.

"Er—no, no," Amplett replied, hurriedly. "No, certainly not." And he turned again to his wife, whose grievance about his absence from the committee meeting was only just coming to its full flower.

Jack and Edna looked at each other with a rueful grin as they closed the gate behind them.

"Will you grow thin and vinegary like her?" Jack asked in mock uneasiness. "Really, it's a fearful thought that one doesn't know in the least whom one's marrying twenty years from now."

"I shall be fat and dimpled," Edna said with certainty.

"Then Howard's quite right. I oughtn't to think of marrying you." But there was vexation in the young man's laughter. "Fortunately Mr. Amplett seems to be always on the side of lovers. I suppose because he's so happily married himself." Jack gave a faint chuckle. "Poor wretch! But give me time and I'll make good yet."

Edna said nothing. She was looking at a stile that gave on to the road along which they were walking. There was some one getting over it, or lying across it, but what was wrong with—

Jack leaped in front of her, spreading his arms wide in a futile attempt to shut out the sight.

"Back! Keep back! There's been an accident'!" he called, and Edna stood where she was. Jack rushed to the stile across which Howard Cautley had apparently been climbing when his gun had gone off, blowing half his head away.

"Go to the Cottage and get Harbord here. Tell him Howard's had an accident and that he's to bring something we can use as a stretcher."

After the second's dead stop of horror she was off, running for the Cottage. It was much nearer than back to the house, nor did she want to burst in on the Ampletts with the dreadful news.

"Mr. Harbord! Mr. Harbord!" she called as she ran down the little lane. The windows would be open. He would hear her and hurry out.

Even in the turmoil within her she heard a window hastily banged shut in the Cottage and welcomed the sound. It must have slammed behind Harbord as he ran to meet her. But there was no sound of any footsteps—no sign of any one as she flung open the tiny latched gate and rushed for the nearest windows, those of the living-

room, which were never closed except at night or in
bitter weather. But they were shut now, all three of them.
She called again, and rapped on the glass with her
knuckles. On the instant she heard the front door open—
to one side of her and hidden from view by the trailing
clematis that covered the little porch.

"Is any one calling me?" Harbord asked.

Edna thought that she had never heard a sillier
question.

"Quick, Mr. Harbord!" was her only answer. "Jack
wants you. The Major has had an accident with his gun in
getting over the stile. He's dead! What can we get to carry
him home on?"

Harbord stared at her as though, for a moment, at a
loss. She would have expected Jack, poor darling, to need
time to collect his wits, but not alert Frank Harbord.

"We'll manage him on the shed door," he said with a
gasp.

"And while you're getting it off, I'll telephone to
Doctor Blackie." She would have stepped into the little
lounge-hall, but he blocked the way.

"Just a moment!" he begged. Speaking suddenly very
loudly, "I'll want your help at the shed to get the door off.
That's more important than telephoning under the
circumstances."

She quite agreed, but she would have thought that his
clever hands would make light work of a shed door.
Harbord looked as though he could lift an ox unaided.
And yet he seemed oddly slow, as well as very swift. He
would pause for quite a second before tackling another
screw which, when he started in on it, would be out in a
flash. He had hardly begun and had asked her to hold the
door tight in—a quite unnecessary help, she considered—
when she heard steps crunch on the path outside. Could
it be Jack? She would have hurried around the corner of
the cottage which screened the front door and the path to
it from her view, but for an almost peremptory word from
Harbord.

"Hold it pressed tight—as tight as possible!" he commanded.

"I thought I heard some one—"

"Press it in with all your strength," he urged, and he did so. Whoever it was whose steps she heard it was not Jack. They were going away from the house. But for the moment she had no attention to spare. Now, at least, Harbord was working as swiftly as any man could. The door was suddenly off, and he turned to Edna.

"By the stile, you said? The stile just over there?"—he motioned with his head. She nodded.

She carried one end of the door. They found Jack walking up and down. It seemed to her that his face had changed in some indefinable way, that he was not quite the same young man that he had been early this morning; or was it merely that some new emotion had taken possession of him? If so, it did not look like grief, though, remembering the Cautleys' way of hiding their feelings, she told herself that it might be that.

The two men lifted the body on to the stretcher, after asking Edna to go on to Fairlawn and break the news. Jack called after her to tell Amplett that he himself would see about letting the police know.

For once Edna was glad that Mrs. Amplett was of the managing type. She quite took charge of the death, issuing all orders as to where the body was to be laid, who was to be notified at once, and who could wait.

The stretcher was not long in getting to the house. A couple of passing farm laborers had been hailed, and now carried it. Jack Cautley hurried off, as soon as he was relieved of his end, to inform the police of the tragedy, so he called back to the other, who agreed to go on to the house alone.

Harbord was able to supplement Edna's few words as to what they had found at the stile. The Major, he said, had obviously been getting over it with his gun in his hand, the safety-catch off, and the trigger must have caught in his waistcoat buttonhole.

"The one he always wears open?" Amplett murmured, nodding his head to himself.

"The bottom one. And as the gun had gone off at close range it had practically blown the side of his head away. He must have been dead some little time when Jack found him. He says he was quite cold even then."

"Jack says Lionel had only just left them," Harbord went on. "He thinks he will be making for town, and that he may be able to catch up with him in a car after a word to the police."

"If it's an awful shock to us, what must it be to his cousins!" Amplett said finally, after more questions had been asked and answered. "What about Fabian? Does he know?"

"Unfortunately he intended to go for a long ramble this afternoon; I haven't seen a sign of him since we left here after lunch. Neither has Jack."

"Very awkward," Amplett said truly enough, then, after seeing Harbord to the gate, for the young man seemed oddly inclined to linger, oddly slow to take a hint. Amplett went to find his wife.

Superintendent Wanklyn, at the Woodhampton police station, was sincerely shocked at the news brought him by Jack Cautley. Every one who knew the Major in the days when he lived down there, liked him. Hard as nails on a liar was Howard Cautley, harder still on a coward, but he had ever a generous and lifting hand for the lame dog.

"Half-past six just gone." The superintendent entered the hour in his book. "And you found the Major about when, sir? I'd like the times as exactly as possible for the coroner." The superintendent was a youngish man with an alert, keen face and observant eyes.

Jack thought back. "Let me see, I dropped into Fairlawn at half-past five. The church clock was striking as I opened the gate. I expected to find the Major finishing his tea. He and I had been out shooting together. After lunch I went to the Cottage for the guns and Lionel stayed talking to Howard until I joined them. Then he dashed off up to town."

"About when did he leave you?"

"He only walked for a few minutes with us, when the Major remembered that he had left something he especially wanted up in town. Lionel said he would run up and fetch it. He hopped back to where he had left the car and drove off. The church clock was just striking half-past two, we all looked at our watches to compare them as one does, you know, when any one talks of being in a hurry and a clock strikes."

Wanklyn nodded. He was taking notes very carefully, more from habit than for any especial reason.

"I went on with the Major, but I was shooting so badly that by half-past three I had had enough—so had he! I took the dogs back to the Cottage, where Lionel turned up just after four. He hadn't been able to get the lens the Major wanted—it's a lens used for inspecting aeroplane fabrics, especially doped cottons.

"He was going up to town again and hoped to get it then. We stayed on chatting and loafing in the garden until it was time for him to set off about half-past five, just a few minutes before, for I got to Fairlawn at half-past five, and it takes quite ten minutes to walk by the road, which is the way I came. It's a pity, or else, if I had come by the stile, the Major's body would have been found earlier."

"Supposing he was dead by then," Wanklyn put in.

"Oh, he must have been. He was beginning to stiffen and was already cold when I came on him, you know."

"And—that was a quarter to six, I understand?" Wanklyn found the exact times hard to get clear in his mind.

"Well, perhaps that's a little early, say nearer six... somewhere around six, earlier rather than later. Then Miss Edna hurried along to the Cottage to get Harbord and a door. It took Harbord some time to get one off its hinges, and then we lost more time getting the Major on it—we wanted to be sure that Miss Upjohn was well out of the way—it was a sickening job—" Jack's hands quivered a second as he lit a fresh cigarette.

Wanklyn murmured a word of sincere sympathy.

"And then, after getting a couple of passing laborers to carry him, I went back to the Cottage, thinking that Lionel might not have started for town at all. He wasn't very keen on his engagement—nor very sure that the lens would be ready before seven. He wasn't there, and after waiting a bit I came on here."

"And Mr. Fabian?"

Jack explained, as Harbord had to Mr. Amplett, that there was no possibility of reaching his other cousin until he himself should see fit to return after his afternoon's ramble.

Jack and the superintendent were walking up to Fairlawn as they talked. At the house, the police surgeon, a tall, elderly Scot, was already waiting for them. Wanklyn had telegraphed to him at once on hearing of the accident.

"No difficulty about the cause of death," he said under his breath, and the superintendent nodded with a shudder as he turned away after replacing the sheet over what lay on the bed.

"How long ago did it happen, would you say, doctor?" he asked. "It's now a quarter to seven."

"Three hours ago at the very outside, with two and a half as a likely possibility."

"Not earlier than four, and possibly half-past four," the superintendent jotted down.

The three of them looked at the gun. They all agreed that the wound was the sort that might be expected if it had been discharged fully loaded straight into the Major's face. The weapon itself was an Anson and Seeley, hammerless, long-range pigeon and wild fowl gun, chambered for a three inch cartridge. The Major's name was on it. Jack illustrated on himself how the safety catch had caught in the lowest waistcoat buttonhole, and he showed by means of a chair, and table how the Major was lying when he had come upon him.

Miss Upjohn would be questioned later, but as she had stood still when the body was first sighted lying sprawled across the top of the stile, it was not likely that she could add anything to Jack Cautley's carefully detailed account.

"I wonder if the Major was on his way here, or to the cottage when he had his accident," asked the doctor, washing his hands.

"Here," Jack said promptly. "He always liked lashings of hot tea at five—quality immaterial; quantity, and above all temperature, the main things."

The doctor hurried away to say a few words downstairs as to how greatly the Major would be missed by every one who knew him, even though nowadays he only came down for odd moments.

Jack went in search of Edna. The superintendent stayed a moment longer making his notes by the body, then he called Constable Todd to accompany him, and made for the stile, with Jack beside them to show once again how the Major had been lying.

He would have taken the exact position, but Wanklyn stopped him and told him not to step on the earth by the stile, nor to lean on it. A description would do quite well. Jack gave one which earned him the police officer's thanks. Then he left the two men in blue to take measurements and make a diagram. That done, Superintendent Wanklyn grasped his chin between thumb and forefinger and bent over the stile again. Todd knew from the gesture that his superior was keenly interested. He in his turn had another good look. The stile, so called, was a very primitive affair of two short lengths of wood nailed firmly to the crossbars of a fence, one above the other at a distance of a foot between, in such a way that one pointed east and west, the other north and south. Each piece protruded equally through the sides of the fence. On the top, an upright had been nailed as a hold to grasp when mounting the simple two-step affair. Most men vaulted over. Jack Cautley had described the Major's body as hanging over the top bar, arms and head on one side, one foot on the top cross-bar, the other dangling limply beside it.

Todd saw that the superintendent was concentrating on the top step, the one from which the Major's dying, or dead, foot had presumably slipped as he fell forward after the shot. Todd saw a scrape, a deep, scrape—just such a one, so it seemed to him, as a shooting boot might make if the wearer had slipped or missed his footing. Just such a one, in short, as he would have expected to find.

But the superintendent repeated: "That's funny, my word that is!" and held his chin more tightly than ever.

Constable Todd had a most tremendous opinion of the superintendent's powers. He himself, a lanky giant of a young fellow, was not strong in brain power, and knew it.

"What's funny, sir?" he asked finally.

"This. And it struck me as funny up at the house. Those shooting boots of the Major's were two inches thick with loam and bits of clover."

"Tramped across the field from that corner there, after rabbits probably. He'd have potted some in Farmer Green's field—" Todd began, like a man, reading a chapter aloud.

The superintendent interrupted him promptly. "That's not the point. I could swear those boots had never stood on these little cross struts with a man of the Major's weight atop of them. And now here, as you see, there's no mud on that scrape. No mud on the cross bars—"

Todd peered at both attentively.

"Powerful swipe all the same, sir," he muttered.

"But not made by those boots of the Major's," Wanklyn repeated firmly.

"You're a regular Sherlock Holmes, sir," Todd breathed. He thought himself that he was over-praising Holmes, whose methods he considered very irregular.

"Here's the mark of where he stood his gun," Wanklyn went on.

"I wonder why he used the stile at all, sir. Many's the time I've seen him swing himself over by that upright or the top rail."

"But for the fact that there seems no reason for him to be shot—no enemies— What's that coming down the further end of the road!"

"Looks like a camel, sir, but it's that Father Fabian, as they call him, wearing his white dressing-gown. His hat half-way down his back tied on by a bit of string, and his shoes in his hand. Walking barefoot, that's what he is!"

Todd's height enabled him to get a first view of most events.

"Come back from India mad as a hatter, poor chap," murmured the superintendent, eyeing the advancing white object closely.

"Funny this should happen after he comes down to live at the Cottage," Todd said under his breath. The superintendent had known Todd since the latter was breeched. "There's something about him that sort of curdles my blood, if you know what I mean, sir."

"Tut, tut!" snapped the superintendent. "A constable's blood should never curdle, Todd! Not if he saw a witch riding on a broomstick in the sky."

"Well, it's a feeling like that he gives me," Todd muttered uneasily.

Fabian Cautley, in true pilgrim's garb, though the two police did not recognize it, his hat where it could not shield his head, his boots where they could not save his feet, came slowly towards them. He was limping a little, and was chanting something under his breath, a line from the East, which, properly intoned, could split the atom, according to the Teachers of the Innermost Things.

The superintendent went to meet him. Fabian almost stepped on him before, raising his eyes, he seemed to see him with a start.

"Evening, Mr. Cautley, there's been an accident to the Major, I'm sorry to say. Have you heard of it?"

Fabian stood a moment as though dazed. Then he shook his head.

"Accident? What kind of a one?"

The superintendent told what Jack Cautley had found at the stile. He finished with the usual sympathetic remarks due, in his opinion, to any member, of the dead man's family. The man to whom he was talking received the news oddly. He lifted his right hand high above his head as though taking a silent oath, and the hand shook. Then he turned to the two police officers.

"There is no death, superintendent. You might as well say that the sun dies because it is night, and you don't see it."

"That's as may be, sir;" the superintendent replied stolidly, "but the sun returns every morning, and the sun doesn't leave a dead body behind it. The Major has. So, according to the police regulations, the Major is dead. I suppose you didn't happen to be anywhere around about the time we think it may have taken place, sir? You didn't hear one isolated shot which might have been that one?"

"I heard nothing," Fabian replied very concisely, "after four. Up to that hour I seem to recollect several shots. Knowing that my two cousins were out together after birds I paid no attention. After four I would not have noticed if there had been volley firing."

"Indeed, sir? Why not?" the superintendent promptly asked.

"I was engaged in meditation. You know yourself, I fancy, that if you are concentrating on some knotty point you may quite fail to hear any noise which does not concern you—as you think."

Wanklyn nodded. So did Todd.

"And where were you from four on, sir? It'd be a help to know, a rough guide as to when the shot was not heard, even if you were thinking of other things."

"I don't know in the least," Fabian said promptly, "except that it was somewhere quiet—in a field, or under a hedge. I walked on deep in thought, and probably sat down when tired. I only noticed my surroundings a few minutes ago when I was just past the church—the village church."

The two policemen eyed him doubtfully.

"You don't remember where you were at four?" Wanklyn asked.

Something passed swiftly over Fabian's harsh face; whether shadow, or quiver, it was gone on the instant. "No. Or yes, I know I was in a field when the clock struck. One of Mr. Green's fields. The one where the oak was split by lightning last month."

That was some distance away, half an hour's walk from the stile, and it lay in the direction from which Fabian had been coming.

Glancing at him, Wanklyn noticed that the man's hands were twitching, or rather his fingers were being clenched and unclenched. Fabian had ugly hands though they were strong-looking and thin, and there was something about them, especially now, that suggested talons opening and shutting on their prey. Wanklyn told himself that he must not be affected by Todd's bias against this particular member of the Cautley family, but he also told himself that he must not forget this all but concealed excitement.

Fabian Cautley now dropped his eyes, blinked for a moment, murmured "Peace be with you," and would have passed on, but the superintendent held out something—it looked like a pinch of dust—between his fingers.

"I wonder if you can tell me what this is, sir?" he asked eagerly.

Fabian held out his palm; the superintendent placed on it some road scrapings, at which Fabian stared. He shook his head. "It's just earth, isn't it?" He sniffed at it. Again he shook his head, but Todd was staring as hard as his superintendent, not at the pinch of dust, but at marks of dried blood in the palm of the hand. It was because he had caught sight of this that Wanklyn had held out the dust for inspection.

"Have you hurt your hand, sir?" he asked curiously, peering at the marks. They looked as though the palm, with wet blood on it, had been hastily wiped, leaving marks only in the center and along some of the deeper lines—that line known to palmists as the Line of the Head, for instance, which on Fabian's hands was much too sloping and forked.

The hand jerked as though the superintendent's easy touch had been searing metal. Again the curious sort of quiver passed over the features.

"No," Fabian Cautley said in a very low, very tired voice, "but I cut my foot on a stone back there. It bled."

As he raised his foot and pointed to a recent cut still bleeding in spite of the thick dust on it, they saw that the palms of both hands had the marks of blood which had been wiped off.

"Mr. Fabian, sir, you'll get tetanus!"—the two police were shocked—"if you let earth get into a cut. Why not slip your shoes on again?"

"Have you ever heard of the Kneipp Cure?" Fabian asked.

The superintendent had heard his father speak of it, and not in tones of admiration.

"Something to do with walking barefoot in the wet, isn't it?"

Fabian nodded. "This is also a Cure that I'm undergoing—this walking barefoot along the roads. A very good Cure indeed, superintendent. Peace be with you both," and he plodded on past them.

The two police stared after him. He did not turn back, but limped slowly towards the Cottage gate; and one thing they both noticed—Fabian Cautley walked as undeviatingly as a sleepwalker, or a camel, turning aside for no rough patch of the road, no sharp flint, no large stone. Even from where they stood they could see that both feet were now bleeding from fresh cuts, fresh breaks.

CHAPTER FIVE

SUPERINTENDENT WANKLYN looked at his constable, and Todd returned the look.

"Is he balmy, sir, or—?"

"Or is it part of a calculated effect? That what you mean, Todd? He always was a rum chap, was Fabian Cautley. The first time I saw him must have been nearly twenty years ago. He was drowning a kitten. He had been told to do it, but if ever a boy enjoyed his task young Master Fabian enjoyed that. I was fresh to the place, and if I hadn't been in uniform, I know who would have gone home with a thick ear."

"And I heard about a horse of the Major's that he thrashed that cruel that the Major told Mr. Fabian to pack his things and be off. That was a couple of years back, before Cautley Hall was sold. Hushed up, of course, but they do say that Miss Isabelle Gray as he was engaged to, heard of it and was about to turn him down, but she caught the 'flu and died first."

"You're a regular old gossip, Todd, for a young 'un."

"Still, sir, it's only because Miss Isabelle died and the Major is sorry for Mr. Fabian that he had him down at the Cottage at all," Todd insisted. "Never was two men more different."

"But all the Cautleys are different from each other," Wanklyn pointed out, as he drew out his notebook. "Not a single trait in common, as one might say."

"Bar one, sir. They all four look as though the devil himself couldn't frighten a Cautley. Even Mr. Jack has that in his eyes, smiling though he may be, and a bit on the soft side. It sort of goes under the smile and Mr. Lionel has it clear enough. As for that Mr. Fabian—well, he looks as if it might be t'other way to. As though he could give Old Nick himself the creeps if he tried hard."

Wanklyn pursed his lips and nodded. He was just finishing his sketch of the stile, for the place was a difficult one to photograph until the light should be better.

The next few minutes were spent by him in investigating all the ground around the stile, while to Todd was given the easy task of sitting on it and keeping still. But in a few minutes the superintendent was motioning him to follow along the hedge for a space.

"Look inside that gap!" he commanded in a low voice. "See the depth of that hole? Some one sat there on a shooting-stick. Recently. Not over a couple of hours ago I should say. Medium weight, and only sat there a short time. It's not often used, that gap isn't."

Wanklyn was scrutinizing the ground further. "Whoever sat here smoothed over the spot, but that's where he dug his heels in."

"Does this mean that you think the Major was shot, sir? And shot by some one who sat here in hiding until he heard, or saw, him coming along?"

"You go too fast, Todd." The superintendent straightened his own back and stood, hands on hip, staring intently around him. "But that scraped step— those boots thick with soft loam right up over the insteps—and the front of his waistcoat—remember what it looked like?"

"Bits of woods, and stuff from the top of the stile, sir," Todd said promptly.

"But why? To've fallen as Mr. Jack found him, he must have been standing on that top step, waist high above the top bar. There's nothing on this side of the stile to've made those marks on his clothes. But the cross bars would—supposing he had been dragged up them into the position in which he was found."

"Dragged when dead?" Todd wanted to know.

"Can you see anyone dragging the Major about, alive?" Wanklyn asked, and Todd looked foolish.

"And now these marks in here of the shooting-seat and the toes—Well, it isn't impossible, not impossible, Todd. I don't go farther than that—yet—that some one sat here and waited for the Major, knowing which way he was coming."

"Wonder how any one would know that," murmured Todd; "most people who knew the Major was off at the 'hide' would have expected him to stick there, except for a trot home for tea around five possibly. But I interrupted you, sir. Sorry. I got carried away."

Wanklyn was too deep in thought to have heard half that his junior said. He now went on meditatively: "Yes, it doesn't seem impossible, Todd, that whoever sat here stepped out and met him at the stile, took his gun from where he had placed it—"

"As though to oblige—" nodded Todd breathlessly.

"—And shot him with it while talking to him as he stood on the other side, with his head well over the stile," went on the superintendent. "The man—or woman—who shot him jumped across and hoisted him at once half over the stile, tore his coat lining on the top there, dropped the gun as though from his hand, and left him—to be found by the first passer-by."

"'Tisn't every one who knows of that gap—not by a long way," Todd muttered. "Besides, it must have been some one who knew the Major well, that the Major would think nothing of handing his gun to—"

"He must have had a quick finger on the trigger," Wanklyn added grimly. "The Major wouldn't have let him point a muzzle at him and pull a trigger at his leisure."

"You bet not, sir!" came from Todd. "But perhaps he was calling the attention of the Major to something in the gun—got him to look down a barrel and then fired."

"This is only what 'isn't impossible,' mind," Wanklyn warned him with a frown. "Don't go too fast again, Todd. We'll see if we can find anything to turn what 'isn't impossible' into what's very probable, and then into what's certain. No cigarette ends here that I can see—no further marks—"

Todd could find none either.

The superintendent, sure that nothing had escaped their two pairs of eyes, went on to the "hide" used by the Major. It was on a field of the dead man's that still remained unsold, and was reached across another field in a diagonal direction from the stile. Inside the simple shelter of lathes and boughs they found a couple of shot pigeons which had evidently been intended for decoys. The skewers which had transfixed their dead bodies to the ground, as though feeding, were still in them. A couple of brand new artificial decoys lay tied together on one side, their spikes unmarked by any earth.

"Didn't use 'em. Hadn't time, I should say. Probably thought they'd do better later on when the light was less sharp. And here's his bag with the other birds he'd shot-" Wanklyn counted them; it was quite a good haul. "Wonder what made him leave them here—and the bird decoys. What interrupted him and sent him back along that lane and stile to the Cottage or Fairlawn?—one can't say for which he was heading. Might have been just that he wanted tea early—I'll do a bit more scouting."

Once again the superintendent left the other to mount guard while he searched about. The hedge ran a few yards away from the "hide." After a few minutes he called Todd to the other side of it.

"Look at that oil in the road! Motor car waited here. Look at these tire marks!"

"Smart make of car by the look of them." Todd was examining them carefully.

"Ah!" suddenly came from the superintendent, who had pounced on something in the ditch. "It's a west wind and they had blown under the overhanging edge of the road. Look at these, Todd!"

Todd needed no second invitation. What the superintendent was piecing together on the road were fragments of an envelope roughly torn up. The paper was clean and fresh; no part was missing. In a second it was put together and both read the address:

> Lionel Cautley, Esq.,
> United Empire Club, Pall Mall.

The postmark was legible, and was of that morning's delivery.

"Lionel Cautley!" both exclaimed under their breaths.

"Ah!" The superintendent was putting the scraps away in another envelope of his own. "So he came back here first before going on to the Cottage after he went up to town. Must have fetched this letter down with him, perhaps to show it to the Major, and came down at once to this 'hide.' The car marks show clearly that they turn here and then branch off in the direction of the Cottage."

"Mr. Jack evidently had no idea of this."

"Just so, Todd. That's what makes it look so odd." There was a pause.

"But it was Mr. Fabian who had blood on his hands. One can't get over that, sir."

"Mr. Fabian?" The superintendent shook his head. "Remember the saying: In every crime look for '*quis prodest.*'" The superintendent pronounced the last as though it were the second person singular of the verb *to prod*.

"Mr. Lionel's the heir—though, mind you, he may have nothing whatever to do with his cousin's death. The talk may have been over the contents of this envelope, but it may have concerned a third party, and the third party might have watched and listened and decided to shoot the Major before he could pass on the information in the letter to some one at the Cottage, or Fairlawn, or even to us. But I don't think so. Anyway, the fact remains that the man who is supposed to benefit most by the Major's death seems to've been here shortly before that death, and not to've said a word afterwards about the meeting to their common cousin."

"Not much doubt of its being Mr. Lionel here, that new Vauxhall of his," Todd was thinking too, "has just this make of tires. They must have had quite a few words, that oil didn't drip like that inside of a quarter of an hour."

Wanklyn agreed. "Yes, and it looks as though after the talk the Major picked up his birds and decoys and dropped them in the 'hide' as though expecting to use them again later in the evening. It looks to me as though he had gone back to the Cottage to continue the talk with Mr. Lionel."

"But Mr. Lionel didn't act as though expecting any one according to Mr. Jack," Todd put in. Wanklyn looked at him impatiently.

"Of course not! Wait a bit! The Major takes his gun with him—naturally wouldn't leave that behind at the 'hide'—is met at the stile—a heavy man would only need to have sat a very few minutes to have made the mark we found in the gap—"

"Mr. Lionel is heavy certainly," Todd agreed, "but not so heavy as that Father Fabian. You think he may have left his car close to the stile, nipped into that gap, and lain in wait for the Major?"

Wanklyn nodded.

"And if so," the superintendent added, "he would have been able to step out with some word about having remembered something more—"

"More of what?" asked Todd.

"More of what they were talking about here by the car," the superintendent said impatiently. "The Major would bend forward to hear it and—bang!"

Todd looked impressed, but by no means certain.

"It was Father Fabian who had blood on his hands, sir," he repeated stubbornly.

"He had, but he didn't try to hide it," Wanklyn said slowly, "though of course he might have seen that I had spotted him. He certainly was all of a turmoil inside, and grief wouldn't take that form, not with him. You see, Todd, that's where local men score in an inquiry. They know the history and they know the characters of the people they have to deal with. They can tell what's usual and what's not, what's put on—"

"Like his stuff about the Cure he was taking," said Todd promptly. "If the Major has been done in, Super, I'll bet my new pair of boots that that Father Fabian had a hand in it somehow—"

"He doesn't fit in under *quis prodest*," Wanklyn reminded him, "not so far as we know at present. But we must be off back to the house. Not a word of all this, Todd." He spoke sternly. Todd was rather fond of gossip. The constable looked aggrieved and assured his superior that he knew the regulations, and wouldn't be found drowned talking. An undoubted fact, as Wanklyn pointed out.

Back at Fairlawn, the superintendent asked to be taken again to the bedroom which had been assigned to the Major during his short stay, and where his dead body now lay.

"I'll run through his pockets first of all, sir," he said to Mr. Amplett. "It's just as well to have answers to all questions that the coroner can think of." The pockets yielded nothing.

There was a tap on the door. Mrs. Amplett wanted a word with the superintendent.

"You had better take charge of a valuable pearl necklace that was handed Major Cautley after lunch," she told him, and left the carrying out of her order to the officer and to her husband.

Amplett looked about him for the green case that he had seen only a few hours ago.

"He would hardly be likely to have it with him when shooting." He described the look of what he was after, and the superintendent at once picked up from the mantel a lovely box of a soft green that shone as though enameled.

It was the shagreen case which had been dropped by
Magic Airways into Major Cautley's pocket.

"That's it!" Amplett nodded to the superintendent,
who pressed the spring. The case was empty. For a
second Amplett stared, then he said: "We shall find the
pearls in one of his pockets—wrapped in tissue paper—or
in his suitcase, still more likely."

It was in none of these places.

Amplett stepped out and telephoned to the Cottage.
Harbord answered. Jack Cautley was out, he said.

Amplett hesitated a moment, then he asked whether
by any chance Jack had left anything belonging to the
Major at the Cottage, a package, say, or anything of that
sort?

Harbord was very voluble. He said that he himself
had been away from the Cottage until just before Edna
ran there for him to help in carrying the body, and could
not be sure, but, as far as he knew, Jack had brought
nothing back to the Cottage save his gun, a cartridge bag,
the two dogs, and a couple of birds, very much shot to
pieces, one of which was a large black hen.

Amplett evaded Harbord's questions by finding it all
"very awkward" and hanging up. Then he returned to the
bedroom. The police had not found the pearls meanwhile,
and the superintendent was looking very grave. He asked
the probable value of them, and Todd silently whistled at
the sum named. Wanklyn wanted an immediate
description of the necklace, but Amplett was quite unable
to furnish one worth having.

"You're not imagining that it has been taken?" he
finished in tones of horror. "Oh, that's quite impossible,
superintendent! Our servants are both of them far too
incompetent and lazy to be able to bring off a coup like
that. Besides, how would they know that the Major
wouldn't be able to find it gone and send for you—as he
would have done on the spot." Suddenly Amplett drew a
deep breath. "I see your idea. You think that since it's
been known that he met with his fatal accident, some one

may have come in here and taken the string? Well, unfortunately, it's only too true that none of us thought about pearl necklaces. It's very awkward, but of course the room hasn't even been locked. But there again," Amplett's worried frown smoothed itself out, "there again, superintendent, we have no strangers in the house—no guests even. Just my wife and I, Miss Upjohn, and her sister who is engaged to be married to Mr. Lionel Cautley." He stopped and listened. Downstairs a voice could be heard speaking which he seemed to recognize and recognize with surprise.

"Why, that's Mason, surely!" He opened the door and stepped on to the landing. The superintendent followed him. He saw that Mr. Amplett was right. It was Mr. Mason who was speaking to the servant—Mr. Mason, the leading solicitor in Woodhampton. Looking up, Mason recognized Amplett.

"What's this I hear?" he asked in shocked tones. "I've just come from Cautley's Cottage, where a young man told me that the Major's had an accident while out shooting—a fatal accident. How d'you do, superintendent. I'm afraid your presence here means that the dreadful story is true! Not that I doubted it. People don't make jokes of that kind."

Amplett was shaking hands with the tall, slightly stooping figure.

"Yes, I'm sorry to say it's only too dreadfully true, Mason. The Major was found lying over a stile near here. His gun caught in his waistcoat and went off, blowing half his head away. Of all the terrible things to have happened!"

Mason asked a few horrified questions. The three talked over all the details which would shortly be public property.

"It'll be a fearful shock to his cousins," Amplett wound up. "They were more like sons to the Major than mere relatives. Jack wasn't at the Cottage, you say? Had Lionel returned yet?"

"I saw no one but a good-looking young fellow who told me that—well, that poor Cautley was dead. Dreadful! Dreadful!"

"Good-looking fellow—that would be young Harbord— Frank Harbord, the agitator. But what brought you out here in the first place? What made you go to the Cottage?" Amplett asked.

For a moment Mason eyed the two men in front of him with a look that suggested that something interesting was coming.

"I drove over in reply to a telephone request to that effect from Cautley himself. It reached me just before half-past four this afternoon."

"Indeed!" came from Amplett, and inwardly from the superintendent.

"The exact time was twenty minutes past the hour by my watch. You see, the Major wanted me to come over immediately, so we discussed the best I could do to meet his wishes, which is the present time."

"So we know he was alive at twenty minutes past four and had to walk from the telephone to the stile. How long were you talking, sir?"

"A good five minutes, superintendent; not more, I know, because when I hurried in to my partner and told him of the message, he looked at the clock and said it was already nearly half-past."

"I should say if we allowed—" The superintendent checked himself. It was no use trying to make out a time-table of the Major's doings between the telephoned message and his death. He might have stayed for many a trifle, matches, cigarettes, his decoys...

"Why did Major Cautley want to see you, sir?" asked the police officer. "Did he give any definite reason?"

"None whatever."

"But what were his exact words, sir?" Superintendent Wanklyn pressed.

"Rang me up, asked me if I could manage, as a great personal favor, to come out at once to the Cottage where he wanted a word with me. I was able to arrange this with my partner, and I came as soon as I could. I had told the Major that I could not be there before seven."

"But did you expect the call, sir?"

"Not in the least, superintendent.

"Did his voice sound urgent or worried?" Wanklyn next asked.

"Not in the least; but then I can't imagine Major Cautley's voice expressing either of those emotions though the house were burning down around him. But I had an idea—I thought he said something about 'we'll be there' as he hung up, after I had told him that seven was the earliest I could do."

"He meant Jack Cautley perhaps," Amplett suggested. "Jack had only parted with him an hour or so before he found him dead. It was a frightful shock to all of us, especially the women. Daphne Upjohn burst into tears when she saw his body being brought in. Quite broke her down."

"Oh, by the way," Mason put in, "your speaking of Jack Cautley makes me think of Lionel. I wish you'd remind him about the Cautley pearls that were lent his mother—" He got no further. Amplett told of the handing back of the string at noon today and of their disappearance since then—"temporary disappearance" he put it.

Mason made no comment, but sat with pursed lips, running his finger tips together as though counting them over and over.

"No suspicion of foul play, I suppose?" he asked abruptly.

Amplett jumped.

"My dear Mason!"

Wanklyn replied that of course when a gentleman used to firearms as was the Major was found shot dead, every possibility had to be borne in mind and investigated—the possibility of suicide, and the possibility of foul play.

And now, he went on, could Mr. Mason tell him how the Major's will ran? Was popular rumor right in thinking that Mr. Lionel Cautley was his cousin's heir, since he was his next of kin?

Mason did not reply directly. He began with the statement that he had drawn up the Major's last will some four years ago, when the aeroplane works began to develop into the big thing they were today. A codicil had been added only a month ago. "The codicil is quite simple. It leaves to Mr. Fabian Cautley, besides a legacy mentioned in the will itself, a house called Dunnottar, vacant at the time the will was made, owing to the death of its tenant, Major Barstairs, Fabian Cautley to enter into possession of it immediately on the Major's death without waiting for probate—which would be possible, as the Major intended to offer it him at once at a very small rental, so small that both the Major and the solicitor had been certain that Fabian would accept with pleasure.

"Now as to the body of the will itself. It's a very complicated document, but all that concerns the present situation is that there is a sort of entail of the bulk of the property for twenty years, during which the income is to be paid to the next of kin or the next of kin's children. Should Mr. Lionel have died childless before the Major, or within the twenty years, then Mr. Jack would inherit. Failing him, or his issue, it would be Mr. Fabian. Should all three have died childless within the time, then the works were to become a sort of co-operative society, full details of which are given in the will, and the money would become a trust fund for old-age pensions and family benefits. Frank Harbord, whom I've apparently just met for the first time, though I've often heard of him,"—Mr. Mason made a face "had a good deal, indirectly, to do with this part of the will, or rather a book of his had—*The New Gospel of Work and Capital.*"

"Never heard of it!" murmured Amplett.

"The Major considered it the only constructive, workable theory of its kind and went by it; and,"—here

Mr. Mason gave a little apologetic smile, as though to recall to his listeners that he was talking of a dead man—"actually made this stranger, this young Harbord, principal trustee in this case, and endowed him with a handsome salary. But to come back to actualities, after twenty years the kinsman to whom the income is being paid, inherits the capital with many restrictions and regulations. You, Amplett, are an executor, and the head of the works, the Director as he's called, is another. There are two more besides. Each of you has a small legacy to gild the pill. Other legacies, of a thousand, are left to Jack Cautley, to Fabian Cautley, to myself, and to several people at the works—smaller ones to workmen there."

The superintendent made very careful notes of this will, was given an idea of what the death duties would probably amount to—at least the sum which had been arranged to cover them—and felt more than ever sure that *quis prodest* was certainly the right line to take here. The Major, was an even richer man than rumor said. But *quis prodest* applied to the pearls, too.

He next asked for a description of them. Mason promised to return to his office at once when he left Fairlawn and telephone the particulars to the police.

"Did he have them in his pocket?" he went on, turning to Amplett, who said it was all dreadfully awkward, but that, thinking it over, it looked to him as though he must have had them with him, have been found dead by some passing tramp, been searched and robbed."

"Only robbed of the pearls, Mr. Amplett," the superintendent reminded him; "as far as we know, nothing else is missing. Certainly he had nearly two pounds in change on him, besides over ten pounds in one pound notes."

"I don't like it," Mason said, as had the superintendent before him, "I don't like it at all, Amplett."

Amplett retorted plaintively that no one liked it.

"You have no idea, sir,"—the superintendent turned to
the master of the house—"what it could be that the Major
wanted to see Mr. Mason so urgently about?"

Amplett looked as though he found the question
"rather awkward," but he said that he knew of nothing
whatever to explain such a request. Beyond that, he
seemed unable to go. Wanklyn had a feeling that Amplett
could at least give a guess as to what the summons might
have meant, but if so, he must tackle him about it when
alone. Also, the superintendent wanted to get into touch
with Lionel Cautley as soon as possible. True, the fact
that Major Cautley had telephoned at four-twenty and
that, according to Jack Cautley, Lionel had been at the
Cottage from around half-past three till nearly half-past
five, removed him from the position of Criminal
Apparent, yet his explanation of what it was which,
unknown to Jack Cautley, he had talked over with the
Major before he went on to the Cottage, might be of the
very greatest interest and information.

One thing seemed certain, it was not to get to the
police station that the Major had left his birds and
decoys, for since he had telephoned to his solicitor, he
could have telephoned to Wanklyn. Then what had taken
him to that stile? His talk with Lionel? Those missing
pearls... the cousin in whose charge they had been—the
same cousin who had just handed them back to the
Major... Wanklyn was sure that here was something
which, properly unwound, would lead to the heart of what
he believed to be a crime.

CHAPTER SIX

IT was close on eight when the superintendent got to the United Empire Club, and Lionel Cautley was just crossing the hall on his way to dinner. He was alone, and Wanklyn hurried after him.

"Mr. Cautley," Lionel wheeled. "You may remember me, Mr. Cautley, I'm Superintendent Wanklyn—from Woodhampton."

Instantly the face looking level with his stiffened. Otherwise Lionel Cautley gave no sign, only waited.

"You have heard by now, I suppose, of the accident to Major Cautley?"

Lionel Cautley opened his eyes. "Accident? To my cousin?"

The superintendent wondered whether the show of amazement and anxiety was not overdone—for the man who was exhibiting them.

"We'll go to my room—I happen to have taken one here for tonight—and you can tell me about it," Lionel said swiftly, leading the way to the lift and up to an upper floor. Here he showed the other into a bedroom and closed the door. He had a flat elsewhere, but he had lent it for the week-end.

"Now, then, what has happened?" he began in his quick, imperative way.

The superintendent told him. He only spoke of it as an accident. Lionel Cautley listened with an expression of horror on his face, which again the superintendent thought too strong, too visible, for Lionel Cautley's usually impassive features.

"Now, sir," the superintendent said finally, "this accident has some peculiar points about it."

"Ah!" Lionel Cautley gave him a very probing look. "Such as?"

"Well, several little things, sir, which may neaten themselves out, so to speak, on examination. When did you last see the Major?"

"This afternoon at four o'clock. He was in the 'hide.' Jack Cautley had just left him. The Major had asked me to run up to town and get him a package from an optician which should be ready by noon. I found that it wouldn't be there till seven, so I drove down and let him know, then I went on to the Cottage where I met my cousin Jack Cautley just bringing the dogs home after a rotten time missing birds. He's a frightfully poor shot at the best."

The superintendent nodded with quite unconsciously warm agreement. He had seen Jack Cautley's shooting.

"He and I loafed about until he went over to Fairlawn for tea around half-past five, expecting to meet the Major there, and I buzzed up here again after that package, which was still not ready!" He made a little gesture of disgust at the dilatoriness of the firm in question.

Wanklyn felt suspicions prickle at these details. They were not like Lionel Cautley's usually rather curt way of talking, any more than was the exactitude of his timing. The other now went on to deepen the superintendent's mistrust by giving the hours at which he had looked in at the optician's, and the name of the firm.

"Did the Major seem in his usual spirits when you parted from him? Was he excited in any way, so that he might have been careless of how he handled his gun?" he asked, after a pause.

"Nothing about him made me think that he would have an accident," Lionel said slowly. "I suppose there's no doubt but that it was an accident? You speak of curious details?"

"You think he may have killed himself intentionally?" the superintendent asked quickly.

"Not at all! Anything but!" Lionel said shortly and very decidedly. "Only one always wonders in such a case whether there could be any question of foul play: that was why I asked." Again his eyes bored into the superintendent's face. The latter felt a profound distrust of the man.

"You evidently know something," he said briskly. "Come, sir, you evidently have your suspicions. What rouses them?"

"Your way of talking," Lionel said, his powerful, compelling gaze on the other. But Wanklyn was police-trained. No man's gaze could affect him except in as much as he thought it suspicious or not.

"Hardly sufficient, sir, unless you already had reason to think of foul play in connection with the Major's death."

"Look here, superintendent," Lionel said, "don't let's go walking round and round like two cats with a plate of hot stew between them. All I know is that the Major had been trained to shoot by my grandfather, and that it was instinctive with him to be careful of how he handled a gun. He wouldn't have clambered over a stile carrying a gun in the first place. His invariable practise was to stand it on the further side and vault over."

"There's the mark of where he stood it down," Wanklyn said to that, "but what was to prevent his catching sight of a bird and letting fly at it while standing on the stile? And after that making some awkward movement to reach it as it fell, or clamber over the stile hurriedly..."

"Did you find the bird?" Lionel asked.

"No, but he may have missed, or the bird may have dropped into the undergrowth."

"I don't think that my cousin would have fired on an impulse like that—unless at woodcock, and there are no woodcock down there. I don't see him snatching up his gun while half over a stile—nor, as I said, do, I see him clambering over a stile at all."

"That's what made me wonder whether he hadn't stepped upon it to get a better aim—but suppose there was no bird in sight, then his having the gun in his hand or on his arm must have been due to some worry—being lost in thought—"

There was a short silence.

"All you've suggested seems very unlikely to me," Lionel said finally, "very. But, of course, I only know what you've told me. I'd like to help you, superintendent, and just go over the place with you to see if there's anything that strikes me as odd. I might be able to settle my own, and your, doubts once and for all—"

The superintendent meditated on the offer. He thought that Lionel Cautley had some definite purpose in making it. The ground had been thoroughly searched. On the whole, Wanklyn decided to accept it. He did so with quite a passable show of enthusiasm and gratitude.

"He was my cousin as well as a pal," Lionel said simply.

"I wonder if you could tell me anything about his will?" the superintendent asked, "whether he's made one recently, and so on—"

"I haven't the slightest notion," Lionel said, as though the subject were distasteful.

It was arranged that they should travel down to Woodhampton together in half an hour. Lionel said that he had a few things to see to, if the other would wait for him downstairs, or join him at the club garage.

Wanklyn seemed to think this latter suggestion excellent. He left the other and walked briskly to the lift, to circle back again by another corridor. There was no one in sight. He set his ear to the door panels and listened intently, a key ring in his hand should any one pass along. The telephone was not being used but he heard a crackle-crackle of paper; yet nothing was being wrapped up—the sound was too indefinite for that. It seemed more like the turning of pages. Another will? When the sound ceased, and he heard the man inside begin to move briskly about as though putting things together, Wanklyn hurried downstairs and to a telephone outside.

An inquiry told him that the chief constable was at New Scotland Yard at a meeting. No message save the most urgent ones would be delivered to him.

Wanklyn felt that his vague uneasiness could hardly come under that heading. He had no proof that the missing pearls were connected with the Major's death, though if Lionel Cautley's alibi were genuine, he saw that they constituted the most likely possibility of a motive for a crime, and one which threw the field open to many suspects. He had not yet mentioned them to Lionel Cautley. He preferred to do so when the latter would be where he could not reach a telephone or send a message.

Lionel accepted the superintendent's offer to drive him down in the police car, as his own, he was told, needed some repairs.

The superintendent swung the side mirror a little so that it showed him his companion's face if he leaned to one side. Then he told him of Mr. Mason's arrival, and what he had to say about a telephone message from the Major. There was a hold-up at the moment, and the superintendent leaned well across to his little square of glass. He saw no change in those virile, sunburned, rather predatory features, and yet he felt sure that his words had excited the other deeply. He seemed to feel the man's whole body tense beside him on the seat, he could have sworn that Lionel drew, in a deep breath between teeth clenched till his cheek muscles bulged.

"And there's one other thing, too, Mr. Cautley, which in a way I should have told you before if I had been going by the order of importance in which the things, are listed. The pearls which were handed back to the Major at noon today cannot be found anywhere."

And on that the superintendent did see a change in Lionel's face. It grew wooden in its intentional impassivity.

"How odd," was his only reply.

"They, apart from other things, might suggest that this is something more than an accident," Wanklyn went on. Lionel only nodded and refused to be drawn to give any opinion on what had just been told him.

They finished the short drive in silence, and stopped at Fairlawn. Amplett and Mason, who were still discussing the dreadful affair, came out of the library to speak to Lionel. He waved to one side their expressions of shock and sympathy, and asked whether he could still see his cousin's body. He was taken to the room where it lay and left alone with it.

Wanklyn went on to have his interview with the chief constable, who had now returned to his own home. He found Captain Fairchild quite unimpressed by his facts.

"Quite right to take the line you're doing, superintendent," he said approvingly, "but, personally, I think you'll find everything peters out. I don't believe there's a crime here. I think the Major was deep in thought and forgot to put on his safety-catch, and, accustomed to its always being on, handled his gun carelessly—with the usual result, and in falling have raked his waistcoat a bit."

"And the missing pearl necklace, sir?" Wanklyn asked meaningly.

"Ah, that's a different pair of shoes entirely! If that's gone, it's been taken, stolen. But as he wouldn't have gone shooting with fourteen thousand pounds worth of pearls on him, if stolen, they were stolen while he was out of the house, and that being so, the last thing the thief would want to do would be to kill the Major and bring down all this inquiry. Fortunately, in working along the loss of the pearls, you can satisfy yourself completely that the Major's death was an accident."

Wanklyn thought a moment. He could see that this loss of the pearls, if it proved to be a real loss, might do just that, give him an excuse for looking very carefully into the Major's death without seeming to consider it a crime. He believed the two were linked, or at least, he thought it very improbable that there should be a theft and a murder on the same afternoon connected with the same man—Major Cautley.

It looked to him as though the thief knew that the Major would instantly suspect him, and would at once send for the police. Major Cautley would have done just that, the superintendent fancied; the Major was the kind of man to whom a theft would be so abhorrent that not even a blood tie would avail to let the thief escape. He would, the superintendent believed, consider it his duty to have the thief unmasked, taken from the ranks of unsuspecting men and women, just as though a relative of his had developed leprosy—the superintendent noticed with a faint smile at himself that he was already thinking of the thief of the pearls in terms of a close relation of the Major's. He had very little doubt in his own mind as to whom he would ultimately find was both thief and murderer, but the difficulty would be to prove it. In some way, so Wanklyn believed, Lionel had hoodwinked his cousin Jack. Those hours in the Cottage garden—if the younger had fallen asleep—they had probably had some drinks—what about a pinch of something or other—an explorer would know of many such—Jack Cautley might have been lost to the world for an hour, and ten minutes, or fifteen, could have done the trick—three to get to the stile, five to ten to wait for the Major, one to kill him, and two to get back to the Cottage. But how to prove this? Fortunately there were those missing pearls, and in proving who had taken them, where they had gone, might lie the straight and royal road to the darker crime, as the chief constable said.

Meanwhile Lionel Cautley had asked for a word with Daphne, but Edna, looking very pale, had told him that Daphne had locked her door and said that she would see no one, would not even reply to any inquiries. All she wanted, she had said, was to be left alone till tomorrow. Lionel's face was more impassive than ever when he got this message, but he stood a moment as though thinking it over before he turned away with a smile of thanks to

Edna. She was not smiling, but looked a little frightened, Jack thought, who was watching the two of them as they, stood talking in the garden.

"Anything wrong?" he asked as Lionel turned away. "Daphne isn't ill, is she?"

"No." Edna repeated Daphne's message and then hurried back into her own room as though unwilling to be questioned further. Jack frowned as he watched her go. He felt that Edna was keeping something back, but he also knew from experience how futile it was to try and get anything out of her that she wanted to keep to herself.

He heard a voice that he did not recognize. Going back into the library, where he knew that Mr. Amplett and the solicitor were talking, he found Captain Fairchild.

"Yes," Captain Fairchild repeated to the room in general, "it seems clear that the accident was due to a moment's forgetfulness on poor Cautley's part. The last thing in the world to have happened to him, one would say, and therefore it does happen! Just like life. Thank you,"—to Amplett—"I know what your Madeira is like. I've never drunk any to touch it—" and Captain Fairchild seated himself with a glass of the wine to his hand.

"Now about the pearls," he went on, "we must first of all wait and see if the Major didn't post them to you, Mr. Mason, possibly. He was using the post-office telephone he told you, and that very fact, with Fairlawn or the Cottage 'phones nearer to him from the 'hide,' makes it look as though he had posted something, and used the opportunity while there to telephone. If not posted to you, what about his own flat in Chelsea? We shall know by tomorrow morning of course, but until then, as I see it, nothing can be done." And on that note of resigned standing to attention in respect to the pearls, and calm acceptance of Divine Will in regard to the death, Captain Fairchild drank his one glass and took his leave. He was always a busy man.

The superintendent came back after seeing him into his car, and looked very wise. While Mr. Amplett had been saying a last few words from the steps, he had had a brain-wave. The inspection of the stile by Lionel Cautley and himself could not take place until morning, and meanwhile...

"It's a pity we can't have a photograph taken of the stile and the ground around it till morning," he said now, as though rousing himself from deep thought, "but in this light nothing would show."

"Do you think there is anything to be shown?" Mason asked at once.

"Captain Fairchild seemed quite satisfied," Amplett murmured.

"He is—we are supposing the photographs which will be taken about nine tomorrow morning—I think that's the best hour for lighting the ground around the stile—show nothing to make us alter our opinions, but it's surprising how a camera, like a microphone, will pick out things one doesn't notice. "However—" The superintendent, having planted his little seed, also said good-by in his turn.

CHAPTER SEVEN

AS soon as it was dark, Superintendent Wanklyn and Constable Todd made themselves comfortable on their ground-sheets, and took turns at watching, or rather listening. They had placed themselves under some bushes close to the stile where Major Cautley had been found shot. They were both awake when they heard the crack of a twig, then the swish of grass; then they saw what looked like a very large firefly near the ground moving in circles. It was a powerful electric torch. Apparently the wielder of it saw nothing to interest him, for after a very few minutes the light, played up and down the stile. After a short time the light wobbled away and seemed to be lost in the hedge.

"Stay here. He's making for the gap," murmured the superintendent. He used the masculine pronoun because once the light had shone on a pair of stout field boots, unmistakably a man's.

He followed the torch. He was but a step behind when it was shining on the ground inside the gap. The holder of it seemed fascinated by the mark of the shooting-stick, for he bent forward, peering intently at the mark and at the ground around it. Then Wanklyn flashed his own light over the searcher. To his great surprise it was Mr. Amplett. Amplett blinked for a second, then stepped aside and in his turn shot a beam of light on Wanklyn.

"Coming to have a look around too?" he asked amicably, making room for the police-officer.

The superintendent did not tell the other that he had been under police supervision for some minutes.

"What made you come here, sir?" he asked, instead. "We wanted the ground left as it was, you know."

"And I touched nothing just because of that," Amplett assured him, "but—well, it's rather difficult to say why I came—curiosity, I suppose. If you thought there was something here worth photographing, why—well, the Mayor was my guest, you know, Wanklyn," Amplett finished up with dignity.

Now that would go down all right—possibly—with a man from the Yard, according to Wanklyn, but he knew Mr. Amplett too well to be satisfied. "That might explain it by day, sir, but to come out at this time of night—I think I must ask you to explain more fully sir. Because—"

He wheeled. Something moved swiftly behind them in the lane.

"Got you!" came exultantly in Todd's voice, to be followed by a strangled howl and a thud, and no more remarks from the police constable.

"My goodness, whatever is the matter?" gasped Mr. Amplett. Wanklyn hurried to where his light showed him something dark, and found Police Constable Todd lying prone in the road.

"Another death?" Mr. Amplett asked in aghast tones as Wanklyn knelt down.

Wanklyn shook his head. He ran his fingers over a gash on his subordinate's chin and examined it intently. Todd, he saw, had been knocked out, hit fair and square on the jaw—a lucky blow purely, seeing the darkness, but the man who struck the blow had been wearing a ring, a ring with a rather high setting. Lionel Cautley wore a signet ring, so did Jack Cautley. And suddenly the superintendent saw with his mind's eye another ring, a high gold circle and a cross with a loop at one end inside it. It, too, might have made such a mark as this.

A moment more and Todd was sitting up, another, and he got to his feet, breathing rather heavily, but manfully trying to hold himself very straight.

"I saw a head peering into the gap after you. There were two of them. Not that I could see the second, I only felt him," he began to report.

"Two heads and you felt only one," murmured Wanklyn with relish.

Todd needed a moment's breathing space. "No, sir." The constable pulled himself together. "I saw one head, and grappled with it—I mean it's holder—I mean the man who had it,"—Todd was evidently not yet quite at his best—"when another chap knocked me out."

"Did you see absolutely nothing of either chap, Todd?"

"The man I caught was wearing thin shoes. I felt them when I stepped on his feet. I stepped hard." Todd's voice suggested pleasure. "As for the second bloke—I didn't see him, I only heard and felt him. Fist like a steam-hammer."

This was not very much help for identification purposes either. Wanklyn decided to return to his bird in the hand.

"You still haven't explained, Mr. Amplett, how you came to be examining that stile and the gap—especially the gap. Why should that interest you? Come, sir, suppose we sit down here and you clear this up."

For a moment Amplett seemed undecided. Then he appeared to make up his mind. "Well, superintendent, 'it's a fair cop,' as the criminal always says in the films. I had no idea, of course, that you were watching the place. It's uncommonly awkward—but having been caught out, I'll lay my cards on the table. Don't blame me if they're not worth looking at. It's just that this last week or so, the last two times that I've seen him, there's been something on the Major's mind. He'd fall into a brown study unless he himself were talking. After a long speech you'd find that he hadn't heard a single word. That wasn't in the least like him. And last time when he was down here, that would be about three days ago, he and I were out walking, and we passed this very gap in the hedge here. He dashed in. It wasn't on our way, and I said so. He then told me that he thought he had seen some one crouching down there and wanted to find out who it was. Now, an odder speech than that from Major Cautley could hardly have been imagined!"

"Just so, sir," agreed both the superintendent and Todd. "That's where knowing the dead gentleman comes in," the latter added, true to his teaching.

"Didn't he explain what he meant?" Wanklyn asked.

"No. Only repeated that he thought he saw a man hiding there, and wanted to find out who it was."

"Not why he was there, but merely who he was?" pressed the superintendent.

"I don't think he was giving me the real explanation," Amplett said to that. "I think he said the first thing that came into his head. Another very odd thing to imagine about the Major!"

"You're right there, sir!" agreed both his listeners.

"And then, too, there was the way he stood looking about him and listening intently, as though to hear if any one was moving away—it was so unlike him to care, or stop, to listen, that the whole little incident stuck in my mind."

"I wouldn't call it a little incident, Mr. Amplett," Wanklyn said. "Seeing what has just happened I should call it very significant. Very important possibly."

"Then you do think there's something wrong!"

"I think you think so, sir," came promptly from Wanklyn.

"No, no!" came defensively and hurriedly, from Amplett. "I simply wanted to make sure. You know how a vague thought can chafe one. I wanted to make quite sure, that's all."

"And you are sure—?"

"I see nothing to suggest that his death wasn't an accident—barring your presence—yours and the constable's."

The three smiled, but the superintendent was a dogged man.

"That's all very well, sir, but for you to get out of bed and come this distance—"

"Short distance," Amplett reminded him.

"At this hour of night, means, to any one who knows you, sir—excuse my frankness—that there is something more than just a memory; something definite, I should say."

Amplett was silent. He had the harassed look that usually with him accompanied a remark to the effect that it was a bit awkward. As the superintendent patiently waited for a reply, he said finally:

"I thought I heard our front door shut, superintendent, shut very softly and some one walk—very carefully—to make no noise—down the drive. I didn't mean to get up, but somehow, lying there thinking—thinking over many things, old days together with the Major, old talks with him, one thing and another, I couldn't sleep, and got up. Once up, I had a feeling that I must come here and see if something was wrong. There isn't anything to see. I've had my walk for nothing. And now I must get back at once, or Mrs. Amplett may wake up and miss me."

Todd was behind the superintendent, and used his position to give a grin in the darkness.

"It would be very awkward if Mrs. Amplett did wake up," Amplett repeated with something like a tremor in his voice. "I think I'll be getting along now; at once." He suited the action to the words and turned away after a couple of "good-nights" to the two police. Suddenly, watching him, they saw the torch rocket up to heaven and fall with a clatter, while Amplett gave a full-throated yell. It sounded like a howl of fright.

"Coming, sir, coming!" came from the two members of the Force, but Wanklyn pressed his subordinate down on the ground-sheet with the iron hand of authority. "You stay here! This may be a scheme!" and Wanklyn sprinted off in the direction of the yell and the torch still lying prone on what looked like a patch of emerald painted on a black drop.

He found Amplett, very white and shaken, peering down at a figure, a figure sitting on the ground, knees wide apart, toes tucked under him, his head sunk on his breast, the white folds of his loose cloak covering his hands. It was Fabian Cautley. He seemed as rigid as a stone image, and looked not unlike one with his shut eyes and a faint grin on his harsh features—a grin of derision Wanklyn called it to himself.

On the front of the white robe was a piece of paper with something written on it in large printed characters: "I am under a vow of silence for the time being. Do not expect me to answer you."

This was too much for the superintendent. He grasped Fabian's shoulder firmly. It remained rigid in his grasp. The superintendent had an odd feeling that by it he could lift Fabian Cautley up, had he the strength, just as he could lift up a carved statue.

Instead of trying, he shook it gently, and Fabian rocked lightly back and forwards again, just like an image. Then he grew calmer. After all, the man had a perfect right to sit still and grin if he wished. He was doing no harm. He was not trespassing. He was simply aggravating—that was how Wanklyn put it to himself.

Even the fact that from where he sat he might have been able to hear all that Amplett had just said was not in itself a punishable offense—though aggravating. A sudden thought struck him. Stooping down he lifted the fold of the robe that covered the clasped hands, which were oddly bunched and touching each other. On the little finger was the gold circle with the ankh. Throwing the light of his torch on it he scrutinized it closely. There was dried blood in the cross..

How long would Constable Todd's blood take to dry, supposing that this was the ring that had cut his chin? An absolutely baseless, perfectly unfounded, supposition. The robe parted to show that under it Fabian was dressed in a flannel shirt and dark gray trousers. The shoes placed beside him were ordinary shoes, but rather light in weight.

"What's it mean?" asked Amplett in a whisper. "Is he in a cataleptic seizure? Is he sleep-walking?"

"Or rather sitting," Wanklyn suggested with a wry smile, "I don't know, sir. Funny! But don't you stop here, sir. You go on home. I'll see to Mr. Fabian."

"He ought to be seen to with a rope's end. I nearly broke my neck over him, sitting here in the dark," Amplett said viciously, and Wanklyn quite agreed.

"I might try him with a lighted match," Amplett suggested. "I'm told that it's a sure test as to whether they are really in a cataleptic seizure."

Why, thought Wanklyn, did Mr. Amplett and his like always have to ask advice, wait for approval, before putting their ideas into action? He would very much have liked to see the end of a lighted match just touch that grinning figure, but being able to stop it, he had to do so.

"Better not try it, sir. It might hurt him," he said solemnly, and picking up Mr. Amplett's torch saw that ruffled gentleman around the nearest corner. Then Wanklyn debated a nice little point. He wanted to whistle Todd to him, but what if this grinning image—his own expression—had planted himself here with just that purpose in view?

Wanklyn put temptation from him. Picking up the shoes he left Fabian Cautley sitting on his crossed ankles, the fingers and thumbs of each hand joined into a circle, knuckles touching, his lids closed, on his lips, a curious half smile of utter withdrawal from a world of trouble.

"These anything like the shoes you stepped on?" he asked his attentive henchman. Duty had been hard for Todd, too. He wanted very much to know what had caused Amplett's howl and the superintendent's delay in returning.

"Very much so, sir, but I couldn't swear to them. All I can say is that there's nothing against their being them." Todd was not at his clearest tonight.

In a few words the superintendent told of Fabian sitting close to the hedge a little further down the road in a place where, with good hearing, he might have learned all that Amplett had to say.

"And probably hoped it would be more, sir. Was his hand swollen?" Todd asked, feeling his chin. "That blow was a good 'un. Got his distance worked out all right."

"Lucky fluke, that's all, probably," Wanklyn said.

"Lucky? Did you say lucky, sir?" Todd was a good-tempered lad, but for a moment words failed him. "From his point of view. Now then, I'll return these shoes to the Sleeping Beauty. Wait for my return." He came back in a very short time. "He's gone," he said curtly.

"That shows how little there was in his being asleep," Todd said in great excitement.

"Yes, but it would also seem to show how little there is in his brains, to give himself away to me like that! And yet we both know Mr. Fabian Cautley belonged to the Indian Civil—The Woods and Forests—and that you don't get half-wits in that Service by any means."

"The sun may have addled 'em. That's what they think around here."

"Umph!—I'm not so sure. I wonder—he's his cousin, too."

"The Major's? Yes, sir. Distant cousin."

"No, no! It's Mr. Lionel Cautley I was thinking of—" and for a second there was silence. "I mean, if he suspects him too... there's no love lost between them... But that would suggest, Todd, that Lionel Cautley was here tonight too. Say it was Lionel on whose toes you trod..."

"But why would Mr. Fabian have given me that jolt, if he's not a pal of the other chap whom I had all but nabbed?"

"We don't know that he did." Wanklyn's tone was impatient. "The main point just now is one about which we are certain and so can theorize. Why should Mr. Fabian Cautley have tried to overhear what was said, unless he suspects some one whom he thought would turn up here tonight?"

"Mr. Amplett?" Todd seemed surprised.

"That jolt you got hasn't brightened you any," Wanklyn said emphatically. "No, Lionel Cautley, of course!"

"Well, he may well, have been here. All the world may have been here. Come to think of it sir," Todd's tone grew still more animated, "that friend of Mr. Jack Cautley's, Mr. Harbord, he wears a seal ring which looks its though it felt like this." He touched his chin.

"And why should Mr. Harbord mix in to this? He's Jack Cautley's friend, and Mr. Jack Cautley certainly had no hand in it—at least, that's how it seems so far."

"That's where knowing the people helps," came Todd's dutiful assent.

Wanklyn shot his subordinate a keen glance, but Todd looked quite innocent. The superintendent decided that it was time Todd had a nap in order to be fresh enough to relieve him in a couple of hours from now. As a matter of fact it was well past dawn when anything new happened. It came in the shape of Lionel Cautley.

He gave a call from the road before he got close to the stile near which the superintendent was sitting.

Wanklyn stood up and moved forward. The superintendent had just been thinking that there is nothing to equal an autumn morning when the songs of the birds at dawn are not drowned by the young ones shrieking for food, a clamor which had never charmed the ears of Wanklyn.

It had been a very peaceful two hours, but at the voice of Lionel the last remnants of dreamland were swept away.

"I wondered if I could have a look—with you—at that stile," Lionel said. "Of course, I'm no detective, but we explorer chaps have to have keen eyes. To notice on which side of the trees moss grows has saved a life more than once. I offered to help last night, you know."

Wanklyn murmured something civil. He was wondering whether Lionel Cautley had helped last night by a vicious undercut to Todd's jaw, and if so, whom he had helped. Wanklyn moved aside to let Cautley have a look at the stile. Together, the two vaulted over and Wanklyn showed him where the body had been lying when found.

Lionel eyed the scrape on the step.

"Where did he slip to?" he asked.

Wanklyn's eyes asked his question.

"Where did my cousin's foot slip to? There isn't any mark on the ground where it fetched up. It should have gone half way through to China from the depth of that scrape. See what I mean?" He illustrated it in pantomime. "It's a funny scrape, anyway," he went on, bending low over it.

"In what way, sir?" There was reservation in the superintendent's tone, watchfulness in his fixed stare.

"This mark wasn't made by a slipping foot."

"Then what did make it?" the superintendent asked in his dullest manner. His mind was not dull. His thoughts were very much on the alert.

"Heaven only knows!" Lionel, walking round and round in little circles, now stood away from the stile, looking at the ground. The eyes of the superintendent circled with him. Suddenly Lionel stooped and thrust a hand into some stinging nettles. He fished out a broken brick and laid it against the scrape. It fitted exactly, even to some peculiarities.

"There's what scraped that step! I'll wager we could see brick dust in those marks if only we had the eyes to see."

The superintendent said little. He had searched those nettles himself last night, true only with his stick, but just to stoop down like this and lay your hand on the thing that fitted... "Them as hides can find" was in his mind as he looked into the face turned towards him; and which of the two faces, his own, or Lionel Cautley's, was the more watchful, it would be hard to say. Neither seemed to feel enthusiastic over what it read. As for Wanklyn, he was aware of recklessness, a love of danger for its own sake, which he felt rather than saw. This man would love to play with peril, love the feel of its inspiring touch as another man would love the feel of a warm fire on a cold night.

"I searched those nettles yesterday and found nothing," he said slowly.

"Ah, but I was looking for just exactly a half-brick, and the break in the nettles told me where to find it. That's what I meant by the explorer's eye."

The superintendent made some non-committal answer as he carefully wrapped the brick up. *If* a real find it was a help, a great help. It proved that his own idea was right that the scrape had not been made by the Major's loamy boots, and the suggestion of examining the step for brick in the scrape marks was acute too. Wanklyn would be relieved by Todd shortly, and he would himself arrange for the wooden cross-bar to be taken off, after it had been coated with some transparent fixative, and its marks analyzed.

Lionel stayed a few minutes more, trying to get some information from the slow-tongued and apparently slow-witted superintendent, but gave it up at last and turned back towards the Cottage.

CHAPTER EIGHT

LIONEL CAUTLEY when close beside the Cottage gave a sharp glance around him and, suddenly swerving, darted across the lane and started off towards Fairlawn in his long swift stride, resolute yet unhurried. He evidently did not intend the police, who might be watching from the stile, to see that he had not gone straight home. At Fairlawn he made for the window of Edna Upjohn's sitting-room. She was an early riser, he knew. There she sat working over some plans for her colored borders. She was very pale, he thought, but Lionel was not of those who spend any time on the troubles of other people.

"I want a word with Daphne," he said peremptorily, stepping in.

"There's nothing like not being able to come to the point." She shot him an indignant glance.

He took his cap off and apologized, but with a look that suggested that Edna was wasting precious moments.

"I'll see if she's awake." She rose, for Edna was a kindly creature.

"If she's asleep, then wake her please. I must speak to her at once. I would go up and say as much through her door but for Mrs. Amplett, who is an insufferable busybody."

Daphne and Edna came in together. Daphne had on a dressing-gown which for once seemed not to suit her. At any rate she looked older than her age this morning, and as though she had slept badly, but she ran to him very charmingly and flung herself into his arms. Edna had left them alone together.

"Lion, darling, let's get married and go away—on a long, long trip. I want to forget it all."

"Where were you last night?" he asked harshly.

"In bed. Why?" She looked the picture of surprise. "I saw you let yourself into the house a little before two o'clock," was the answer.

"Me? You may have seen one of the maids who looks like me from a distance only, I hope. I've given her a couple of my frocks. Darling, what on earth makes you say such extraordinary things?"

He stared at her, suspicion in his eyes. She looked back with a glance that never wavered.

"Harbord was with you," he went on through set teeth.

"With her," she corrected. "How do you know?"

"I saw him standing at the gate. Now, Daphne, don't lie to me. It was you!"

"Lionel! You brute!"—but she clung the closer. "I do believe you'd be jealous if it were true! What a pity it isn't. I went to bed and stayed there. Ask Edna. Though I'm foolish to love a man who won't believe me—who tells me that I'm lying." She hid her face on his breast.

His arm tightened, but somehow its grip suggested one who detained rather than one who clasped. "Daphne," his voice was a whisper now and his eyes were steel, "how did you come by that shagreen case?"

"Shagreen case?" she repeated in a tone of bewilderment, closing her eyes as though these complicated matters were very tiring.

"The one the pearls were in—the pearls that are lost. I saw it in your handbag when it fell open on your arm just after you and Howard had been talking together in the conservatory."

"He gave it to me," she said with a limpid look like a child's. "I had told him what a lovely thing I thought it— lovelier than the pearls, because they could be imitated but it could not, and he promptly took it out of his pocket and said I might have it."

"But he couldn't give it away. It goes with the pearls, and is listed with them, with the few entailed pieces of jewelry my grandfather named in his will."

"Well, he gave me that case!" she retorted, pulling herself free, or trying to. There was a frightened pallor about her reddened lips.

"Yet it was lying on his dressing-table later on. Lying empty, of course."

"Yes, when he had that dreadful accident I couldn't bear the sight of it. He was killed only a few hours after giving it me. Don't you suppose I have any imagination, Lion, any—any—?" She could not seem to find a name for the quality she had in mind, and fell silent.

"You didn't tell me of the gift," he said, still in the tone of an accuser, still with the look of one, too.

"Why should I have?" She looked angry now. "What does all this mean, Lionel?" Then the angry look was smoothed away, her voice grew caressing again. "Surely you know that I'm frightfully easily worried by trifles. The idea of a present from a man who was found dead a little later! I couldn't bear the sight of the case. So of course I put it back on his table."

He stood with folded arms looking at her. There was a great longing in his eye, and with it something distinctly hostile.

"It won't do, Daphne. Why should you have put the case back instantly? You must have done it while Howard's dead body was being carried upstairs and the room put to rights to receive it. Why should you do it?"

"It was still in my handbag," she retorted, "and filling it up frightfully. I opened it, the bag, to find my handkerchief"—her voice trembled, but his glance did not soften—"found the case and just laid it on his dressing-table without another thought—only a shudder!"

At that his face did soften. He drew a deep breath.

"And what do you mean by these questions?" she asked in her turn, now assuming something of his pose and look.

"I wanted to be sure that Harbord—" He stopped, not from indecision—indecision would never be a quality of this young man. "That way of giving back the pearls—" he began again, and again he stopped. "You and he—" Again came the pause. He looked at her moodily. Finally he gave a little sigh. "Well, we can talk about this later. The Orientals are right. Women should be kept in harems. You still assure me that it was not you I saw coming in last night, having obviously just parted from Harbord?" Once more his gaze, piercing, almost inimical, rested on her. Once more she met it with a glance of sweetest innocence as she shook her beautifully waved and cut hair.

For a second he looked as though he would like to refer to Oriental methods again, but if so he said nothing more, only rather moodily added that he wouldn't keep her any longer. He walked out into the hall with a dark look on his face, to find Edna writing by the front door with a pad on her knee. He barely nodded to her as he stalked away. She watched him go.

There was always something about Lionel Cautley that frightened Edna, or rather there was something in him which she always felt could frighten her if she caught a good look at it. And he was treacherous, or he wouldn't have got Daphne away from Jack. Daphne could be swayed by any young man who took her flitting fancy. She could no more help it than a kitten could help purring to the hand that stroked it. Yet, oddly enough, pleasure-loving Daphne seemed more really caught by the impossible Harbord than by Lionel Cautley, else why should she be so mad as to flirt with him while engaged to Lionel? Last night, for instance. Edna knew that her half-sister had been in town with Harbord and had come back after midnight. She had not questioned her, she had not let her know that she knew, but Edna had lain awake most of last night listening to the odd sounds in the house. She had heard Mr. Amplett come down very shortly after Daphne had closed the front door, letting it slip with rather a bang, as the front door had a trick of doing. Fortunately he could not have known who it was. Edna felt miserable today. The death of the Major yesterday, dreadful in itself, seemed to have lifted the lid from other dreadful things, seemed to have let loose poisonous vapors. She went back to her room, where she found Daphne crying as though her heart would break. Edna could not remember having seen Daphne cry since she had had a tooth out years ago.

"Oh, life is horrible! Horrible!" Daphne would give no other explanation. "All the time you've got to keep on doing what you don't want to do, and—and—" she took refuge in her handkerchief.

"Did he know that you were in town last night?" Edna asked.

Daphne nodded miserably.

"With Harbord? Does he know that?"

"I'm hardly likely to go roaming round at night alone!" came from the folds of the little square of pink muslin and lace. "He's a jailor, Edna. He's not one of us at all. He's a mediaeval monster! All the Cautleys are horrible. Pleasant enough outside and stone inside—stone and steel and—horrible!" and Daphne, looking, for her, quite wild, broke from Edna's hand and rushed to her own room, where she again bolted herself in.

A couple of hours later Edna came unexpectedly on Frank Harbord bent over a photograph album and scrutinizing a picture in it with a magnifying glass. As soon as he heard her step and before he turned to see who it was, he shut the book and slipped it with almost guilty speed back into its place again in a bureau bookcase which was given over to family "no-longer-wanteds." She had noticed that the page open before him had a bright green card of some kind in it. Harbord began talking to her about the Major's death, but he said no word as to what he had been looking at. She rather fished for it, but he carefully made no mention of portraits, yet there were only family portraits in that book, as she well knew.

"This is the lens, or rather one of them, that Lionel Cautley brought down with him last night. They're used in pairs for examining aeroplane fabric, it seems, and apart they make quite good lenses, though with a very small focus. I was just trying this on various objects."

Why on family portraits? she wondered. He knew what that book contained, for he and Jack, Lionel and she had spent the last wet afternoon at a hilarious game of Lionel's inventing called Family Bridge. You played it with the family portraits, following man, woman, girl, boy, or baby, each with its own kind, and the ugliest took the trick. Afterwards when the four of them had laughed themselves almost ill, Edna had replaced the portraits, carefully tucking their corners into the little slits left for them. Harbord had helped, and very neatly and swiftly he had worked. She remembered now the one mounted on green board, a man in an Indian uniform, Mrs. Amplett's father, if she was right—some one quite dull. She was about to ask Harbord point-blank about his present interest when Jack called to his friend, and Harbord hurried off as though eager to get away. She had the album out again in a moment. Yes, on the page in question was the portrait. Above it was a sweet-faced woman, Lionel's mother. They had left her out of the game. Any member of the family, according to Lionel's rules, could except any portrait as not to be used. Edna stared at the two again. At what had Harbord been looking?

Just then Daphne came into the room. She bent over the page in her turn. Edna expected a question as to why she was so interested in these faded pictures, but Daphne instead drew her away from the book, closed it, and put it into its place, talking rapidly the while of a proposed party to the Engadine for the coming winter. Wouldn't Edna like to come out too for three weeks' tobogganing? Even though the Cresta was no longer open to women, there were quite fair ice runs to be had, and besides that, where would you find better skiing in the Alps? Edna was good at skiing. The mother of a friend of Daphne's talked of taking a chalet just above Maloja. They wanted a party of young people good at sports, and she, Daphne, was to bring another girl and two men out with her. Harbord had promised to come, if the idea materialized. Lionel, of course, would be there too. What about Edna?

Edna was delighted at the most unexpected invitation. It would suit her very well. Portraits and magnifying glasses were forgotten, and the two went out into the garden full of talk about plans and clothes.

Daphne left Edna rather abruptly, but the latter had just caught sight of the gardener's lad at work and stayed to explain to him hotly what she meant by trenching and what by slacking. That good deed done, she went back to the book of portraits. A thought had struck her. The man in the colonel's uniform was wearing a row of ribbons, but the woman—Mrs. Cautley—that string of pearls wound round and round the slender throat, with the handsome clasp well to the front, surely that must be the Cautley string. Could it have been at that that Harbord was staring so hard? She opened the book at the green card. It was now the only photograph on the page. Some one had torn the book itself in jerking the other out. Who?

Harbord came in at the moment, rather hurriedly, rather as though intent on doing something quickly. He stopped when he saw her with the Book spread out in front of her. Jack was with him.

"What have you done with my Aunt Emmeline?" Jack asked lightly, coming to look at the book. Harbord came too.

"Her picture was here just now. By the way, she is wearing that Cautley necklace in it, isn't she?" Edna asked.

"My dear girl," Jack spoke with his pipe between his teeth and in a nonchalant manner, "you don't expect a mere man to know what the lady was wearing, do you? I wonder how they ever managed to get through a Court in her days. The train itself must have taken a good hour to rustle past the throne." And with that he began to talk about the coming inquest.

It struck Edna that Jack wasn't as good-looking as usual this morning. He had lost, or mislaid, that cheery beaming glance of his, that merry, though rather idiotic smile. There was something about him just now that she didn't quite like, it reminded her too much of Lionel and his effect on her. She gave him an answer that was no answer, and went on out to see whether Horace, the gardener's boy, had really dug two spits: deep this time, and not merely forked over the top soil a bit.

Superintendent Wanklyn did full justice to his breakfast when he got it at last. He had sent Todd off first to have his, and then get a couple of hours' sleep while another man took his place. The chief constable came in while Wanklyn was finishing his fourth kipper, and to him Wanklyn related the strange events of the night.

"Nothing really suspicious in all that," Fairchild said finally. "One must beware of getting 'Policeman's Mind,' you know, superintendent. It's worse than housemaid's knee and caused by the same sort of thing—too much of one kind of work. Amplett's curiosity was natural. So was Lionel Cautley's. And you've only to read his book *The Everest Effort* to see how quick he is at getting the facts of a case. Those two men with whom Todd had that little engagement—well, that's not exactly proof of a crime either. Pounced on by a man in the night, of course one would defend oneself, or one's friend."

"And leave a policeman lying knocked out in the road, sir?" Wanklyn asked.

The chief constable frowned, and said he didn't like the look of that either, but what he was trying to get the superintendent to see was that it was not necessarily a token of any connection with the death of Major Cautley.

"I've got the autopsy notes here. It's all just as we thought. Everything fits, the gun wound and the idea of an accident—"

"And I'm as certain that it was no accident as I am that you're there and I'm here, sir," Wanklyn said doggedly.

Fairchild frowned again. It was no sign of ill-temper with him, but of thought.

"There are some obscurities, I grant you," he said finally. "As to your fixed idea that Lionel Cautley was the criminal—I think that's impossible, seeing the alibi that Jack Cautley gives him. And you, like me, are prepared to accept Jack Cautley's word, I see."

"I am, sir. Yes, undoubtedly. But"—Wanklyn spoke hesitatingly—"these Cautleys always hang together, sir," he added in explanation of the tone. "I don't say that if Mr. Lionel Cautley went to his cousin with some cock-and-bull story about being innocent but in an awkward position, Mr. Jack wouldn't stretch things a bit to shield him—believing firmly in his innocence."

"Umph! Well, of course you'll have to look into the business relationships of the Major and his heir." And Wanklyn knew by the words that he had scored.

"Odd that the Major seemed to have rather a fancy to Mr. Harbord." Wanklyn murmured, reaching for some more marmalade. His mind had gone off at a tangent.

"Not a fancy! Merely saw that one of his ideas was well worked out and could—possibly—be tried at his works. But I understand that he had intended to give it up; so Colonel Blackmore told me last night when I had a word with him about the Major's death. He has invested heavily in the works and takes an interest in them. He had just got the Major to promise to alter the clause in his will about—possibly—trying out Harbord's theory of wage and capital sharing. Probably the Major told Harbord as much when he dropped in to the Cottage before lunch, but evidently there was no ill-will over it.

Anyway, it's a most unlikely contingency that all four Cautleys will die childless. Hello, here is Lionel Cautley!"

Lionel was shown in a moment later. He said that he had merely dropped in to know whether the step of the stile had been examined yet, and whether his certainty that brick dust would be found in the marks on it had been born out.

Wanklyn told him the results of the examination were not yet to hand. It would be noon before the superintendent could know whether Lionel's odd guess— if it was a guess and not actual knowledge—was right or wrong.

Lionel thanked him and left, to walk back to the Cottage, with his erect carriage and long step which suggested that nothing but an express train could stop him. A man almost ran into him from a turning of the little lane and stepped back with an apology only to step forward again with a:

"Surely you're a relation of Major Cautley?"

"My name is Lionel Cautley. I'm his cousin," Lionel said instantly, looking at the man in front of him with a quick but very friendly glance. Every explorer meets strangers with a friendly glance, it's part of his equipment.

The man who had stopped him wore a parson's collar. He was a stout, middle-aged man dressed with a shabbiness which suggested that he was certainly not laying up treasure for himself on earth, but with a face that indicated the probability of quite a good balance standing to his account in heaven. He was Mr. Tunbridge, the rector, who had just returned from a holiday in a miners' camp in Wales. Lionel had never met him, but he was quite a friend of Major Cautley's.

Tunbridge proceeded to introduce himself as such, and say some words of sympathy at the Major's tragic end.

"It was evidently you to whom he was referring the very last time I had a talk with him," Mr. Tunbridge went on, falling into step with the other, for they were both going the same way.

Lionel turned his head and shot him a keen, inquiring look.

"He asked me if I had ever met in my rambles a man who resembled him, or whom I could mistake for him in the dusk, say, or in foggy weather," went on Mr. Tunbridge.

Lionel seemed to have grown taller, more rigid, as he walked on in silence.

"I told him I hadn't, except perhaps Jack Cautley. There is a sort of family resemblance there which now you see and now you lose. Don't you think so?"

"Perhaps there is," Lionel agreed courteously. "What did he say to your suggestion?"

"He said he didn't mean him, but had I seen any stranger lately who might be mistaken for himself. I had not—then"—here Mr. Tunbridge made a sort of half bow—"and said so. Evidently, however, you must have been in his mind."

"I wonder how he came to ask you the question, Lionel said, lighting a cigarette. "Seems rather a roundabout way of asking you if you had met me. Nor do I agree that the likeness is as great as all that."

"The likeness is striking to a stranger," Mr. Tunbridge assured him. "As to how your cousin came to speak of it? Out of the blue. We were looking at the Vita glass windows in the school. Don't you agree that sunlight is the greatest of Heaven's gifts to us mortals?"

Having traveled—which Mr. Tunbridge had not— having seen Arabs and Africans roasting under red-hot suns and yet a prey to every ill that we have to endure, plus several more; having seen market women abroad spending their lives out of doors in the sunshine and yet not one whit the healthier for it, or the longer lived, Lionel Cautley was not silly enough to agree. He made some remark about Baal and Moloch, and in a second the two were in an animated talk about sun myths and sun worships. But through it all there was something impenetrable in his eye which had no part in the cheery talk, and meeting it full as he said good-by, the parson thought what a dark, forbidding face this cousin of the dead man had, and he wondered how he could have thought the two so alike at a first and casual glance. Well might the Major have made his qualification about a foggy day or the dusk being necessary to mistake the one for the other.

CHAPTER NINE

MEANWHILE, back at the police station, which the chief constable himself had left shortly after Lionel, there was a laborer, stolid, heavy-footed, shown in to the superintendent's room. Wanklyn looked him over carefully. The man's name was Hammersley. He lived in the village and was employed at various odd jobs, such as thatching, hedge-cutting and the like, which younger men no longer know how to do nor care to learn. He had a fairly good reputation with his employers, and would have had a better had not his skill depended too much in inverse proportion on the number of glasses of beer which he had absorbed. But the police had a black mark against his name, a very black mark—unknown to Hammersley. He was suspected of holding dog-fights in his cellar, fights to the finish, where only one dog could be the winner. It was not merely the brutal fights, but the preparation of the dogs—starving them to the requisite ferocity, letting the food placed before them just out of reach be eaten by other dogs, until their tempers were those of fighting cannibals—which the superintendent, along with his men, loathed. Only the hope of getting a conviction made the police civil to the man, but let him suspect that their eye was on him and there would have been no chance of getting at the truth. Two men had come down from the north recently who were suspected of plying the same trade, this of dogs which tore and rent each other until only one was left alive. The police believed that some one with more money than Hammersley and his like could produce, was behind the men. Hammersley himself always had a dog in evidence which he was willing to sell. He had a couple of kennels at his cottage; the dogs, unknown to him, were watched, but, so far, it had been impossible to prove where the missing ones had gone.

Hammersley now touched his forehead and took off his cap. He was a brown-faced, blue-eyed, rather personable-looking man, with nothing in his features, not even when he smiled, to suggest that the police could be right in their suspicions.

"The sergeant was giving it out last night that he wanted to hear of any one as saw the Major yesterday afternoon. Well, I heard un as well as saw un. Having a scrap he was." Hammersley passed and cleared his throat importantly. Hammersley was quite a help to the police. The man was very anxious to stand in well with them. Observant and accurate, he had helped to make rough the path for more than one poacher. He always took good care to assure the police that all he cared for was to see wrong-doing stopped, that rewards meant nothing to him.

"Yes?" Wanklyn now said, showing his interest. "A scrap? With whom?"

"With his cousin, the gent as was here just now. Yes, sir. Half and half. Not a regular one I wouldn't call it. Not a scrap I don't. Not a real, regular affair, but I thought every second as it was a-coming. Which was why I lingered—to see what was a-coming. But after making as though they would clinch, the Major he pulls himself up and makes off into the field, the one where his 'hide' is, and t'other chap, his cousin, the gent as was here just now, kept dancing about on his toes, shouting, 'I'll make you hear reason!' A roaring, rearing rage he was in, and t'other, the Major, just slings back over his shoulder, 'You can do your damnedest!' Nasty tone, sir, and nastily meant."

"Did he get into the field where the 'hide' is by the gate?" asked the superintendent.

"The Major?" Hammersley laughed. "He did as he always does. Stood his gun down and swung himself over by the top board. Light on his pins as a lad, the Major. And a punishing fighter."

"What did Mr. Lionel Cautley do?"

"Hopped into his car and drove off. I couldn't stay no longer though I felt sure I hadn't seen but the beginning. Stands to reason it was but the beginning. But I had a job to do for old Mr. Burton, who won't put up with no waiting."

"When was this talk?"

Hammersley went on to explain with great detail that it must have been just after four and that he had stood listening and watching for quite a quarter of an hour. His detail was convincing and careful. He was not to be shaken in it, nor in his certainty that he had seen what in men of his own class would have ended in a first-class, "proper" fight.

Mr. Hammersley was thanked, offered a drink, which he accepted gratefully; whistled his dog, who seemed devoted though perhaps a thought too obedient to him, and plodded off.

"Now, here again is where local knowledge helps," the superintendent finally said, and Todd, who had come in, nodded. Hammersley was a man who loved a fight. Without being quarrelsome he would offer to fight for his opinion any time, just as another man might offer to back it with a bet. "Fight you for it!" was his favorite offer. "Come now, fight you for five shillings. Well then, fight you for a bob! Come on then fight you for nothing! Come on!" and it was possible that he had watched the scene between the cousins through colored glasses. But Hammersley was by no means a fool, or a liar. He might have read something much more hectic into what he saw than belonged there, but he would not have imagined it all.

"If he's right, and Hammersley generally is, then Mr. Lionel Cautley can't have spent all the time with Mr. Jack they both insist he did."

The two checked over again the various ways in which Hammersley had arrived at his certainty as to the time—ten-past four. No, unless deliberately lying, Hammersley must be right, and the superintendent was sure that he was not lying.

"Local knowledge again. Hammersley wants to stand in well with us and has never made the slightest mistake in anything he has told us yet. He hopes that if things ever go wrong and we catch him at one of his dog-fights, things will go easier with him. They won't. If we can only catch him! Only find out where he gets the money to keep them up!"

For a few minutes the superintendent and the constable talked warmly of how this most desirable end could best be achieved. Then they returned to Lionel Cautley.

"So that alibi's a fake. I felt it. But how to prove it, Todd, that's the difficulty in this case."

As Todd had no ideas on this knotty point he only shook his head and murmured: "Just like Mr. Jack to help any one out of a hole."

"It's a very serious thing to do when the person is a criminal," the superintendent said gravely. "Accessory after the fact, Todd, is what Mr. Jack has made himself. That's the worst of a family affair. The Cautleys, all four of 'em, would stand by each other through thick and thin, no matter how they might fight among themselves. Well, I'm off to town to see what can be ferreted out about the missing pearls. That's the end of the string we hang on to, as the chief says, and we'll see if we can't get home to the murder by it."

Looking very resolute, Wanklyn gave his orders as to what was to be done during his absence.

The postman came in as he was finishing. He had some letters to deliver. Wanklyn, who was in the outer room and saw him was struck by an idea.

"Did you have any letters to deliver at Bunch Cottage yesterday afternoon, Mr. Robey?" he asked. "The three-fifty delivery was what I was thinking of."

"I had a registered letter for Mr. Fabian Cautley," the postman said promptly, swinging his bag off his shoulder for a moment. "No one in. Rang and rang and rang!"

"What time was it when you reached the Cottage?"

"It was gone the quarter-past four, sir," Robey replied promptly. "I marked the time on the envelope and took it back. It got delivered by the later, seven-forty, delivery. Why, sir? Any complaints been made about it?"

"I simply wanted to be sure that you had done your best to deliver it," Wanklyn said in a very official tone.

"Done my best!" repeated the indignant Robey. "Why, I battered on that door with the knocker until my arm got tired. Then I rapped with my stick on the panel, then I opened the door a bit and called, 'A letter for Mr. Fabian! Registered letter for Mr. Fabian" I walked through the little passage into the garden, but when there's no one there what are you to do? I had to take it back and bring it by the next delivery."

"You did quite right," Wanklyn said pleasantly, and Robey's face grew calmer.

"But Mr. Jack Cautley says he was in the garden at the hour when you should by rights have delivered it." Wanklyn seemed to be glancing at a note on the sergeant's desk.

"Then he was hiding up in the one and only tree is all I can say!" Robey said it with heavy sarcasm. "Mr. Fabian likewise."

"And Mr. Lionel likewise?" asked Wanklyn with a smile.

"Mr. Lionel? He wasn't there. His cap wasn't hanging on the peg. He always hangs it up when he comes in. I've had a lot of letters to deliver for him, many of 'em registered, and I've never known that to fail. No cap means no Mr. Lionel."

"He must have other hats or caps." Wanklyn seemed amused.

Robey shook his head. "He wears that cap or nothing."

Wanklyn and Todd both shot each other a swift glance. Neither could recall ever having seen the explorer in any other headgear than a light fawn tweed cap. As Robey said, he either wore that or went bareheaded.

The postman left on that, after being assured that the superintendent considered the non-delivery of the registered letter fully explained.

"They hadn't any right to come to you about it," said Robey with rather belated dignity. "They should have sent in a complaint to the Postmaster-General. After all, Mr. Superintendent, no offense, but you only wear your uniform in the name of the Law, I, mine, in the King's Name!" and with a really magnificent swagger Robey went out, leaving two grinning men behind him.

"You're right, sir!" Todd said almost reverently, following his chief back into the latter's private room. "It is Mr. Lionel! And my feeling about Mr. Fabian was just feeling—nothing to it!"

"And nothing to my suspicions of Mr. Lionel as yet, Todd," Wanklyn said ruefully, "or rather my certainty that it's him. This postman—well, they've only got to say they were both on their beds fast asleep, and who's to disprove it? Robey didn't search the rooms."

"Still, sir, add Robey to Hammersley, and you get two witnesses," Todd said meaningly.

"Yes, and add Mr. Lionel to Mr. Jack, and you get two denials," came the reply. "No, I think we'll let the inquest go through without offering any suggestion of foul play. After all an inquest is only to determine the nature of the death. Meanwhile we must see—you, if you can find some one else who also saw Mr. Lionel talking to the Major at the time of the so-called alibi; I—about the pearls. I shall get the chief's permission to go to the Yard about that and tap their brains. Jewel robberies are their daily bread up there."

At Fairlawn, while the postman was undermining Lionel's alibi, that young man was trying to induce the two Upjohn girls to leave Fairlawn and stay for a while in town.

"I hate my Aunt Violet, darling thing," Daphne said promptly, "she's cut too much on the pattern of a wardress."

"Still, she asks you to come to her—"

"Yes, but I stayed with her before coming down here, and I had to account for every moment as though I were a factory hand. I wonder she doesn't install a time machine in her flat. And Edna hardly knows her. While you've told me that you loathed her."

"I'm not fond of her," Lionel granted reluctantly, "but at a pinch— No one else would put you both up, you think?"

"My prehistoric monster, no one nowadays puts two girls up—unless it's Aunt Vi. You carefully take a house in town nowadays that won't let you put any one up. Never!"

"Still, I think, seeing what's happened down here, that you two oughtn't to stay at a hotel, even if you had an old dame with you. After all, this aunt of yours means well, and she stands for protection—safety—"

"I believe you egged her on to ask us!" Daphne spoke as though her aunt had been incited to a crime. "I wondered how she came to do it!"

"Don't you think it would be rather unbearable for Mrs. Amplett if we both left her—just now?" Edna asked. "It's a frightful shock to her, all this, though she does always act as though made of cast-iron. She likes Daphne, and wants her to stay on. And I'm an 'employee' here. I shouldn't like to ask for a holiday just at this dreadful moment—not unless it was absolutely necessary."

"Of course it's not necessary. Not at all!" Daphne said firmly.

Lionel did not respond. He looked moodily, darkly, at her, as she reached for a flat bottle behind a woolly terrier on the narrow mantel ledge. "I'll take an aspirin," she murmured, "or two would be better." She shot him a reproachful look as she did so, a look that said that he was the cause of her headache. He did not catch it, as he stood there his eyes for a moment fixed on a distant sky-line out of the window, apparently deep in thought. Lionel Cautley never gave the impression of being lost in thought, or lost anywhere.

Edna went out as a servant came in. The superintendent would like a word with Mr. Cautley, if it is convenient.

"He's come to ask some further questions about those pearls," Lionel said, when the door had closed again and they were alone. He gave Daphne a searching look.

"Naturally!" she retorted, "they were in your possession until they were handed back. Who should know as much as you about them?"

"Mason," was his reply to that, and there was meaning in the tone.

"The solicitor?" she drawled.

He nodded. "Yes. He has the paper giving the correct weights and description of the pearls and navette fastening—I think that's the name for it."

Amplett entered with his apologetic air.

"The superintendent is here again. He wants a word with you, Lionel. It's rather awkward, the way the police have of dodging in and out of the house. One never knows whether to offer them a drink or to pretend not to see them. My wife is getting rather—er—worried. The fact is"—Amplett came closer—"the police aren't quite satisfied. At least, that's how it seems to me."

"You surprise me!" Lionel said caustically. "What unreasonable people they are to be sure—"

"Unreasonable?" Amplett looked puzzled. "I think they're reasoning very hard in the matter. They ask no end of questions—odd questions too—rather awkward to answer, some of 'em."

"Such as?" Lionel wheeled to face him directly, a light in his dark eyes that made them flash.

"Well—about those pearls, for instance—and where everybody was all the time—and why Harbord gave them back in that funny way—"

Lionel listened intently; he was standing very rigidly, almost as though to attention. But Mrs. Amplett could be heard above, apparently in urgent need of Mr. Amplett, who called his customary "Coming, Malvina, coming, my dear!" and hurried away.

The superintendent appeared at the door.

"Mr. Mason wants you to help us in going through Major Cautley's papers. He thinks that you, as the head of the family, the Major's heir, ought to be the one to look through his letters and so on at his house in town."

"Of course, I must be there. Want to do it now? I'm quite ready."

Wanklyn explained that they had telephoned for him to the Cottage, but that there seemed to be no one there, so he had ventured to make an appointment for Mr. Cautley with the solicitor an hour from now.

Lionel nodded. He was watching the police officer closely in spite of his impassive face and undisturbed manner.

"Perhaps we might drive up together," Wanklyn went on, and Lionel said that that would suit him perfectly.

"By the way, sir, are you sure that you and Mr. Jack Cautley were together yesterday afternoon at exactly the times you gave? And left the Major when you thought you did?"

"I think so," Lionel said with apparent ease. "True, one does sometimes make mistakes about minutes. Tel] you what, superintendent, I'll think it over, and work it out and let you know this afternoon before the inquest, shall I?"

Wanklyn said that he would not be present at that function, but that if Mr. Lionel Cautley would let him have a line, or a message, to the police station at any time, it would at once be read.

"The fact is," he also spoke casually, as casually as had Lionel just now, "the fact is, we have just had a piece of evidence—some one who saw you and the Major talking together, Mr. Cautley, which doesn't seem to fit in with the hours you gave. So I should be much obliged if you would go over the times again in your mind and let us know them very exactly."

"Right," Lionel, said with a pleasant smile that for a moment made him look like his cousin Jack, only it was not quite so merry. "Right, superintendent. I'll think the hours over again and let you know the result." He looked at his watch. "I've time to step over to the Cottage and see whether there are any letters for me," he went on easily. "Will you pick me up there in your car?"

Wanklyn said that he would, and Lionel, catching up his cap in the hall, strode off, but not before he had stepped back to where Daphne was still eyeing herself in the mirror without any of her usual look of pleasure at the sight.

"Daphne," Lionel said in a low, curt tone, "watch your step! No, don't talk to me,—or any one. Only watch your step," and with that he was out into the hall, again, and this time off, down the drive.

At the cottage he found Fabian sitting under a tree, one finger laid to the side of his nose in quite a knowing way; but Fabian's eyes were closed, he was breathing in through one nostril at a time, four seconds to draw in a breath, sixteen to hold it, eight to expel it. Lionel stared at him for a moment as though longing to burst out into some form of violence, then he hurried on.

Jack was writing in the one large sitting-room of the Cottage, where the inmates had allocated one corner to each member; one for Jack and one for Fabian, and one for any visitor—in this case Harbord. It was an untidy room, rather as though a couple of young cyclones lived there.

"Jack, we made a mistake," Lionel began, closing the door behind him, but characteristically leaving the window open. "I'm going to confess to the police about that alibi of mine. I know it's awkward for you, but you only did it to help me out of what you thought might be an embarrassing situation."

"Going to give yourself up to the police?" Jack said with unexpected dryness. "You're making a mistake, Lionel, that may cost you your life—or liberty."

"I'd rather tell them the truth than have them tell it me," Lionel replied in the same tone as the other, "and I feel sure that they know it, or at least know something about that last talk I had with Howard."

"What makes you think so?"

"Partly something the superintendent just said to me, partly something Amplett let drop just now. And, besides, I'm being followed—all the time. My things have been gone through twice over." He spoke indifferently as always, but his keen eyes were on the other. Hard, bright eyes had Lionel Cautley.

"Well do as you think best, of course." Jack spoke as though dismissing the matter. "When are you going to confession?"

"I want to put my things in order tonight, but I don't think I shall be arrested." Lionel spoke confidently.

"I do."

"Not if I'm able to give them a useful hint as to where to look." Lionel's face was very grim, very dangerous. Jack studied him carefully. He himself still wore that pleasant, rather silly smile of his that so rarely came off his face.

"I suppose it's no good asking you to be more explicit? No? Well, don't do anything until we have each had time to sleep on it,'" Jack said after a rather tense little pause. "Of course, if you're right, it's the only thing for us to do, but it will place you in an awkward position."

"It will. Both of us."

"Ah, but you're the next of kin, as you seem very persistently to forget. I've only an indirect interest in

Howard's death—you a direct one. It was because of that I suggested the plot, if one can call it a plot."

"Because of that, eh?" There were several things in Lionel's voice, but conviction was not one of them.

"Where are you going now?" Jack asked, as the other got up.

"To town. The inquest is tomorrow, you know."

"Look here," Jack put his hand on the other's arm. Lionel moved away; he disliked being touched. "I want you to promise me that you'll do nothing until we have another talk together—after another think, separately. You can always say tomorrow what you haven't said today, but you can't unsay tomorrow, or ever, what you have said today."

Lionel looked hard at him, seemed about to speak, but only nodded, and went out as the superintendent's car drew up.

"Peace be with you!" murmured Fabian, as he passed him, still sitting in the garden.

CHAPTER TEN

"I'LL take the right-hand drawers," the solicitor said, "you, Mr. Cautley, will perhaps look through those in the left. We will each lay on one side purely unimportant letters, and place on the table in front of the superintendent any which seem to us out of the way or peculiar—should there be any, which I doubt. But I see the Major kept both sides of his writing table locked."

"I'll take the right-hand side, if it's all the same to you," Lionel said easily, "the light's better, and one of my eyes is giving me trouble. But what about the superintendent?"

Wanklyn answered that by pointing to a bureau against the wall.

"I'll look through those. I may have to look through everything, but your preliminary sorting out of the papers will save time before tomorrow's inquest."

Wanklyn had chosen a bureau behind which was a flat, long mirror, enabling any one writing with his back to the door to see who entered. He kept his eyes on the glass as much as on the papers which he was fingering. They were mostly household accounts, he found. One of them was rather difficult to decipher and the superintendent concentrated his gaze on it for a minute. That was when something crackled under Lionel's hand. A glance into the mirror showed Wanklyn that Lionel Cautley was picking up something from the floor with one hand, and that, apparently to support himself, he had his right hand crooked into the drawer, like the fluke of an anchor.

In an instant the superintendent had his hand on a paper which was under Lionel's fingers and half pulled out of the drawer. He had an idea that some sort of disappearance was being staged. It was to frustrate such a trick that he had chosen his place in front of the mirror.

"You'll upset the drawer, sir," he said lightly, laying the paper in question back in its place and bending over it. "This seems to be in your handwriting."

"That's why it's not going on the central table," Lionel said casually, but the superintendent was reading. The letter was a request from Lionel to be released from work at the aeroplane works, and for funds to finance a desert expedition. Across the letter Major Cautley had scrawled "Unreliable."

"Not my character, but the information as to the gold," Lionel said, tapping the word with an apparently indifferent pipe-end. Wanklyn nodded as though satisfied.

When the papers were sifted, when he had seen those on the table safely sealed and put away in his case, Wanklyn asked the butler-valet for a word. He seemed to have nothing to tell them.

But the porter downstairs stopped the trio on their way to the superintendent's car and Mr. Mason's taxi. He asked if the burglary last night at the Major's flat had been duly reported.

"First I've heard of it," the superintendent said promptly.

"Just what I thought! Mr. Chinnocks, the manservant there, was caught napping, that's plain, and doesn't want to make a fuss about it, but I've my duty to the landlord to think of. I saw a man with my own eyes as I was coming home. I'd had a breakdown in my son's car—he's a motor mechanic and was a-testing of a car, and it didn't stand up to it. Well, we crawled home on one flat tire after another, and it was nearer three than two last night when I slipped through the front door and across the courtyard, and what should I see but a man dropping out of the Major's library window on to that lead roof and into the next street. Like something in a film it was. I gave a shout and tried to run round to head him off, but my sprinting days are over, and when I got there I could hear a car, though I couldn't even see it. But my shout had made him lose a shoe. I saw him trying to get his foot out of something—stuck between the wall and a pipe in getting down he had—and there we found a shoe right enough. Gent's evening shoe. Mr. Chinnocks has it. I wanted to notify the police, but he says nothing was took and he wasn't going to have 'em in. Well, any one can understand that—no offense, gentlemen—but he had ought to have mentioned it to you. It's the shock of the Major's death what has gone deep. He's all broken up over it. Been with his gentleman for twenty odd years. Never expected to leave."

Wanklyn asked several questions. According to the porter, Chinnocks was fast asleep when finally roused by him. Chinnocks was a hard sleeper, once he got asleep, he added. The servant and the porter had gone carefully over the flat, but, apart from the open window, nothing seemed amiss, though some of the plate had been stacked on the floor, evidently in preparation for carrying it off.

The superintendent with his party returned to the flat. Chinnocks rubbed his chin and shook his head in apparently genuine self-reproach.

"There, to forget to mention a thing like that! But nothing was taken. Nothing whatever. He was after our plate—I found it stacked on the floor—but something must have disturbed him. I'll get the shoe for you, sir," and he brought in a man's shoe a minute or two later.

The superintendent studied it. The shoe was quite neat and good in its way, but its name suggested mass production, and its size that of any man around five foot six or seven. From the look of it, it had seen wear. He wrapped it up after the butler had initialed it inside with indelible pencil.

A few more questions were asked of the porter, who could only guess that the fellow was young and athletic from the way he negotiated the road, very anxious not to be caught from the way that the loss of his shoe did not stop him from running over very rough cobbles indeed. "Must have left his skin on every one of them," the man said cheerfully, "unless he was used to running barefoot, and he didn't look it. Toff by the outlines of him. All in black. No hat, but a cap on, but somehow I think he would have looked all right in a topper."

Chinnocks shook his head disparagingly.

"Very common footwear, this," he murmured. "What you bin doing to it?" the porter said good-humoredly. "Must have left it in the cinder-box since I gave it to you. It was well polished then, like patent leather."

"I've handled it a bit of course," Chinnocks agreed. "That stuff it was blacked with came off in flakes. Cheap stuff, like the leather."

That was all. When the porter had waddled downstairs again, the solicitor looked meaningly at Lionel and the superintendent.

"Plain to see what the man was after—the pearls! His information was all right up to a point, but insufficient. He seems to've known that the Major would have the pearls given him back by you, but not where they would be handed him. Or else he thought you had already done that, and that the Major was keeping them here for the night, before letting me have them to put with the others."

Lionel did not agree. He thought it much more likely, he said, that the handsome family plate which adorned the flat in Chelsea Embankment was the attraction—not the pearls. Then he, too, had to go on with Mason to the interview with the insurance company's solicitor.

Wanklyn stayed behind for a while, looking over all the papers in the flat, those not set apart for him as well as those which he had put into his bag. Then he stood a while looking into space.

"He's a fox!" he was saying to himself, "and the Major seems to've known as much; but even the cleverest of foxes makes a mistake one day, misjudges the pace of the hounds, or finds an earth stopped—."

In his own mind, the reason for the burglar's visit was, undoubtedly the pearls. Wanklyn had all along agreed with the chief constable, that Major Cautley was posting something when he had used the post-office telephone to send a message to Mason. As he intended handing over the pearls to the solicitor, it seemed odd that he should have sent them to himself at his flat, but he might have done so for some as yet hidden reason. A reason connected with his talk with his cousin Lionel? Suppose the Major suddenly believed—rightly—that the pearls were in danger—after that talk... Because of that talk?... Was he trying to throw the thief off the scent by those words about handing them over to Mr. Mason next day? Or had he sent them to Chinnocks?

Wanklyn himself spent the next hour in finding out beyond a doubt that no registered letter or parcel had been sent to the Major's flat. It seemed out of the question that the Major should have trusted so valuable a string of pearls to the ordinary post, though Wanklyn knew that jewelers often prefer to do this rather than call attention to the value of what they are sending.

As far as could be traced, no letters or parcels seemed to have been delivered at the flat on Chelsea Embankment last night. Wanklyn believed that possibly the thief, too, had misread Major Cautley's going to the post-office—which now seemed to be merely in order to telephone to the solicitor—and that he, too, had assumed that the pearls would be sent back to the flat. Why had a thief thought that this would be done? It sounded to Wanklyn like an accomplice, like some one who imagined that the Major would act on advice given him, or a warning given him—advice or warning which had after all been disregarded.

Wanklyn felt that team-work was now needed. He went on to what he called briefly "the Yard." The chief constable had already had a talk over the telephone with the authorities there. As a murder might be linked with the missing pearls, Wanklyn, after a short wait, was shown into the room of one of the chief inspectors. Wanklyn knew him by name and by reputation as one of the Yard's best men, and he also knew that among his underlings Mr. Pointer was immensely popular. Wanklyn, meeting him for the first time, looking at the quiet gray eyes, had an impression of a personality, of a character quite out of the common. He sensed that here was a man whom you could trust in large or in small things—a man who would never play for his own hand. A pair of very fine dark gray eyes unspoiled by any blue, looked out of a sunburned, grave face. They were pleasant eyes to meet, but, as Wanklyn found after talking for a while, absolutely inscrutable. So was the whole face. Wanklyn was quite good at reading expression, but here he knew any effort in that line would be doomed to failure. Yet in a few minutes he found himself talking easily, freely, to one of the best listeners he had ever met.

"The trouble is this," Wanklyn wound up, "I know who's guilty, but I'm hanged if I can see how to bring the murder home to him. The only chance, the chief constable thinks, is to prove the theft of the pearls. If we can do that, we may be able to link them up with the shooting of his cousin. He's got an alibi which, as I've told you, we believe false. I rather think he himself will alter the hours of that. He may have seen Hammersley too, or remember now that he heard some sounds which makes him think that some one may have been there at the time—"

The chief inspector touched a bell. Wanklyn was passed on to Inspector Watts, who would see to it that he would have the services of a man who was an expert where jewel thefts were concerned. Wanklyn spent a day of swift rushes and descents here and there, but the upshot was that no trace of the pearls was found, and the Yard man believed that he would have come on some word of them through his select corps of double-crossers had they recently been added to the stock of illicit jewelry in London.

They reported the double failure to the chief inspector. Pointer looked at his shoe-tips.

"What makes you certain that the string was real?" he asked.

Wanklyn bit his lip. It had not occurred to him to doubt the Cautley heirloom.

"You say Mrs. Cautley had the loan of the pearls for Court wear, then possibly Mr. Lionel Cautley allowed Miss Upjohn to wear them on some special occasion?"

"Yes," Wanklyn said. Though neither would own to having done so, seeing the kind of girl Miss Daphne Upjohn was, and seeing how head-over-heels in love with her was Lionel Cautley, he felt sure that she had worn the string more than once.

"Umph! Well, I think, if I were you I should make some inquiries among artificial pearl makers, copiers of genuine things. There are only a small number of good workers."

Wanklyn obtained their names, and another expert to open other secret doors. He found that the fact that it was evening meant no slowing up of the inquiry. On the contrary, Detective-Sergeant Yates seemed to think evening a better time than day for the visits he intended to pay.

"Secrecy is the essence of this sort of thing, naturally," he remarked, as the two walked towards the Tube station. "At the same time, as far as we know, all the people capable of making a really first-class imitation of a string of pearls are quite genuine artists in their own line, not crooks. There are just eight of them in town, and, other things being equal, I should expect that if Miss Upjohn or Mr. Lionel Cautley wanted a substitute for the real thing, the job would be given by them to some one in town. Now, who is the special jeweler each goes to?"

A telephone talk with Todd told Wanklyn that Miss Upjohn had several boxes marked with the names of the larger jewelry places in town, and also three which bore the name of a little shop off Sloane Street specializing,

Wanklyn found from the Yard expert, in very good repair work. This, Yates now thought, would be the most likely place for her to have had any copying work done. Todd had not found any boxes in Lionel Cautley's possession. His studs and links bore the mark of one of the large London men's shops where it was hardly likely that he would have given the order to copy his cousin's pearls, even had he wanted it done. Wanklyn believed that he might have wanted this.

Chief Inspector Pointer's words had slanted an entirely new line of light on the problem. If Harbord, by his sleight-of-hand display, had distracted Major Cautley's attention from the pearl string, the latter might have accepted an imitation as his property, might have found it out later—might have taxed Lionel with it during that interview which Hammersley, swore had taken place, and taken place so stormily. Lionel might have shot his cousin in desperation. But, after finding that the latter did not have the pearls with him—a possibility which he could hardly have expected—Lionel had not returned to Fairlawn, which, as a guest in the house, he could so easily have done. Had he preferred to arrange with some one there to take the string of sham pearls from the case and destroy, or hide them? Was Miss Daphne in this much of the crime? He would only have needed to meet her outside the house. There was no proof of when Daphne had returned to Fairlawn in the afternoon, except her own words. She could easily have had a hand in the whole affair.

However, these were but so many variants of the real theme, and for the moment it hardly mattered which one had been played. Wanklyn felt convinced that Pointer had, as usual, seen into the core of the ball of tangled possibilities. The motive was probably a double one. The pearls themselves, and the prevention of Major Cautley finding out the truth or taking steps to have the person who had substituted the false for the real pearls arrested. Here again, Wanklyn said to himself, his personal knowledge of the dead man helped him. Had such a substitution taken place, had some one foolishly thought to hoodwink the Major by handing him back a spurious for a real thing, he would have received no mercy. There was in him, as in all the Cautleys, a streak of that which would not let him, even if he wanted to, give way to weakness in such a case.

Meanwhile, the expert had taken Wanklyn to a woman who worked for the little shop off Sloane Street. She was a thin, elderly-looking person with bright, keen eyes and noticeably fine hands, but she refused to give them any information whatever. Her orders were strictly confidential, she said, and she could only give any information with the permission of "The Trinket Box" as the firm called itself.

The Trinket Box belonged to a Mr. Diamond, though his wife and daughter usually ran it. The police had nothing whatever against the firm—quite the contrary, it had a first-class reputation. They found Mr. Diamond to be a stout, elderly Jew, who lived over his shop with his family.

Yates was quite straightforward. He had told Wanklyn that any effort at finesse would defeat their own ends. He explained to Mr. Diamond that a pearl necklace was missing which they, the police, believed might have been only a copy of the original, and have been substituted without the real owner's knowledge. Had Mr. Diamond ever copied a pearl necklace belonging to Major Cautley? Mrs. Diamond, a stout Jewess and her pretty, still slim daughter, were present at the interview. Wanklyn noticed that mother and daughter looked tremendously interested in the question, but that is a national trait, and explains in part what makes them such good salesmen and women.

All three Diamonds assured Mr. Yates and the superintendent that they had had no copy made of the necklace in question. Wanklyn had the particulars as furnished by the solicitor, and Mr. Diamond proved from his books that the necklace had never passed through his hands.

The detective and the police officer left finally, and decided that next morning they would tackle the big establishment from which Lionel Cautley occasionally bought things. No inquiries there were possible after seven in the evening, so Wanklyn returned to the Yard, where he learned one unexpected fact. He had brought with him the pile of silver plate which the burglar of the night before had stacked, ready for taking away with him, it was believed. The only finger-prints found on any piece were those of the butler himself. Wanklyn had secured his by the simple means of having him hold a card with some writing on it which he thought might be the Major's.

"Well, well!" murmured Wanklyn, not quite seeing what this meant. "He looked an honest man, and too good a servant to need to do this sort of thing, especially as it's all only plated stuff."

As the chief inspector made no remark, Wanklyn looked at him.

"I should be awfully obliged for any suggestions you care to make," he said honestly.

"Well," Pointer said promptly, for no one ever asked him for help in vain. "Doesn't that shoe suggest to you a middle-aged man as its wearer? A man who is great deal on his feet, addicted to walking on the outside edges? Very short and stout I should expect to find—at any rate takes very short steps."

Wanklyn stared, first at the chief inspector, then at the dilapidated shoe still standing on a table behind them.

"Mind explaining the magic?" he asked, grinning. But he had turned the soles up and saw for himself. The spread of the feet did, suggest middle-age. The wear of the shoes, especially on one side, the outside, the distention of the leather around the top edges, told of fat feet. But the short steps? He asked how this last was arrived at.

"No worn edge to the back of the heels," Pointer said. "Your long stepper always wears his shoes down there, the longer the stride the more the heel takes the first thump of the body's weight."

"You've described Chinnocks pretty closely," Wanklyn said, putting the shoe back. "I had noticed myself that it was of a size to fit him, but that only meant it's of a size to fit nine men out of ten. Well, I'm surprised. I frankly confess it. He struck me as a thoroughly reliable sort of man. Thoroughly devoted, too, to his dead master."

"And possibly also to that dead master's family," Pointer finished.

Wanklyn fixed an attentive, inquiring, stare on him.

"The pile of plate with the butler's fingerprints all over it, the shoe which fits a man of his age and build, and not at all the kind of young devil who scrambles over roofs at night, both suggest, off-hand, that the man is shielding some one—some one who broke in last night without his knowledge or assistance, but whom he recognized by his shoe. The shoe very likely had the name of a place, or maker, in it which meant something to him. Or—you said that he was the only man-servant in the flat, didn't you?"

"Yes, they're service flats. He was butler-valet to the Major."

"Then he would probably know shoes particularly well. Recognize them at a glance. Under the circumstances, I think he did the best he could by piling up that plate, and changing the shoe for one of his own, to suggest a robbery which was frustrated by the porter's unexpected return."

"Mr. Lionel! That's why he didn't go on to Fairlawn! He knew the pearls were sent off by the Major, but, like us, hasn't the foggiest notion of where they were sent. And then that paper too—that paper he tried to get out of the drawer today. He'd have had it if I hadn't been too

quick for him. Paper that shows he wanted funds, and
that his cousin ranked him as unreliable, or his tale as
unreliable." Wanklyn was all on fire with inner
excitement.

"He has a good reputation," Pointer said dreamily.
"Kind of man who never has any difficulty in getting
others to go along with him to the ends of the earth. That
means a lot, Wanklyn."

"Oh yes," Wanklyn agreed, "he's the kind that won't
stop short of success. I've heard that too. Never gives up a
thing he has set his hand to. Never hands on anything to
another to finish, nor lets any one else in on his plans till
he's carried them out himself. That much all sticks out of
his books on climbing. Very nice and useful reputation;
but I think he's a bit overreached himself here. Well,
tomorrow may give me quite a leg-up. Those pearls—that
idea of yours that we ought to look out for imitations, has
widened things tremendously. I shall get my clever young
gentleman though!"

And on that confident note, Wanklyn thanked the
other warmly, and left the Yard, feeling an added respect
for the brains there.

CHAPTER ELEVEN

EARLY next morning Superintendent Wanklyn was at work again. A few pieces of information came to him. The first was that about a week before his death Major Cautley had arranged with a firm of chartered accountants to go through the books kept by Lionel Cautley. The inspection was to be strictly confidential. The accountants added that the Major had written saying that Mr. Lionel Cautley had himself requested the inspection and wanted to be present at it, as he feared lest some inadvertent slip of his—he was unaccustomed to figures—might involve the firm in quite a big discrepancy. This, the firm in question now wrote confidentially, they considered merely a form of speech to shield the Major's cousin. Wanklyn, again basing his guess on his knowledge of the dead man's character, thought this very likely.

So Lionel Cautley's books were to be gone through... Like the accountants, Wanklyn did not for a moment believe in the young man's own desire for this. The news was a help. It would go a long way to prove motive. Just as he hoped that by following up Chief Inspector Pointer's suggestion of the substitution of a false for a real string of pearls, he might yet go all the way towards a really feasible reason for the shooting of the Major.

As soon as the shops opened, Yates and he unearthed yet another strand which would, Wanklyn believed, finally be woven into a rope around Lionel Cautley's proud neck. At the big Stores, as they liked to be called, of King and Court, they found an assistant who had arranged for a duplicate to be made of the pearls which interested Wanklyn so greatly. There seemed no possibility of doubt. Most careful details had been entered. Receipts for both real and imitation strings were to hand signed *Lionel Cautley*. The real pearls had been returned to him at his rooms, while the imitation string, by request, was left in the shop to be called for. And it had been called for by the same very charming young lady who had brought the real pearls. The firm's receipt had not been given to her on that first occasion, but posted to Lionel Cautley along with an acceptance of the order for a copy. She, when she came for the imitations, had brought with her a receipt for them signed in the same name—Lionel Cautley. It had taken a week to make the imitations, and, even so, the salesman now acknowledged that the color was not as perfect as it should have been. There was one flawed pearl in particular, whose streaks of vivid pink had rather baffled their usually clever copyist. He, the salesman, would always be able to identify their copy at a glance by that particular bead, the second from the navette end of the clasp. In the real string, the streaks were very sharply striated in the copy, blotched.

The manager, who was present, explained to the two inquirers with a little smile that it was more difficult to copy an imperfection than a perfect pearl, and, as the salesman acknowledged, in this particular case the copy was not at all good. But the rest of the string was quite fairly well done, though not up to their man's usual standard. They had learned since that he was having some trouble with his eyesight at the time, and should have refused the work. The charge for the copy was twenty pounds. Had it been really first-class it would have been nearly double.

The salesman, whose memory was getting clearer, said that the order was placed with him on a Saturday morning quite early. The young lady had seemed in a great hurry, but absolutely above suspicion. Moreover, the fact that the receipt was to be sent, and the real pearls were to be returned to Mr. Lionel Cautley at his own address—whereas it was only the beads which would be fetched from the shop a week later—had made it all seem quite beyond suspicion. The firm had had intermittent dealings for many years with Mr. Lionel Cautley. One of their departments had done most of the outfitting for him and his friends on his last expedition. The question of anything wrong had not entered the head of the salesman. Copies of valuable jewelry were being made every week. Many people preferred to lock away the genuine article. At least, that was the explanation given, and if the firms entrusted with such work occasionally wondered whether the heirs to the pieces in question always knew of what was going on, it was not their place to institute inquiries.

Wanklyn had a word on the telephone with Captain Fairchild after this interview, and laid before him all the facts of the imitation string that had just come to light.

"I've seen the receipt for the real pearls," he wound up. "The Stores won't part with it yet awhile, but there's no doubt about its being Mr. Lionel's name which is scrawled across it. Well, sir, it seems to me that I've proved my belief now."

"Possible defalcations at the works—selling or pawning the pearls—that your idea, Wanklyn?"

Wanklyn's reply was to the effect that he didn't see what other idea was capable of being held by any reasoning animal.

"He's not particularly short of funds," Fairchild replied to that in a ruminating tone. "He has a small income of his own which is intact—according to the bank manager."

"A small income isn't much use to an explorer, is it, sir?" Wanklyn pointed out, "especially when he's going to marry a very smart young lady whose dresses—well, they look expensive to me."

"Look here, Wanklyn, what about calling in the Yard?" Fairchild said after due reflection. "The case with its ramifications of possible duplicate pearl strings made, and probably disposed of, in town, needs town help. Also

it would please people down here at Woodhampton.
Fabian Cautley, it seems, has been stirring up a strong
feeling that Scotland Yard should be called in to make
quite sure that Major Cautley's death was purely
accidental, and his own accident at that."

Wanklyn was more than willing. Chief Inspector
Pointer himself would probably be given the task.
Wanklyn hoped this would be the case. He would enjoy
working under Pointer, he knew, or rather, technically
speaking, working with him, for the Yard is still only
supposed to "advise" the local authorities as to the best
steps to take.

On proceeding to the Yard, Wanklyn was taken at
once to the assistant commissioner. Major Pelham, a
rather soldierly-looking, youngish man with a bluff face
and manner, did not greet him any too warmly. The
executive head of the Yard had strong opinions about
calling in specialists to "cold" cases, and this certainly
was that. However, he finally instructed Chief Inspector
Pointer to a look into the affair, and, if he thought that he
could do any good after all these hours, to take it over.

Pointer spent the time in Wanklyn's car in going over
with him all the facts of Major Cautley's death and
circumstances.

"Since Captain Fairchild telephoned to the A.C."
Pointer went on, "we've had the Cautley records looked
up. Nothing whatever in Major Cautley's to suggest any
reason for him to be murdered.

"Nor, I'm bound to say, in Lionel Cautley's, to suggest
this tangle of possible theft and possible murder. John
Cautley, his cousin, seems all right. The usual easy-going
young man who feels that there's no real necessity for
him to work hard. The only one of the family, in fact,
against which we can find out anything is Fabian
Cautley. He resigned from the Indian Forests under an
unpleasant cloud. He resigned, in short, because he was
asked to do so. There was a hint of one of his Indian
servants being pushed by him into a river full of

crocodiles. There was no evidence available. In fact, Delhi would have taken no notice, but for certain other rumors which had reached them from time to time—vague rumors, but always hinting at cruelty. The government snatched at the opportunity of the missing gun-bearer to let Mr. Fabian know that he had better leave them immediately of his own accord.

"Mr. Fabian went to Benares for some time and then turned Buddhist and went on to a Tibetan monastery. He came back into the world some six months ago, and made for his only kinsmen."

"What are his private means?" Wanklyn asked without much interest. "No one down at Woodhampton seems to know."

"He must, as far as we can gather, have saved about half his pay every year. That would mean that, unless he has lost it in some way, he has about three or four thousand put by. Not wealth, but not penury. And the Major has left him a house and its furniture, I believe?"

"Yes. That's right. Dunnottar it's called. It once belonged to a Colonel Barstairs—a friend, of the Major's and of Amplett's. He was a bit cracked and the house is full of the most extraordinary gadgets. The Major had just let Mr. Fabian have it for this School he talks of founding when he was shot. I think he was sorry about that girl Mr. Fabian was engaged to. It was through him in a way it was broken off. How Mr. Fabian is going to keep up Dunnottar is a puzzle.

"If what he talks about his plans is true it will take a good twenty thousand," Wanklyn went on. "No one likes Father Fabian, as he calls himself, except women. They fall for him. There's something about him—he's very pleasant and all that, but there's something about him you can't like and can't name, either. But there it is. That's why Todd, whom I told you about, pins his faith to Mr. Fabian being the murderer. But where's the motive? He's not the heir, nor near it. Mr. Lionel is. As for Mr. Jack, he's the only one of the three we haven't any doubts

about, though he has bolstered up Mr. Lionel's lie. Sort of
thing Mr. Jack would do. He'd help any pal out of any
hole, though he had to stand in it himself chin deep to do
so."

They drew up at the police station.

Meanwhile at Fairlawn, Lionel Cautley had arrived
about noon and again asked for Daphne. Daphne had
sent word that she didn't feel well enough to see any one.
The inquest would be this afternoon and she too had been
summoned. She had just taken two aspirins and intended
keeping quiet until lunch.

Edna did not look at him as she gave the message.
She knew, and she was afraid that he knew, that Daphne
and Frank Harbord were having a long talk in the room
which was supposed to be her own sitting-room, but
which Daphne had appropriated.

She herself had been out in the sunken garden, really
enjoying herself as she looked around at the results of her
labors, but an angry shout of Harbord's, "Photos don't lie,
though people may!" followed by an equally angry, high-
pitched sentence from Daphne to the effect that she didn't
care what he thought he had seen in that damned picture
which he had stolen, had sent Edna inside.

She was no sentimentalist. She did not feel in the
least that she was "nearer God's heart in a garden than
anywhere else on earth," she knew how many snails—
Edna thought a baby snail one of the most beautiful
sights in the world, as it is—how many doubtless worthy
slugs would never return for another meal, how many
high-hearted young leather-jackets would never become
Daddy-Long-Legs, how many battalions of greenfly she
had swamped only that morning, how many earwigs she
hoped to trap in those neat little painted match boxes of
hers slung so invitingly among the dahlia leaves... To
Edna to have a good garden was the mark that you were
a first-class fighter, and absolutely adamant, absolutely
without pity where your hobby was concerned. A
detective too, and a strategist. But the high words had

distracted her from her work, and moreover were all too evidently not meant for a third person's ears, so she had come inside to clear off some circulars which she had not yet opened.

She hoped Lionel would not stay around waiting for Daphne to change her mind. Lionel would not shout, but he would, she felt that odd certainty as to his capability, be very nasty.

"Amplett in?" he asked now, to her relief. Edna knew that Mr. Amplett was dictating letters to Miss Smith in the library. Miss Smith would be shooting up coy little glances from her big black eyes and pouting with her red, red lips. Mr. Amplett, Edna acknowledged the truth with a half smile, would be looking very pleased with the young lady's evident interest, but would be trying to hide that pleasure by extra insistence on the work being carefully done. Miss Smith's efforts to vamp Mr. Amplett amused Edna. Personally, she would as soon have tried to stir Mr. Tunbridge to a romantic passion, but perhaps Miss Smith looked on every employer as so much practise, until one day she would strike the right combination of a soft heart and a soft head.

She mentioned, without looking up, in which room Mr. Amplett would probably be found. Her eyes were on a delphinium which had somehow got loose from its stakes, and unstaked delphiniums can come to such sudden and dreadful ends. She heard Lionel cross to a side table and pour himself out a glass of water and return to his place on the hearth rug.

"I'm afraid I must interrupt his very pleasant labors," Lionel had said with a sneer, "and so I'll fortify myself with a couple of aspirins too."

Edna did not hear him. She had already hurried out to render first aid to lovely, brittle *Norah Ferguson*. She should have seen to this before, she told herself, as she tried to straighten up one bent spike of blossoms, but Jack had been in this morning very full of a request from some city magnate to call and discuss plans for a new

office building. Jack's car for once was out of action, and
he wanted to find out the best train. Together he and she
had made out a time-table, and Edna was more than ever
certain that Jack needed a clever wife as a partner.
However, at last they had got things straightened out,
and Jack had hurried off, calling back to her to tell
Lionel, if she should see him, that he had intended
having a talk with him, but that the letter postponed
that.

Edna spent nearly an hour in the garden, and only
left it finally in charge of the boy while she went to see to
some cuttings that should be sent off. She sold quite as
many plants and seeds for Mr. Amplett as she bought.

When she came in again it was lunch time. Lunch at
Fairlawn was still at one o'clock. Mr. Amplett was
walking up and down the lounge, looking very bothered,
she thought. She saw him go to the door of the morning-
room. He turned the handle. The door was evidently
locked.

"Come, come!" Amplett called through urgently, "you
can finish after lunch." There was no answer. Amplett
turned to meet his wife's stare as she came sweeping
down from the landing above.

"Who is locked in there?" she asked promptly. "Lionel
doesn't want to be disturbed," he said hesitatingly.

"Is he alone?" came the next question, at which Jack
would have exploded had he been there, Edna thought.

"I'm certainly not in there, if that's what you mean,"
came Daphne's light, cool voice from farther up the stairs.
Mr. Amplett hurried into the gardens, through a door,
and round to the windows. They were shut, but he tapped
on the pane. There was no reply. Staring through the
glass he could see nothing. The net curtains veiled the
inside. He tapped again on the panes, but nothing showed
itself.

Daphne joined him almost instantly.

"He won't answer. It's very awkward."

"What is?" Daphne asked him in a hard, level voice.

"Lionel wanted to write a letter, be quite by himself," he said. "He's locked the door. I hardly like to keep on badgering him, but it is lunch time, and, as you know, Malvina—" Amplett, his head held more on one side than usual, drifted slowly back into the house.

Daphne did not waste any time tapping on the panes. She slipped around to the door, tried it very quietly. Amplett stood watching her with a puzzled frown on his face. A minute later she ran up the stairs to her room. Something in her manner suggested that she was going in search of a definite object.

At that moment Jack's voice hailed from the open door and Amplett came forward to meet him. Edna, too, came out again into the lounge at the sound. She was eager to know how the important interview with the city magnate had gone off, but Jack would only say that things seemed very promising. Then he looked at the clock. "As usual, my watch has stopped. I see it's past one. Is Lionel still here? Fabian told me that he was coming up here."

"He's locked in the study writing a letter," Amplett replied.

"Which is evidently in Sanskrit, from the time it's taken," Edna added, "and which has still to be translated into Chinese. I could hear him taking aspirins at the rate of one a second as I passed just now. Please talk low. Sanskrit is quite a tricky language. And Chinese is catchy, when it comes to writing it."

Jack lit a cigarette. No, he wouldn't stop for lunch, but he would wait for a word with Lionel. He couldn't be much longer now. His glance told Edna that he hoped she would stay and talk to him while the rest went in to lunch. She was sure that he wanted to tell her all about the interview.

"But I intend to have a word with Lionel first," Daphne said sharply. She passed on apparently ready for another effort on the locked study door. It so happened that none of them could see it from where they stood.

It was perhaps three minutes later that they heard her cry out. The sound came from the study itself.

The door was now wide open, and inside stood Daphne bending over something on the floor. Something quiet and twisted. Something with a white, distorted face.

It was Lionel Cautley, and he was already chilly to the touch, with that growing coldness which is unmistakable.

For once Amplett did not say anything about things being awkward.

"What have you done to him?" he asked instead, in a tone of horror and suspicion. She began to scream at that, and the room filled with the people in the house. Amplett himself, without another word, went to the telephone, brushing even his wife aside to get, to it quickly.

"Dr. Doubleday in?" they heard him ask, after he had given a number; and then, "Please come at once to Mr. Lionel Cautley, doctor. He's here at Fairlawn and apparently his heart has given out. He's quite dead. Yes, he—well—he looks as though he were dead."

The last avowal came almost apologetically. Then Amplett hung up.

"Don't touch him!" he said sharply. But Jack had put his hand inside the waistcoat, and did not seem to hear him. Amplett looked uncomfortable, but made no further protest.

"It's not beating, is it?" he asked instead. Jack did not reply. He looked strangely broken, genuinely stricken, as he withdrew his hand and knelt beside the body, staring into the altered face of his cousin.

Daphne had tottered to Edna and clutched her arm. She was not screaming now, but her eyes were wild.

"Fabian's face!" she gasped. "I knew, when I saw Fabian's face that—that—"

Edna could not think beyond the nearest thing, which was that Daphne must not break down, must not lose her self-control again. Edna was a herbalist as well as a gardener. She opened the French window and picked a stalk growing close to it, for it was valerian, the *officinalis*.

"Here, chew these leaves! Don't mind the taste. They'll help to steady your nerves."

Daphne snatched at it and then dropped it to the floor.

"Don't leave me, Edna! Don't let them talk to me," she began, but her half-sister silenced her with a squeeze on her arm not very different from a pinch.

CHAPTER TWELVE

THE doctor happened to be just starting out to see a patient and was able to be at Fairlawn almost before Mr. Amplett had replaced the receiver.

Doubleday knew the Cautleys and the Ampletts well. He wasted no words as he strode to the twisted body on the floor and bent over it. He sniffed the face, he lifted the eyelids—and seemed struck by what he found.

"What happened?" he asked the Ampletts, for Jack had turned away as though speech was beyond him.

Mr. Amplett explained that Lionel wanted to write an important letter and said that he did not want to be disturbed. He, Amplett, had left him screwing the cap off his fountain pen... This was how he had next seen him.

"Is he taking any medicine, or drugs of any kind?" Doubleday asked.

Amplett looked towards Jack, who shook his head. "Not as far as I know. What killed him?"

"Heart failure," came the instant reply. "What caused the heart failure is the question. There'll have to be an autopsy, of course."

"Not in here!" came firmly from Mrs. Amplett. Doubleday reassured her.

"Sent word to the police yet?" he asked.

Jack said that he would do so, but Amplett shook his head for once and himself reached for the instrument. He very briefly asked the sergeant to let Superintendent Wanklyn know that Mr. Lionel Cautley had just been found dead in one of the rooms at Fairlawn.

"What a ridiculous way of putting it!" Mrs. Amplett began to recover herself again. "It sounds as though we had something to do with his death!"

"Well, he did die here!" her husband reminded her, rather tartly for once. "It's very awkward," he breathed into the telephone, "not being able to touch him or move him. He's lying on the floor! It's a very trying sight for us all. Please come as quickly as you can!"

There was no need to add that. Todd set out at once at a sort of jog-trot for the house, while the sergeant stood in the road and watched, shading his eyes, for the superintendent's car.

To Wanklyn, leaning out for a perfunctory question as he drew up with Pointer, the sergeant hurriedly told the news, and Wanklyn, after one incredulous start, fairly churned up the road ahead. Todd was caught up with before they reached the gate, and jumped on the running-board.

"He's escaped us!" was all Wanklyn said between set teeth.

They were taken at once to the room where the doctor and Amplett still stood talking in low tones. Jack Cautley was not to be seen, nor were any of the women present. Daphne was on her bed having a sort of shuddering fit, and Edna, white and silent, was trying to soothe her.

Wanklyn would have left it to the chief inspector to take the lead, but the other directed him by a wave of the hand to carry on for the moment. He himself stood back and a little apart from the group, letting his eyes rest first on the dead, then on the living.

The door opened noiselessly and Jack Cautley looked in. Pointer placed him from a family resemblance to the dead man, and from Wanklyn's description, but his face was not pleasant and smiling now; it looked deeply shocked. Then the door closed once more, and Amplett continued his short account of how the body was found, by whom, and when.

"What do you think caused the death?" asked Wanklyn of Dr. Doubleday, or, as he liked to be called, Colonel Doubleday, R.A.M.C.

"As I was just saying to Mr. Amplett, it takes me back to my time in India. *Bikh* or *Vikh* is what I put it down to, and I ought to know. It has a dozen other names as well. The hill tribes use it constantly. It's one of the ingredients of the poison used for the blowpipe arrows. Aconite in our language would be it's nearest equivalent. And, by jove, some of the finest aconitum I've ever seen are to be found in the corner of the gardens here near the old stile. The true *Aconitum Ferox* too. Well, we shall soon know if I've guessed wrong," and he offered his help at the p.m. The police doctor was a friend of his.

For a moment, while the superintendent, a clever photographer, took some photographs of the body, they stood looking down at it. By the look of him, Lionel Cautley must have died in great agony.

"Is this poison that you suspect quick-acting?" Pointer asked.

He was told that it was not comparable in that respect with strychnine. Like arsenic, all would depend on the amount taken, on the strength of the dose in other words. The room was cleared of all but the police officers and the doctor.

The body was next stripped. There was not a mark or a bruise to be seen on it.

"Queer!" Doubleday said aloud to the room in general. "One cousin found dead lying over a stile after shooting himself, or being shot. The other cousin found dead in a room after having taken poison, or having it given him..."

Finding that he got no answer, for he was not the police surgeon, but, as Wanklyn knew—and there again he held that he scored—one of the greatest gossips of the place. Dr. Doubleday rather bruskly took his departure.

Wanklyn looked at the chief inspector with eyes that were alight. "He's slipped through our fingers unfortunately, but his killing of himself shows I was right."

"Painful death to choose," Pointer said looking at the awful face on the floor with deep pity. "His face shows

him to've been a man of unusual imaginative powers..
Apart from the fact that he's an explorer. You have to be
imaginative to leave your own hole and corner."

Any objection on Pointer's part, like any suggestion,
was met with great respect on the part of any member of
the force.

"Granted. But he was pressed for time. The insurance
company's solicitor was starting to make himself nasty.
And after that—we find this. Pretty conclusive, I call it.
He had the stuff on him, ready."

"Painful   stuff   is   all   I   say.   And   not   even
instantaneous."

"You don't agree with me?" Wanklyn looked surprised.

"I neither agree nor disagree yet," Pointer murmured.
"All that one can say so far is that, supposing the doctor
is right, and supposing the poison to be obtained,
possibly, from those aconitums in the garden to which he
referred, then any one in the house, in a desperate hurry,
might have thought of them too. Whereas, frankly, I don't
quite see why Mr. Lionel, who, if guilty, must have known
that he would have to see the insurance company more
than once about those missing pearls, should have chosen
just that form of death. It's just because I, too, think it
looks like haste that I don't see that it points especially to
Lionel Cautley."

Wanklyn was uneasily conscious of the truth of this.
As the chief inspector spoke he was looking over the dead
body again.

"He seems to've been doing something with those
flowers," he now said again in a tone of triumph. "There's
earth under his nails and some scattered on the carpet.
By heavens! I wonder if he had the pearls on him all the
time and tried to hide them—" Wanklyn took one stride
towards where, against the wall, rose a tall, oblong
mirror whose foot rested on the floor. Against this foot a
row of hothouse flowers and ferns were planted in a gilt
flower-box.

Pointer restrained him with a glance. "Better have another look. I wouldn't touch those pots for a second."

"Why not?" Wanklyn asked in surprise.

"Well, don't you see that Mr. Lionel only has earth on the very tips of his fingers, the very tips of his nails, one might say. There is none in the quicks, none, above all, on the palms, which isn't what one would expect to find on the hands of the man who took out that cineraria there and plumped it down again. Look at the earth around that fern. It's been pressed in by some one's knuckles—there's no soil on this man's."

"You think?" Wanklyn asked, stopping dead where he stood.

"Well, it rather suggests that another pair of hands than this poor chap's did the gardening in this room—and this rather suggests the same sort of an idea." Pointer held up a waistcoat. "See the way these papers have been thrust into the pockets, jabbed in anyhow as into a paper bag. Yet they show that a rubber band was once around them. There's no band in his pockets. There's just a dust of earth on this one... and the confusion, the way they're jumbled..."

"Does it mean anything to you?" Wanklyn asked. He was wandering in a dark labyrinth, but he felt that the man with him would always have a light to go by, the light of his reasoning powers.

Pointer straightened up and looked at Wanklyn's furrowed brow.

"They suggest that some one has been in here before us. Either he noticed the earth marks on the dead man's fingers, or he had reason to suspect that something might be buried in those flowers or carried in Mr. Lionel's pockets."

"'He'? Not 'she'?"

"It might be a 'she,' but, if so, she has wide knuckles and a very firm fist thrust. For which assertion see that earth around the fern there."

Pointer now had stooped to one side of the mantel-shelf of polished oak and getting his eye on a level with it, was looking along it. Wanklyn followed suit on the other end, and gave a grunt of suppressed excitement and pleasure.

"Those marks in the dust there by that picture! By jove, they look just as though made by round beads."

Pointer agreed that the three marks in question and the sort of vague scumble around them did suggest beads. Certainly something of that shape had lain there not so long ago. A wood fire coats mantel and room in a couple of hours with a cloud of fine ash. "Those marks were made by the Cautley pearls!" Wanklyn said in a low but assured voice. "By the missing pearls. I knew I was right! He got them away from the Major, and now some one's taken them off him, and he's had to pay the same price himself—his life. Looks to me as if he had known his danger and tried to hide them. Yes,"—Wanklyn was warming to his work—"it looks as if he had laid the pearls down on the mantel, and then something happened, or some one came in, and he had to try to hide them. Or burn them... but they were gotten away from him in the end, Can you burn artificial pearls, I wonder?" he asked the chief inspector.

Pointer knew the answer to that question. Heat would probably turn the beads into a sticky, smelly mess of melted, blackened wax and soap. No such marks were to be found among the ashes on the hearth, of that the two men made quite sure.

"I think that much of it is clear," Wanklyn said.

"Have you any idea why Mr. Cautley didn't wait and do whatever you think he did to, or with, the pearls at the Cottage rather than here?" Pointer asked. "Assuming, for the time being, that the marks on the mantel were really made by the pearls?"

"I think it's time we have a word with Mr. Amplett," Wanklyn said to that. "We may learn something from him that will make it plain."

They asked for the master of the house. Wanklyn often called him that in irony when referring to him. Just at the moment they could hear him being violently censured by Mrs. Amplett for allowing Lionel Cautley to lock himself in. She seemed to think that he should have foreseen all that had happened, which she appeared to consider as the direct result. She came in with Amplett now, and briskly mentioned a few of her hopes. She hoped that the police would not be long. She hoped that as little as possible would be disturbed. She hoped that the ambulance would not delay in coming. She hoped that the inquest would show the truth, which was, "of course," that poor Lionel Cautley had a weak heart. She hoped that... She was finally shown into another room, to her intense indignation, as soon as the detective officer and the superintendent had made quite sure that she had nothing but hopes with which to regale them.

Amplett drew a deep breath as she disappeared, and promptly offered his companions something in glasses. They refused, but he took a whisky and soda himself.

Both thought that, considering Mrs. Amplett, he did well.

His story of what had happened was this:

Lionel Cautley had dropped in around twelve to see his fiancée. "Something about those pearls, so she has told me—preparatory to getting everything all clear before the insurance company's solicitor should be here again. His train was due at five-thirty. As Miss Upjohn is staying here, it had been thought best to have the solicitor in question come here instead of going to the Cottage. Well, they had their talk. Oh, yes, Mr. Harbord was here too. He had come earlier—on the chance that the solicitor might come this morning. Well, where was I?" Mr. Amplett plunged into his glass again, to return to the surface refreshed and to continue. "It's all dreadfully awkward. I mean about those pearls—and that idea of giving them back to the Major like that... Oh, yes, and Fabian Cautley dropped in too. Just to ask a question about the estate and Mason. Mrs. Amplett was in Woodhampton for the morning. My secretary had brought me down some rather important papers to sign. We were working through them when Lionel came in and asked for a word alone with me. Well, of course, people usually want to see Mrs. Amplett. I mean—well, it's often a bit awkward getting away by oneself, but as she was out. I took Lionel into the morning-room. This room. He was looking very odd. Very. It's difficult to express it in words, but he seemed to have shrunk. You know, Wanklyn, Mr. Lionel Cautley's way of carrying his shoulders, his head up and back, his eyes on a level with the chimney pots?"

Amplett looked across to Wanklyn for support. The superintendent gave it at once. "I do, sir. Like the Major. In fact, from the back you might mistake one for the other."

"Well, that was all gone. He dragged his feet, or seemed to. His shoulders were almost hunched. He walked as though dog-tired. When we were by ourselves and the door shut—oh, and also the window—he closed the catch of that himself, I remember—he seemed—" Amplett took a deep drink this time, "he seemed to collapse, inwardly if not outwardly. He sat and stared at me with a face older than his grandfather's. Lined and haggard. At last he said he would like to write a long letter. Could he do so where he was? Of course I said that he didn't need to ask. And he didn't. But he only said in the same low, hollow tone that he needed quiet to write what he was going to. So I left him, after seeing that there was plenty of paper on one of the tables by the window."

"By the window," Wanklyn repeated in the tone of one who intends to remember the position—one which might explain a good deal.

Amplett nodded. "After a few minutes I stepped back for another word, but I found the door locked. I'm bound to say I thought that just a bit awkward. I mean, my wife often goes in there. Her work-bag is still hanging on one of the chair-backs, and had she wanted it—" His expression finished the sentence better than words— "Still, I couldn't very well say so. But I was a bit anxious. I mean, Mrs. Amplett might well have thought he ought to use the study, my room, not a general room... I tried the handle more than once, hoping that he might take the hint and hurry up. I even went to the window and tapped on it. I couldn't see into the room and I hardly liked to be too fussy. After all, he was my guest..." and Amplett murmured something out of which they caught the words "very awkward."

"But where is the letter he wrote?" Wanklyn asked. "We found no trace of anything written. Nor papers in his writing anywhere."

"I don't know," Amplett said very slowly. "I wondered whether he found that he couldn't, or didn't want to, write anything. From his face and the way he sat slumped in his chair as I went out, I shouldn't be at all astonished if he had just sat on—desperate—or whatever he was—until he jumped up and took something..."

"Aspirin?" Wanklyn asked sharply.

Amplett only looked unhappy. "Whatever it was he did finally take," he said with a sigh. "It's all horrible! Horrible! I thought at the time that he was right not to try to talk just then. I had no idea what he meant to write down, but I think if I had stayed... Only at the time I never thought..." Amplett let his sentence die away.

"Who was in the house when you left Mr. Cautley?" Pointer asked. "I mean, whom did you yourself see in the house? And whom in the garden?" And Amplett was taken backwards and forwards over the people under his roof. It finally seemed clear that practically every one in the house could also be in the garden at any time, that only Mrs. Amplett was definitely away from Fairlawn for the greater part of the time during which that door had been locked, although Mr. Amplett did not know at what time Jack Cautley had got back from London—he had not

seen him come in—that Mr. Amplett had no idea when
Fabian left, or Harbord, or what the girls were doing.

"Now what made you think that Mr. Cautley locked
himself in?" Pointer asked when the question of
everybody's whereabouts had been thoroughly gone into.

"I found the door locked," Amplett repeated in a
wondering tone.

"Yes, but did you hear Mr. Cautley turn the key at
once after you left him? The point is," the chief inspector
explained, "was it Mr. Cautley who locked the door from
the inside, or some one else who locked it from the
outside?"

Amplett looked taken aback. "But you found the key
in his pocket when you examined the body!" he protested.

"A key, yes. There was also a key in the outside of the
door when we got here," Pointer said.

Amplett explained that the key of the bathroom door
fitted the room in question.

"I confess the idea of trying whether one of the other
keys wouldn't open the door never occurred to me at the
time. I don't—always—think of things at the right
moment," he added, apologetically.

"How could Miss Daphne Upjohn know about it
fitting?" Wanklyn asked.

"As it happens we had mentioned it, my wife had, only
yesterday—apropos of reading in the paper about some
one who had died in his bath before the door could be
broken open. Mrs. Amplett had said that she always tried
to give elderly people a certain bedroom because the
nearest bathroom could be opened by the study key, and
she always asked them not to bolt, only to lock the door,
so that in case of an accident it would be a simple matter
to help them."

"So that any one could have let himself into the room
where Mr. Lionel Cautley was lying dead and have put
the key of the room into Mr. Cautley's pocket. They could
then have left by the door, locking it behind them with
the bathroom key?" Pointer said.

Amplett looked appalled. "I never thought of that," he murmured. "Of course I took it for granted—you do when you find a door locked—that the man inside has locked it—but, now you put it to me, I didn't hear him turn the key!"

"When you came back to try the door, did you hear anything at all from inside the room?" Pointer wanted to know.

"Nothing whatever."

"By the way, we found an empty bottle of aspirins behind a portrait on the mantel. Do you know how it got there?" Wanklyn asked.

"That belongs to Miss Upjohn. Miss Daphne Upjohn. She swears by aspirin. So does he. They take it as other people take cocktails."

"How did it come to be in this particular room?" Pointer wanted to know. Amplett explained that the room was used of an evening as a sort of general sitting-room, as well as of a morning. "It's far and away the most comfortable room in the house, except my library," he finished. "But I'm safe in saying that there's another bottle of aspirin standing behind the Chinese dog in the drawing-room on a little table. Mr. Cautley got into the habit of taking the stuff because of his malaria. And apparently Miss Upjohn takes it whenever she feels nervy or worried—when she finds a ladder in her stocking—or her frock doesn't suit her," Mr. Amplett added dryly. "Mr. Cautley gave her that very bottle. I remember Jack asking if it would figure among the presents from the bridegroom to the bride.'"

When Amplett had nothing more to tell them, they asked to see Miss Daphne Upjohn. She sent down word that she was not well enough. Edna brought the message. The police had to let it go. They had no right to insist. And if ever a girl might be supposed to have had a shock it would be Lionel's fiancée today.

"The trouble with Mr. Amplett is, even if Mr. Lionel had let a word drop about what he meant to do, he wouldn't let on. Not ever! Old friend of the Major's. But one thing seems to be certain, that is that the pearls have gone on another journey. Those marks there in the dust—" Wanklyn was deeply puzzled.

"Suppose we have another look at them," Pointer suggested. Wanklyn wondered why? He could have drawn the little round spots of clear wood among the gray ash dust, but they went into the morning-room again.

Wanklyn strode to the mantel and gave a snap of his fingers.

"Some one has been dusting in here! Aggravating things servants are!"

"Only dusted the mantel-shelf, I see," Pointer said meaningly.

Wanklyn stepped out again. A word with a constable, unobtrusively watching the room, told him that only Miss Edna had gone in since the body of Lionel Cautley had been carried out. She had stepped to the hearth and stood there a moment, then taken the ornamental feather-duster down that hung beside the mantel, and just flicked it over the woodwork. She had not touched anything else, and had left the room almost at once.

Wanklyn asked for her. She came in immediately. Had she by any chance seen a pencil lying on the mantel-shelf just now? Edna mentioned her dusting with what seemed indifference, but Wanklyn stared at her. This death of Lionel Cautley—one could understand that it would be a most terrible shock, but even so—the skin of Edna's brown little face seemed tautened like the skin of a drum. Her very lips, were drawn and pale. Was it possible that she had cared for the man who was engaged to her younger sister? Why had she dusted those marks away, those suggestive marks in the dust? She said that she constantly dusted in here, that a wood fire made this necessary... But just after a death in that very room? However, there was nothing that could be said. Until they had the doctor's report in their hands, the police could not move. Lionel's death might prove to be heart failure pure and simple, brought on by the over-exertion of his last climbing expedition and his cousin's death.

"Nothing else, is there?" Wanklyn asked the chief inspector after Edna had been allowed to return to her half-sister upstairs, and return with a hurried stumbling headlong gait very unlike Edna's light, gay step. "Nothing else changed in the room?"

"Nothing. I wanted to see if by any chance a ball of wool had been returned, supposing, as I think very possible, one was taken away."

Pointer was looking through Mrs. Amplett's workbag hanging on a chair-back. The chair itself stood beside a little table to which was screwed a circular wool-winder on which the last of a skein of wool was still stretched.

"This wool was violently pulled, not cut—" Pointer held out the dangling end from the winder. "A few more turns and the skein would have been finished. Where's the ball into which it was wound? There's a brown very like it indeed, but not quite the same shade, not the same—"

Wanklyn was turning them over. The balls of wool were large, almost as big as small coconuts, oval in shape, very loosely wound. Pointer parted one with his fingers and showed it to be wound around a cone of tissue paper.

"I follow your meaning!" Wanklyn murmured, dropping his voice and keeping one eye on the closed door. "Suppose some one wanted to get the pearls out of the room—they tugged at the ball until the wool finally broke, stuffed the pearls into the paper core and took them off in it. Not one person in a hundred would have noticed that there was no ball in the bag that exactly matched the wool on that winder." He spoke in open admiration.

"The trouble is that not one person in a hundred would notice whether the ball was attached to the skein when they were in the room," Pointer added with a wry half-smile. "No one can be questioned directly, and it's not an easy point to clear up by a casual question."

"Well, it's not an important point, fortunately," Wanklyn said, after a moment's thought. "I mean, how the pearls were taken out of the house—barring the fact that it rather suggests a woman's having been here—but the only thing that really matters is the fact that the pearls are gone, and that some one was in the study before we were summoned... That bathroom key had been used before Miss Daphne stepped in, I take it! Unless she searched those plants before letting out that shriek they speak of... no one would notice at such a moment whether her fingers had earth on them or not... Miss Daphne and Mr. Lionel and those pearls all seem to go together... The pearls that lay on the mantel." Wanklyn eyed it hungrily. He felt that he would give five years of his life to see them lying there in front of him. If he had lost the criminal, he would then at least have had the spoils to show for his labors.

He led the way out to his car again. Dr. Doubleday had promised to telephone at once to the police-station as soon as he had anything definite to report from the autopsy.

"I know one thing," Wanklyn said as he pressed the self-starter, "once we know the death to be due to poison, I'll put it to Mr. Amplett that there was something fishy about those pearls, and he'll open up. He's timid, and he's a nervous little man, but he'll help us all right once he knows that there was murder done. He's doubtful about the Major's death, but he'll be certain about this, if Dr. Doubleday was right in what he said, and then we may learn something helpful."

Pointer decided that he would rather walk. He wanted to have a look at the Cottage and, if possible, have a word with the other two Cautley cousins, and the clever Mr. Harbord. Wanklyn had to hurry back to his station, and so the chief inspector stepped lightly out and turned up towards the little thatched roof that he could just see from where they stood.

There seemed to be no one about. The Cottage's front bell evidently did not ring, as a trial showed. There was a tiny brass knocker, more for looks than use. A few minutes' work with, it showed that either no one was in, or that they had not heard the small clatter made by it.

Yet, listening, Pointer thought that there was some one in the little house. He heard, dimly, an odd sound that he could not quite place. Was some one beating out something? No, it was not quite like that. Was it something pattering on leather? Not quite that either. Pointer tried the front door. It opened at a touch. Wanklyn had said that it was never locked except at night—if then. He stepped into a room running across the front of the little building, living-room and lounge in one, evidently. The odd sounds reached him clearer now, but they still baffled him. He was only sure of two things about them, one was that he had never heard just their like before, and the other was that he would not forget them again. Not ever.

CHAPTER THIRTEEN

POINTER went to the little stairs that rose up from the back of the room. Mounting them and following the sounds, he laid his hand lightly on a door at the end of a little passage. it was locked on the inside, with the key still in the lock. Pointer stood for a fraction of a second. He had never heard sounds which, without knowing their origin, he disliked more. Was a child being beaten inside there, for an odd stifled sort of whimpering reached him? On the instant he took out a peculiar tool from his inner pocket, gripped the end of the key with it and turned. The door opened and he stepped in. He was not in the least prepared for what he saw.

On the floor, in the center of the room, knelt a man. He was stripped. One hand grasped the seat of a chair across which he had half fallen, the other was wielding a short stick to which ends of rope were knotted. The ends were stained with blood. Blood was running in little rivulets down the bare back of the man and dripping to the floor. It was Fabian Cautley as Pointer guessed, and he was plying what is called a discipline. There was a look of agony on his face with the lips drawn back from his clenched teeth, his eyes tight shut, but the rope-ends rose and fell with almost mechanical regularity.

To see a body maltreated is a horrible sight— unnatural, and in some deep way impious. But Pointer made no effort to interfere or even question the man. The chief inspector was not in the least psychic. He was far too intelligent for that. But this man was ringed about with an unseen circle that no one could have crossed. Inside the scorching flame of some deep and terrible passion Fabian Cautley writhed and suffered. It was no acting. The back showed signs of many scourgings such as this, half-healed stripes which were now opening

again. And the man was quite unconscious of the
presence of any one else in the room, of that the chief
inspector was certain too. That line of passion and agony
which he had somehow managed to draw around himself
blotted out all the world for him, like the herbs strewn on
glowing embers by a necromancer before he begins his
spells. That last comparison struck the chief inspector as
the right one. This was some ceremony of expiation or
exorcism. He thought the latter. He felt, as the scourge
rose and fell, that the wielder of it loathed that on which
it fell, loathed it and hated it, and feared it.

Suddenly the arm slackened. The scourge dropped to
the floor, the kneeling man turned his head with its
clenched teeth, its look of agony. The eyes, bloodshot and
gray-circled, stared full at Pointer, but blankly. Pointer
on the instant left the room and the house. In another
moment those eyes would focus, and the mind behind
them would register clearly. He himself was deeply
shocked by what he had seen. No man can look unmoved
down into the abyss of a soul. Outside in the garden he
filled his lungs with the cool fresh air. What lay behind
him in that upper room belonged to another world than
this of sunshine and flowers. At the gate a constable
stepped forward and saluted. It was Todd. He jerked his
head towards the little house.

"He's in there, Isn't he, sir? I mean that Father
Fabian? I followed him back here from Fairlawn just now.
He was hiding in the garden there, just where he would
have been had he stepped out of the French window of
that room where Mr. Lionel was found." There was a
world of meaning in the man's voice.

"You think there was a connection?" Pointer asked.
With that dreadful picture of the man upstairs mangling
his flesh, he knew that there must be one.

"I know there is, sir," Todd said firmly. "I never did
think otherwise. We met that Father Fabian with blood
on his hands the night the Major was shot, and we find

him on the spot the day when Mr. Lionel is found dead. And he's the third in the *prodest* line."

"In what line, constable?" Pointer asked with interest.

"The *quis prodest* line, sir. That's what our superintendent calls it, and he's never far out. What I says now is we'll have to keep an eye on Mr. Jack. For his own sake. Or he'll be found next run over by a car, or drowned, or something—"

"Does the superintendent agree?" Pointer asked.

Todd was a democratic soul, who was not even awed by the high position of the man from the Yard, and to whom his own superintendent was but as an admired elder brother. "You may be sure he does, sir," was the diplomatic but fervent answer. "I want a word with Mr. Jack when he comes this way. He's the sort never to think of danger. And it's my opinion that that's a very dangerous kind to be just now." Todd saluted and fell back. He intended to wait on in the cottage garden unless fetched by duty, and the chief inspector promised to explain to the man's superior where he was. He himself walked on deep in meditation. He put the scene that he had just witnessed out of his mind entirely. He went back to the account of Major Cautley's death, and to all that was known of the pearls. Along with it he placed in his mind the death of Lionel Cautley.

The two deaths seemed definitely, indubitably, linked by the common string of pearls. If the two deaths were not connected, or connected by some other motive, then the fact that the "pearl mix-up" had run along at just the same time seemed a singular coincidence. The pearls known to have been copied—the originals and the copy both missing... The owner, and the man who had at least temporarily had them in his keeping, both dead... Pointer saw no ghost of a reason to set such an assumption on one side. But the fact remained that a large fortune had now changed hands for the second time, and that Jack Cautley had no better alibi than had had Lionel when the Major, was shot—than had the third in line supposing

Lionel not to have made a will—this Fabian Cautley
whose dreadful image, pain-wracked, streaked with
blood, rose up before the chief inspector again.

He knew from Wanklyn that, as far as the police could
find out, only Lionel had been seen during the hours of
the alibi which he had given himself and been given by
Jack. Neither of the two other cousins had been proved to
be near the stile or the "hide" at the fatal hour, but both
were known to have been near, or at, Fairlawn just now,
when Lionel was found dead.

No, nothing to lay a firm grasp on. Wanklyn was right
in that much. It was all just suspicions guess-work.

And the visitor down at the Cottage, Harbord, was it
possible that he stood for anything in this tangle? Had
the real necklace ever been in his hands? That curious
way of returning an heirloom, was that Lionel's idea? If
not, whose? Miss Daphne Upjohn had left them to be
copied. She had fetched the imitation necklace... Pointer
began to see a possibility here, but on the other hand, she
and Lionel might, as the superintendent sometimes
thought, have been working together. Who could so easily
have poisoned Lionel as his fellow criminal and fiancée,
supposing him to have died of poison as Dr. Doubleday
believed? Nothing could be done until that fact was
proved and the poison named.

To Wanklyn the two hours that passed before
Doubleday spoke to him on the telephone seemed never-
ending. The aspirin bottle was too coated with a mass of
fingerprints for any of them to be disentangled. The
insurance company's solicitor had been rung up and
explained that his talk with Mr. Cautley had been
entirely unofficial, a mere paving of the way, should any
claim be put forward for the loss of the pearl necklace
which had been insured with them. The solicitor had
mentioned to Mr. Cautley that they had been apprized by
the police of the existence of an imitation of the necklace
in question, and spoke of the possibility of its being only
the duplicate that was missing. Mr. Cautley had agreed

that very possibly this was the case, and had added that, in any event, no claim would be made until the whole affair had been very carefully thrashed out.

He had arranged with the solicitor to call again this afternoon, when he expected to be able definitely to tell him whether or not it had been the duplicate which had been returned in error to Major Cautley. The interview had been most friendly on both sides. Then at last word came from the doctors. Lionel Cautley had died of aconite poison. A pellet of a particularly virulent kind of aconite root, *aconitum ferox*, had been found undigested in his stomach, along with at least an equal amount of aconite which had killed him. So far, no other poison had been tried for, as a fatal dose was clearly shown in the amount already discovered.

The one found whole was dispatched to the police station by a messenger. It was just the size and shape of an aspirin tablet, they found, but its color was light dun.

"And now, I suppose," Pointer said to Wanklyn, "you're going to see if Mr. Amplett will be able to help the inquiry."

"I think he may, must, be able to tell us something about Miss Daphne's movements and possibly Mr. Lionel's. He may have handed the pearls to Miss Daphne. Mr. Lionel may, I mean." Wanklyn thought this very likely. "In that ball of brown wool. No one has left Fairlawn. I couldn't post any one inside, of course, until I got the medical report, but I placed a man back and front to see who came and left. It's my belief—now—that the two of them were in this together. And just as he got rid of the Major when he got in the way, I think she's got rid of Mr. Lionel. It would leave her the pearls—"

"And lose her a wealthy husband?" Pointer asked.

"Ah, but I don't think Mr. Lionel would have married her—not after what they had gone through together. Knowing the Cautleys, I don't for a moment believe that he meant things to go so far. No, like many another man, he took one step, and then found he couldn't stop himself from sliding all the way down. But, as I see it, he wouldn't want to marry Miss Daphne after it. He would have shown this—and she decided to get him out of the way."

And where, thought the chief inspector, did Fabian Cautley stand in all this? The superintendent's idea of how things might be was quite feasible, but why was Fabian Cautley scourging himself till the blood ran? And what of Jack Cautley, the new inheritor?

As they walked up to Fairlawn he told the superintendent of what he had just seen. Wanklyn frowned, puzzled. "May not have anything to do with it all," he murmured, rather half-heartedly. "I can't see where he would fit into this affair of the pearls—You mean?"—he started—"you mean about the use of monkshood root? Same kind of monkshood as Dr. Doubleday says they use to make *Bikh* with in India. And Fabian Cautley was in the Indian Forests... and had to leave them and this brings him forward to the position of next but one..." Wanklyn bit his lip. Things were very complicated.

Meanwhile, as soon as the police had left Fairlawn, Amplett had called Edna to him. Like a pale ghost she came.

"I want a word with Daphne. Immediately."

Edna stared dully. She did not recognize the firm tone and inflexible eye. Fond though she was of her guardian, she rather liked the change, but not the reason for it.

"You can't, guardie. She's really ill."

"I'll give her exactly five minutes by the clock to be well enough to hear what I have to say and to answer my questions," was the reply, and Edna was not so sure that she liked the new Mr. Amplett after all.

"You can't see her in five minutes," she now said in a whisper. "As a matter of fact, Frank Harbord is here, and she and he are talking things over together. It seems that Lionel thought—was afraid that—" she hesitated. Her brown eyes were fixed on his with painful intensity.

Amplett hesitated. "Look here, Edna," he said under his breath, "do you think Lionel killed himself?"

Edna had her back now to him. She leaned her forehead on her arm which lay on the mantel-shelf. Her attitude was one of utter despondency, almost of despair, one would have said.

"She thinks so," she said finally in a stifled voice. "Poor Daphne! She believed that he was so—worried over the pearls that he killed himself."

"How did Harbord get here?" Amplett asked, after a second's pause.

"I sent for him," Edna replied. "She was in such an agony of regret about the way in which the pearls had been given back. It seems that—" Edna hesitated, but Mr. Amplett had a right to the truth. "It seems that Lionel suspected—believed—that whoever put the pearls into Major Cautley's pocket in that way, could have got them out again. He as good as told Daphne that he believed Frank Harbord took those pearls."

"And Daphne?" Amplett asked.

"That was what they quarreled over. And she—that was why she was so keen on seeing him again.' She waited until she couldn't bear it any longer, and then rushed upstairs for the bathroom key to open the door and have it out with him again."

There was a short silence.

"What do you yourself think about the pearls?" Amplett asked. "It's all so awkward—"

"I think Lionel was all wrong. I think he was jealous of Frank Harbord and quite unconsciously believed something—anything—that would put him in the wrong. I think the Major sent the pearls somewhere, perhaps to a jeweler to have some alterations made—I noticed that he looked at the clasp very carefully as the necklace lay with it uppermost in the case. I think in time they'll be found. That's what makes it all so horrible!" There was a passion in the tone with which the last sentence was said that quite startled Mr. Amplett. He noticed now for the first time how ill she looked. She seemed to have grown thinner. But his mind was fixed for the moment on Daphne.

"My talk with her is absolutely necessary," he said now with a renewal of his new manner. "And if Harbord is here, so much the better. We shall know where we stand. Where are they, Edna?"

As though in reply, a door was opened with a sort of bang, and as it did so, Daphne's voice could be heard, imploring and tearful-sounding, "I do love you, Frank, but—"

Amplett turned and stared at Edna, who bit her lip. "Daphne loves young Frank Harbord? Since when?" he asked under his breath.

"She says since she first met him," Edna replied in the same dull tone. "And I think she really does. For the first time. She didn't care a hang for Jack. Poor old Jack had nothing to attract Daphne. And she now says she found out as soon as she came here that she was making a mistake in getting engaged to Lionel. But I think she really is in love with Frank Harbord."

"That's a car coming up," Amplett said half absentmindedly. "Probably the police. I'm too late. I wanted to prepare Daphne. You'd better tell her to expect a grilling interview, my dear," and Amplett went out into the hall, for it was the police who had driven up, and he was anxious for a word first with them.

Edna put her hands over her eyes for a moment, then she went. to her own room, where Daphne was now lying in an armchair.

"I'll never speak to another man as long as I live!" Daphne sobbed. "They're all alike! Horrid things! Only thinking of themselves!"

"You'd better imitate them." Edna's tone was anxious. "It seems that the police are back here, and guardie seems to feel sure they'll want a talk with you."

"I can't see anybody. I'm ill!" came in stifled tones from Daphne.

"You can't get back to your bedroom now, they're in the hall." Edna's quick ears had located the sounds correctly. "Daphne darling, what is wrong? Don't put me off any more. It's too serious. Something terrible is the matter."

"Oh, yes, poor Lionel!" wailed Daphne. "How was any one to know? To guess? He always seemed so strong. And he was so frightfully angry and unjust..." She buried her head in the cushions.

Edna stared down at her with a sort of shudder. There came a tap on the door.

"Pull yourself together," she begged.

But it was she herself whom the police wanted, not her sister. On learning this, Edna did not move for a full second, then she went quietly out of the room and down to where Mr. Amplett, the superintendent and a stranger to her, were standing talking together. The tall, upright, soldierly man was introduced to her as Chief Inspector Pointer of New Scotland Yard.

Mr. Amplett took her hand and held it. She stared dumbly at the expression of pity on his face. Her heart seemed to stop beating.

"My dear girl, prepare yourself for a dreadful shock," Amplett began, "I've asked to be allowed to break the news to you, but I have to do it in the presence of the police. Lionel didn't die from heart trouble " He paused.

Edna turned ghastly white. Without a word, she turned her pallid face inquiringly first to her guardian, then to the police, especially to the chief inspector. She trembled a little as she waited.

"He died from poison," Amplett said finally. "Here, you'd better sit down! This has been too much for you. Small wonder!" But she did not take the chair he moved towards her. She clung to his hand instead, her dilated eyes looking too large for her face.

"Quick! Oh, quick, please!" she said imploringly. "What poison?"

"From a form of aconitum poisoning," he said slowly.
"Now, Edna, these gentlemen want you to show them all
the aconitums we have in the garden." He had to repeat a
second time what was wanted. "Aconitums—garden—"
She seemed to recover herself. "I'll show them the wild
garden where the monkshood grows," she said at once, in
a tone of such relief that the two officers looked at her,
Wanklyn with approval, Pointer more speculatively. And
at a good round pace she led the way. Amplett had been
asked to stay behind. The men wanted Edna alone.

"The monkshood was here when I took over the
gardens. It has never been shifted. They're shut in by a
little trellis fence—it's covered with creepers so that you
can hardly see it as a fence, but it would prevent any
child getting at the plants—" She was leading the way to
a corner of the grounds where stood an ash, a chestnut
and a lime tree, along with lilacs of venerable age. The
vivid, metallic green of monkshood leaves shown from
under the shade where stood an artificial well-head of
brick and thatch, over whose edge bluebells nodded and
ferns showed. Tall Himalayan lilies were in the
background.

"What sort of monkshood are they?" Pointer asked. He
knew a good deal about them from the coastguard's
cottage down in Devon where he had been born.

"These outside ones are *Fortunei* and *Napellus*, those
over there are *Wilsoni*, and the innermost ones are
Aconitum Ferox. Very deadly, but as they're never
handled except with gloves on, and then only to keep
them from spreading too much—" She stopped abruptly
and in a second had swung herself over the three foot
high greenery which ran across the corner from hedge to
hedge. The two men were at her side as she did so.

"There's one gone!" She seemed amazed. "One of the
Feroxes is gone. We had three, two at the back, one a
little in front. The one in front is missing. You can see
where the leaves have been drawn over the place here."

Pointer felt the ground. Yes, it was much looser, much more yielding here than elsewhere. It had quite recently been disturbed.

Edna leaned forward. "The root has been taken away. Look at that wilting greenery. It's been moved. Wait a moment!" A quite unnecessary injunction as she turned and jumped lightly over the fence again, Wanklyn with her. "Let me help you," he offered, "can I get anything for you?"

She only shook her head, but he did not think that she realized that his kind offers were merely to cloak the fact that she was not to be allowed to hurry off like that without supervision. She almost ran to a tool-house, snatched a pair of thick gloves from a nail, and a trowel and small fork from an empty flower-pot and then returned to the corner at a run. In a second she was kneeling where she said the third *Aconitum Ferox* had stood and was digging at the ground with the fork.

"Just as I thought!" She brought up with some effort a long piece of root broken off where it began to broaden out.

"Some one's dug up the plant, broken the root in getting it up, left these bits in the ground and stuck the tops into the earth again." She sat back on her heels and mechanically, filled in and smoothed over the ground.

She had forked up sufficient of the broken root end for the two men, watching her intently, each to take some. Each experimented—with his gloves on—as to how it could be cut. It was like a horseradish root in its texture. A penknife could easily whittle it into pellets sufficiently like those of aspirin. Each had a certainty, since the pellet sent to them to see, that Lionel had so taken, or been given, the two which he had swallowed.

Pointer had already learned that Lionel Cautley was not short-sighted. Rather the other way. True, the mantel-shelf in the morning-room was in the shade. But the pellets must have been coated in some way, Pointer thought, or even a deeply absorbed man might have noticed the look and the taste as strange.

In absolute silence the three returned to the house. For the moment Edna was asked to wait in another room, while the police had just a few preliminary investigations to make. These consisted of a quick tour of the kitchens and pantries. Nothing that suggested sugar coating was to be found. No cakes were ever baked. The cook told them no one at Fairlawn cared for them. Sweets, too, were hardly ever ordered, except fruit dishes. Pointer asked for the dishes served during the last week. Not one, he found, had any meringue coating. But Pointer had not walked by road to the Cottage for nothing. There was a tobacco shop quite close with some stationery piled in one corner, topped by gay packets of soap flakes, and on top of all a little square marked *Glossy Starch*, with the picture of a young man contemplating his reflection in a shirt front.

Pointer stepped inside now, while Wanklyn was questioning the household, and bought a packet. He also asked whether a square had not already been bought for Fairlawn that week. The man could only say that he had lost a square yesterday morning, sneaked from the window when no one was looking. If any one at Fairlawn had bought it, he hoped they would pay for it, but probably it was some woman who had come in for soap... He was asked who had come into the shop, and could only say that all the village, high and low, called in for a paper if for nothing else.

Pointer bought some cigarettes as well and left. Wanklyn, meanwhile, had put things clearly before Mr. Amplett; that the death of Lionel Cautley was due to poisoning by *Aconitum Ferox*, two specimens of which still grew in the garden at Fairlawn; that one plant root had been taken away quite recently; that, in his belief, the deaths of Major Cautley and of Lionel were directly linked with, and due to the missing Cautley pearls.

Amplett listened with a face that grew more and more horrified, but he said nothing.

"Now, sir," Wanklyn wound up, "isn't there anything—however apparently insignificant—which you can tell us that will help to put us on the track of the pearls—which would also lead us to the poisoner of Mr. Lionel Cautley, and, of course, on through him to the solving of the death of the Major, nothing however small?"

"The only thing I know that I didn't tell you, superintendent, is this—and I really don't see how it could have been, or be, of any slightest help to you. Major Cautley was going to alter his will, as well as see Mr. Mason about some property he wanted put on the market. But the only alteration he was going to make was one that couldn't possibly have any connection with his death. You'll see that too, at once, when I tell you what it was. Major Cautley was going to cancel a legacy of a thousand pounds which he had left Miss Edna Upjohn. It was a mere mark of his affection for her father, he had added it as a codicil to his existing testament when I appointed him her co-guardian on the death of old General Vesey."

Wanklyn rubbed his chin.

"Did any one know of his intention except yourself?" he asked finally.

"No one but Mr. Jack Cautley. And as we both know— as every one who knows Mr. Jack Cautley knows—it only made him the more determined to marry Miss Upjohn if she would accept him. They're not engaged yet."

"Why did Major Cautley revoke the codicil, or intend to do so?" Pointer asked.

"He didn't go into it; and thinking there would be plenty of time in the evening after dinner to thrash it out, I let it pass. But on thinking it over I've come to the conclusion that, as he didn't want them to marry, he may have thought it only logical to put every obstacle he could in their path. He had an idea that even a thousand pounds might be a temptation to a money seeker. Which we both know Mr. Jack Cautley is not!" Amplett finished, and Wanklyn agreed with him. But the information was odd. It seemed to lead nowhere, and yet—anything that a man does whom you think was murdered has to be very carefully weighed before it is set on one side.

CHAPTER FOURTEEN

"I OFTEN have said how invaluable is inside or private knowledge of the people," Wanklyn said, after the door had closed behind Mr. Amplett. "Otherwise one would waste time in suspecting Mr. Jack Cautley of heaven knows what."

"What makes you so sure of him?" Pointer asked quietly.

"I'm a good judge of character," Wanklyn said after a pause, during which he tried to put into words his feelings, "and there are certain people who seem to live on a plane above suspicion. You know that they wouldn't be tempted. Take yourself, Mr. Pointer," Wanklyn grinned, "I should know quite well after a talk with you, supposing five or six murders had been committed in your room, and supposing it was quite to your interest to have got each of the murdered people out of your way, that you had no hand in their deaths. I don't say that if you were the only one who could possibly have done it I wouldn't begin to waver, just as I would if only Mr. Jack Cautley could have done these, but I would take you last. Just as I should, and shall, take him last."

"Yet, merely from the point of view of an outsider, doesn't it strike you as odd that he gave his cousin a lying alibi?"

"That was to help him out of a tight place," Wanklyn maintained obstinately. "A Cautley would always help a Cautley."

"And supposing a Cautley—Lionel—to have told a Cautley—Jack—that he was tired of the lie and intended to tell the police the truth, you think still that Jack Cautley is above suspicion?"

"What makes you think that happened?" Wanklyn asked.

"Lionel Cautley, who, according to what you tell me, was a clever man, knew that he was linked with those pearls, knew that he was in a most dangerous position. Either he didn't know about the pearls, or he didn't think that we could find out about them, which latter seems incredible."

The chief inspector was looking at his shoe-tips, his hands in his pockets, his head sunk on his breast.

"You think then?"

"I'm only guessing, not reasoning," Pointer warned him. But Wanklyn had heard about the chief inspector's guesses before, and was all interest. "And my guess is that any man of moderate intelligence would know that the insurance company, if not the police, would find out about that copy of the pearl necklace. That being so, since he gave a false alibi, he didn't know then about the pearls."

Wanklyn frowned disagreement. "Aren't you forgetting that he signed the receipt for the return of the real ones?"

"Some one signed for those pearls, yes," was Pointer's reply. "Some one took them in at Mr. Lionel's rooms, yes. Any one, Miss Daphne, or any other great friend, had only to arrange for the pearls to be sent to his rooms at a time when they had made sure that Lionel and the servant would be out—say five o'clock on the day that Lionel Cautley's manservant has an afternoon off, for which hour she or they—had made an appointment elsewhere with Mr. Cautley. She—I think it's 'she,' you know—would open the door, take them from the carrier, a messenger-boy we have learned, take the paper into a room, scribble Lionel Cautley's name on it, and hand it to him to take back to the shop. Being sent to his rooms, the firm were not as careful as they should have been, and would otherwise have been, as to handing him the pearls personally.

"Then the receipt for the pearls which was sent in the first instance to him by the firm. It was posted, we were told, by the four o'clock afternoon post. It would reach him by six at the latest. Miss Daphne was obviously up in town. What easier than for her to be at his rooms at cocktail time, probably with friends, and obtain the receipt."

"You really think Mr. Lionel may have known nothing about the imitation pearls?" Wanklyn rubbed his chin.

"Since he gave that false alibi, I have privately very much doubted it. Any man, otherwise, in his place would be most scrupulous as to every word—provable word—that he said being strictly accurate. Miss Daphne, when she took the imitation string away from the shop, left another of those easily imitated scrawls of Lionel Cautley's name written beneath some few words on his own note-paper. Any child could have written them, and as any idiot knows, you can't test a scrawled signature and prove it a forgery. Provided it bears a resemblance to the real thing, no expert would give an opinion on it."

"Then it looks as if she—Miss Daphne—did it," Wanklyn said slowly. "Not the first woman to poison a man when he became inconvenient."

"And shot the Major?" Pointer asked.

But Wanklyn was only reluctantly giving up his idea of Lionel having committed suicide. He wanted to be quite sure that he was not throwing away something that might, with a little ingenuity, be made water-tight.

"I suppose he didn't take it himself—intentionally?" he muttered.

"Look here, Wanklyn, this may help you to make up your mind. In that empty aspirin bottle is white dust— most of it saccharine coating from the genuine aspirin tablets, but some of the specks are pure starch and sugar in their simplest forms, just such starch and sugar as I sent up to be analyzed at the same time." Pointer explained about the little square of starch in the shop so close at hand.

"Now, supposing it to be the same, do you think that any man would go to all that trouble, if he were mad enough to give himself such an awful death? There is a bottle of sleeping mixture in his room for use during malaria which is labeled carefully, as it is a dangerous drug when taken in an overdose. A brand new bottle. Half of it would have done the trick for him without any need to dig up roots and then cover them with starch."

"That's a fact," Wanklyn said in the tone of a man who gives up the game. "That really does settle it—that coating business. But you really think that Miss Daphne Upjohn—"

"Suppose we insist on a word with her. As you don't want to trample on the feelings of the family, I'll talk to her."

Daphne came in, painted like a totem pole. Pointer drew a chair forward and then stood looking down at her, towering above her. He was well over six feet.

"Miss Upjohn," he said finally, "it wouldn't be fair to you not to tell you that you're in a very difficult position. Mr. Lionel Cautley has been poisoned, just before a second visit from the insurance company's solicitor, who had told him, for the first time, I think, of the existence of an imitation string of pearls. No, don't speak yet." Pointer intended to bluff. "We know that the Cautley pearls were copied more or less exactly. We believe that you had them copied without saying anything to Mr. Lionel Cautley, and signed the receipt for the originals at his flat in his name; that you borrowed money on the originals, and cannot at the moment make it good; that you had Major Cautley handed the imitation string in the original shagreen case; that he knew it for an imitation, and handed them back to you in that talk with you which he had almost as soon as the sleight-of-hand exhibition was over. Now, all these are things we can prove, so I want you to be very careful how you answer them. I don't caution you formally, so we have not yet decided to arrest you for the murder of Mr. Lionel Cautley—"

"And why should I kill the man I was going to marry?" she asked in an expressionless voice.

Pointer decided that Daphne Upjohn was a difficult young woman to read. Will-power and determination and a hint of arrogance and yet strong passions were to be discovered in her ravaged face, but of moral qualities it gave no sign, not even to his penetrating gaze.

"Because he had found you out and would have exposed the whole business of the substituted pearls. You had lost him anyway. You need not lose Harbord as well," he answered.

Pointer was fishing. He did not doubt that she had cared for Lionel Cautley. But she had used Harbord. There must be some tie there. The chief inspector got a bite at once. Under all her make-up her face reddened.

"I deny everything that you have said." She spoke quietly. "If there has been a substituted necklace, Lionel alone knew about it. I asked him if I could wear it once and he let me have it. I was going to an important party. And Major Cautley had told him that when he married he should have the necklace for his wife's use. I gave it back to him and never thought about it again." Daphne looked as though she took no interest in necklaces, whether real or sham. "Then when he fetched it from town, when Major Cautley's solicitor wanted it back, he suggested seeing what Mr. Frank Harbord could do with its return, just as a joke."

She did not carry conviction. And something in her scornful gaze and curled lip suggested that she did not care whether she was believed or not. Pointer felt sure at that moment that she had some good weapon up her sleeve, that she had not come to this talk unarmed.

"Mr. Amplett believes that Mr. Lionel Cautley killed himself when he learned about the existence of an imitation string," Pointer said gravely.

She was not made of stone, this self-possessed young woman. She flinched.

"But," Pointer said quietly, "your version makes Mr. Lionel Cautley out a criminal. And it certainly suggests a reason for his having murdered his cousin, Major Cautley."

"Lionel murdered the Major!" There was vehement scorn in the tone. "What a damned lie! The pearls had nothing whatever to do with the Major's death," she added with certainty.

The door was hurriedly flung open and Harbord rushed in. He did no more than glance at the two men as he shouted at Daphne.

"I'm done with this business. I wash my hands of it. I'm not going to be dragged into this sort of affair. It would ruin not only me, but the Cause."

"I'm glad you see that, Mr. Harbord," Pointer said at once in a friendly tone. "And I agree. To be shown up as having foisted a sham for a real pearl necklace on its owner would be the end of any man's political career. You would never live it down. And that, as you now know, is what you did do. Do you wish to make a statement? Though I must warn you that as we think that that necklace and the murder of Major Cautley are linked, it is possible that we may feel it our duty to arrest you. You and possibly Miss Upjohn here."

All the red left Harbord's face and he turned pale for a second, before he flushed crimson again.

"I'm going to tell exactly what happened, Daphne.'"

"Why not?" she asked coldly, but her eyes smoldered. "Is that a new departure for you, to tell exactly what happened? You announce it so portentously. Please begin. I shall stay here so as to be sure that it really is exactly what happened!"

Harbord turned to the police, who were enjoying this falling out of what might well be two thieves.

"Miss Upjohn knew that I was skilful at sleight-of-hand, and she suggested that I should come to lunch at Fairlawn, meet Major Cautley again, and amuse every one by doing some conjuring tricks. I agreed. I suppose I'm as fond of showing off as most people." He eyed Daphne, who looked supremely scornful.

"That evening I got a note asking me to meet her outside the church. And when we met she said that she thought it would be such a good idea—" Harbord went on to tell of the return to Major Cautley of the case containing the pearls. He had received it himself from Miss Upjohn during his performance, and had not opened it until he did so in front of every one. He had no knowledge of pearls, and when Miss Upjohn had said it was the Cautley necklace he had believed her. He added that although the Major had received the pearls with apparent amusement he had seen him turn the string over with his finger before putting the case away in his pocket. Edna had thought he was looking at the clasp, but Frank Harbord's eyes were keener.

"Daphne—Miss Upjohn," Harbord shot her a venomous look, "slipped in to the Cottage that afternoon as soon as the Cautleys were away with the dogs. She was in a frightful state."

Daphne blew a contemptuous smoke ring in his direction.

"Frightful state," Harbord repeated. "She said that the Major claimed that the necklace wasn't the right one, that it was an imitation. She swore that she had handed me the genuine one, and actually asked me—me! what happened to the real one, pretending that I must have blundered in some way. I was taken in by her I admit." He scowled. "I thought she wouldn't have said such a thing if she hadn't really believed it! I wasted time assuring her that I had passed on what she had given me exactly as she had given it me. Then she as good as blackmailed me for three hundred pounds. Oh, yes you did!" to Daphne, who made a move as though to spring from her chair. "Oh, yes you did, you cat!" Frank Harbord was entirely the builder's son now. "And when I told you I hadn't more than thirty pounds in the world, nor ever would have, you started in on a tale about your sister and debts of hers, and the pearls, and a jumble that would have mixed any man up. In the middle of it Miss Edna rushed up to the Cottage to say that the Major had shot himself by accident. I wondered at the time why you were so horrified at the idea of her or any one knowing you were there. But of course you didn't want any one then to know we were friends. I was to be made use of first, and then, if need be, thrown to the wolves. You slipped in again that night and threw gravel on my window till I came down and rushed you up to town still bent on saving Edna from her folly about the pearls! You wouldn't explain. You couldn't! I did as you asked, drove you up, waited for you in Sloane Square, and drove you down."

"And of course you weren't keen on having the pearl question cleared up on your own account!" Daphne threw in casually.

"Naturally I was! I'm not a thief. And naturally talk about imitation pearls having been handed back made me frightfully nervous. You said it was all right—that you had arranged matters, that the real string was safe, and that you had destroyed the imitation before leaving Fairlawn, or at least got rid of it by dropping it down a drain-pipe. And you were so dashed charming that you quite pulled the wool over my eyes."

Daphne made a little movement that looked to the chief inspector like a wince of real pain, but Harbord went on in the same furious tone.

"But next morning, when all sorts of whispers about something wrong with the pearls were going round, I began to have my doubts. I remembered a picture I had seen of Lionel Cautley's mother with the pearls on. I found it and had a look at it through a good lens, a lens that Lionel had in his room. I was going to borrow the photo to enlarge it—photography is a hobby of mine—but Miss Edna came up. I hung about, however, and saw you flash back from the garden and take it out and slip it into the pocket of your coat in the hall."

"So you took it from there!" Daphne said, white-hot with indignation.

"I took it from there," he mimicked. "And when I had enlarged it I wondered whether the necklace I had had was that one or not. The picture shows a funny shading in one of the beads, it's black in the photo, but it would be pink in the real pearl, nor was the fastening quite the same and then something—Lionel's death—many things—everything made me think there was something all wrong somewhere. And the more I've thought it over the more certain I am that I don't want to be mixed up in it."

Again, with face aflame, he looked indignantly at the fair Daphne. She looked as angry.

"Oh, do stop making a fool of yourself!" she implored him with fervor. "I'm glad I'm not a man. I'm glad I'm not anything so stupid and so clumsy, Frank. And you thought I was in love with you!" she scoffed.

"Now, chief inspector, you've listened to this dear, chivalrous, loyal knight here—"

"Loyal yourself!" retorted Harbord with fury. "What about Lionel Cautley? You did him down, didn't you? What about Jack—"

She waved a hand at him.

"I suppose you've got us both exactly where you wanted us," she said to the chief inspector and Wanklyn. Neither of them denied it.

"But whatever I may have done about the pearls, neither of us had any hand in the Major's death. And I only hope you'll find out who killed Lionel too!"

Harbord burst out hotly. "I like that! You know who killed Lionel. You did! Oh, I don't mean with your own hand, but when he learned about the pearls—" he stopped. "I don't mean that," he now said hastily, "my temper got the better of me."

Pointer eyed him thoughtfully. How deep in the mystery surrounding the death of the two Cautley cousins were these two? And what was it that Daphne Upjohn had up her sleeve?

"Would you be kind enough to wait in another room for a few minutes?" Pointer asked Daphne. She hesitated—but his eye could be very compelling.

"I think I would rather tell you the whole wretched business myself," she said finally, which was what he wanted.

It was accordingly Harbord who was asked to wait in another room, and a constable remained outside the door. After a moment's pause Daphne Upjohn said "Yes, I'll tell you everything. It's a damned unpleasant tale I have to tell, but at least it's better than letting you hear it from that frightful prig out there. He told me he could handle any affair that needed tact, and like an idiot I believed him! These pearls which we're talking about—well—" She lit another cigarette with an attempt at casualness.

"Really, that's all my fault. Lionel let me wear them once at a smart party. I rather fell for them—nice necklace and I was frightfully hard-up. I make quite a good income at bridge, but of course there are bound to be sandy patches, and I had struck one. I kept the pearls for a week. And I had them copied, at the big stores where Lionel often dealt—King and Court. I had the real pearls sent back to Lionel's flat—I wrote his name on the receipt." She broke off and glanced briefly at Pointer. The chief inspector nodded gravely.

"We have that receipt, Miss Upjohn. And the order for the copy," he said briefly.

"Oh! Yes—well—I took the pearls to a small jeweler's shop off Sloane Street. Mrs. Diamond knows me well. She lent me three hundred pounds on the pearls.   And I haven't been able to pay it back. And since the Major's death she's got hold of the story—she's blackmailing me for four hundred pounds in cash."

For a moment she hesitated. "Lionel knew nothing about the advance on the necklace—nor about the duplicate. When I heard that Major Cautley wanted the pearls back again, or that the solicitor did, I knew there would be trouble. But I played for every minute of time that I could get. I arranged that sleight-of-hand with Frank Harbord. Lionel objected, but he let me have my way. I hoped Major Cautley wouldn't give them a second glance, but he turned them over before he shut the case, and afterwards he called me into the conservatory." She bit her cigarette through and started another.

"He gave me until the next day to hand over the real ones. He rather liked me, really, I think; saw I had brains, you know; and he wouldn't make Lionel break the engagement if I turned over the pearls. I had already tried Edna for the money. I tried Frank that afternoon. But when the Major didn't come back from shooting those wood pigeons, I thought I was saved. That ends the chapter with the Major." Her tone suggested sheer bravado now.

"As for Lionel—" her voice wavered. "Well, when he learned from the insurance company about the existence of an imitation string, and that his name had been used in the affair—" she broke off and stared straight ahead of her for a second. "Whatever I did wrong, and it was such a tiny bit off the straight, I paid enough! If I'd murdered the Major, I should have paid for it twice over in the talk—the last talk—we—Lionel and I—had. He cursed me by book and by candle." Her face was all bitterness now, so was her voice and her eye. "I've not had much experience in being loathed. It was something quite new. Well everything new is interesting in its way. But this way cut damned deep. Oh, he was very different from the Frank Harbord of just now. Frank's like a big blustering baby, but Lionel—" She sat a second looking pale and suddenly haggard. "The Cautleys all have a nasty edge to them," she said finally, as though throwing off some black memory. "I know that he didn't kill himself because of—of the whole tiresome muddle about the pearls. I know he didn't. And I hope to God you'll find who did it! And that's why I've told you all this so frankly. I want to be clear of it all—this pearl business—everything—and leave the field free for the real reason why first the Major and then

Lionel were murdered—supposing that they were murdered?" She flashed a quick look at the chief inspector. Wanklyn seemed hardly to exist now for her. Pointer had rather a way of making the other men with him look like part of the furniture.

"We do suppose so," he said gravely. "And the motive, you say, is?"

"Mr. Jack Cautley said the police wanted to stop some dog-fights that were being held around here in secret?" Now she did look at Wanklyn, who, immensely surprised, nodded vigorously.

"Very much so!" he assured her.

"Well, so did the Major." Again she paused.

"I know. They had started before he left the neighborhood, but only on a small scale—now and again—and nothing like so brutal."

"He found out that Fabian Cautley goes to them." So this was her weapon and her defense. It was a good one.

"Indeed?" was all Wanklyn said, but his eyes were alight.

"Major Cautley had just learned this," she went on "Jack Cautley—"

"Just a moment, Miss Upjohn. This is—or may be"— caution made the superintendent alter the certain to the possible—"very important. You say Mr. Jack Cautley told you this. When?"

"When I was so terrified lest—" she paused. "You see, when the Major was shot, I knew from Mr. Lionel that he intended to have a word with him—he didn't tell me what about, but spoke as though it were over some bother—I jumped to the conclusion that the Major had told him about the pearls not being the right ones, and that he had perhaps got stuffy over it, and said some rude things about me, rude enough to make Lionel have shot him in a fit of temper. All the Cautleys have the temper of the devil, though they won't let themselves go as a rule. You see"—her face was bleak now, she looked genuinely wretched, "I overrated his feelings for me, and quite forgot how sacrosanct to a Cautley—are certain fetishes about what women may do and what they mayn't. The pearls were promised to Lionel for his wife, when he should marry, but I, his future wife, must not act on that promise. Oh no!"

"About Mr. Fabian and the dog-fights—" the superintendent put in; he felt like a man trying to steer a coracle on a swift Welsh current. "When did Mr. Jack Cautley tell you about them, and just what did he tell you?"

"I'm just telling you!" Daphne looked vexed at such extraordinary impatience. "When Jack found me so wretched after the Major's death, he guessed, after a few words, that I thought Lionel and he had quarreled over me. He doesn't know anything about the pearls, of course, and then he let slip that the Major had heard that one of those dog-fights was coming off that same afternoon, and that he had only pretended to be shooting pigeons in the 'hide' so as to burst in on one of them—at a cottage belonging to a man called Hammersley, I think he said— and when I thought that Lionel—"

"About Mr. Fabian and the Major first, please," Wanklyn pleaded. "You say you were told that the Major was going to a cottage of a man called Hammersley. But what has Mr. Fabian to do with this?"

"He was going to be present at the fight. The Major went along to the cottage, found nothing of course—the man must have seen him coming, Jack thinks; but while he stood there—the Major, you know—a boy poked a note under the door from Fabian saying that he would be sure to turn up and would as usual be good for double prize money. The Major went back to the 'hide' to wait until the hour set, and never came back at all. Of course he met Mr. Fabian Cautley on the way there and Fabian shot him in the quarrel that followed. And this morning, just before the end"—her voice shook,—"while Lionel and I were having a terrible scene—he had me by the shoulders and I thought he was going to shake the life out of me—I

saw Fabian Cautley's face looking in at us through the
window and grinning from ear to ear, with the most
malignant enjoyment. I know now why. He hoped it
would be thought that I was the last to see Lionel and
would be accused of having killed him, but luckily I
wasn't the last! Fabian was, though, you may be sure of
that!"

They now had the point in her story which, even if
true, was of the greatest importance—that she had seen
Fabian looking in through the window. If true! As for the
rest, though interesting, being pure hearsay it was not
evidence.

"Here is Mr. Jack Cautley himself," Pointer said
suddenly, and rising was out of the room and down the
path in one swift movement. He had seen Jack Cautley
passing the gate.

CHAPTER FIFTEEN

JACK CAUTLEY came in rather unwillingly, Pointer thought. The chief inspector left the talk to the superintendent, who, as being better known to Mr. Cautley, might be supposed to get at facts more easily. Miss Upjohn had been asked to wait in another room, and Wanklyn at once began with a plain account of what had been told them as to Fabian Cautley's connection with the dog-fights which were in secret disgracing the neighborhood.

Jack Cautley's light eyes opened wide.

"Fabian supposed to have had anything to do with such muck? Rubbish, superintendent! Never! Don't you believe it, Wanklyn!" He sounded almost amused in an angry way at the idea.

Wanklyn came out frankly with the source of his information. Miss Upjohn had not made her statement confidential at all.

Jack Cautley seemed unable to believe it. Wanklyn, nettled, and also rather surprised, because he had credited Daphne's story of what had been told her, sent for that young lady herself.

"There seems to be some confusion about Mr. Cautley's having spoken of Mr. Fabian and those dog-fights and the Major. Would you mind repeating before him what you've just told us?"

"Not at all." And very promptly, with her head defiantly high, Daphne let herself be shown back into the room where now Jack Cautley stood shaking his head and murmuring, "Ridiculous! Absurd!"

"The superintendent here has fixed up something, or you have," Jack began promptly. "What on earth has old Fabian been doing to you that you should get your knife into him? What made you think there was any connection between him and dog-fighting in the neighborhood?"

"Not what, but who!" she replied at once. "You yourself did, Jack. True, it only slipped out, and you immediately said something about its being strictly confidential, but, of course, with Lionel murdered because of it, I can't stop at that."

"Lionel murdered because I told— Look here, Daphne, I quite understand—" his tone was soothing.

She pushed his sympathy, real or artificial, away. "You're playing some game of your own." She faced him hotly. "Defending your family, probably. But Lionel was murdered, Jack, and as sure as I stand here Fabian is at the bottom of it, and of the Major's death—"

Jack Cautley turned to the two officers. Patience and regret were to be read on his face, but nothing else. His glance of pity at the girl and of understanding to the men said that here was a poor creature to be humored.

Daphne flamed. "You know you told me—" and she repeated very exactly what she had just told the police about Fabian, the dog-fights and the Major. Jack listened as one in a nightmare. Then he shook his head, and again soothingly told her that she ought not to be up, to lie down and let Edna sit by her.

"Ah, here comes Mr. Fabian himself! Now we can get this cleared up," exclaimed the chief inspector just then.

Pointer was by the window, Jack Cautley some distance away. The chief inspector bent forward as though catching sight of a figure by the gate, as he had just now seen Jack. His glance was not on the road, but on that young man. Over Cautley's face flashed a look of uneasiness and dismay, instantly repressed, as he hurried forward and in his turn went to the window.

"It wasn't Mr. Fabian Cautley after all... My mistake," Pointer murmured, turning away.

"It was a pity," Jack echoed. "He would have been able to assure you, supposing it not to be one of his silent days, that he knows nothing whatever of these disgraceful fights that we all want to stop just as much as Major Cautley did."

"You humbug! You absolute liar! You are trying to shield him—just because he's one of your wonderful family!" And with that, Daphne left the three men alone.

Jack Cautley seemed to meditate a moment. He sighed finally.

"Miss Daphne Upjohn and I were formerly engaged to be married, as, of course, you have heard. I'm wondering whether this story she's repeating, something that she knows I must deny at once... It's not a bad idea to make me seem a liar."

"By the way," Pointer threw in at that, "we have reason to believe, Mr. Cautley, that your cousin Lionel was about to alter his statement as to where he was during the afternoon that the Major was shot. We questioned his alibi; and we have reason to think he intended to change some of the times given us."

Jack Cautley smiled a rather foolish smile.

"Well, you know, one does often think of things afterwards, doesn't one? I mean, one checks up on one's own impressions and finds one was quite a bit out..."

"Would you like to give us a fresh statement as to where you yourself were that afternoon?" Pointer asked.

"I was coming to that." Jack settled himself comfortably in a chair. "It's been quite on my mind. As a matter of fact I was rather out about my having been at the Cottage so much of the time. I brought the dogs back—that time is all right—but I went for a ramble afterwards and was away until I dropped in for tea at Fairlawn." He stopped as though he had said all that there was to say.

"Then you cannot give Mr. Lionel Cautley any alibi at all."

"No," Jack agreed regretfully. "My memory played me false there."

"But what about after you found the body, Mr. Cautley," Pointer went on, "perhaps you have forgotten your statement, but you were some time in getting to the police station. Now, did you overtake Mr. Lionel Cautley on his way to the opticians and have a word with him?"

Jack eyed him without speaking. He seemed to come to the conclusion that the police knew more than he had thought.

"Yes," he said finally. "Yes, chief inspector. When I found the Major dead, I did not think he had shot himself. I knew his ways with a gun too well, and I rather fancied that Lionel might be in a rather awkward position. I knew he had intended having a word with the Major. The engagement wasn't exactly to the latter's liking. Lionel was not the kind to stand criticism of any action of his, or intended action. I thought it would be just as well if Lionel were beyond suspicion. He profited directly from our cousin's death. I did, as you say, race on up towards town and overtook his car, had a word with him as to his danger, and suggested that in order to keep the police from going astray, it would be as well for us each to give the other an alibi. He was not keen on the idea. I still think it a good one under the circumstances."

Wanklyn could not trust himself to speak. But he looked as though he would have liked to let himself go.

"But, as you say, the circumstances have altered," Jack finished.

"Are you prepared to swear to this new statement and sign it?" Pointer asked.

Jack Cautley said that he was. He would come down to the police station tomorrow and have it carefully taken down, giving hours and, where possible, minutes. Then he looked at the clock, and apparently recalled an important engagement.

"Well!" Wanklyn said, "I give him up! Mr. Jack, I mean. It only teaches you never to believe any one! Never to take any one on trust! This alters everything!" Wanklyn would have continued in the same ejaculatory strain but for having to return to his station, and the chief inspector, after agreeing with the other's sentiments, went on out after Jack Cautley. He thought it possible that that young man might stroll in the direction of his kinsman Fabian, and that their first words might be informative.

As he walked away, well behind Jack Cautley's tall, erect figure, nearly as tall and erect as his own, the chief inspector turned over in his mind the interview of just now. He had come so late into the case, he had missed so much that to him would, have been of the greatest help, that he walked warily, even in his thoughts. The pearls seemed a good foundation, seemed part of the very crux of the problem, but Daphne Upjohn denied this—as she would do if murder had been the result of her action. But there was one oddity in the case which the pearls—so far—did not cover. Why had the Major telephoned from the post-office? They could not learn of anything that he had posted. There seemed nothing so urgent in his request for the solicitor to come that he could not have sent it from the Cottage or Fairlawn. This new idea, that of the Major suddenly learning that Fabian Cautley was connected with those vile dog-fights, learning it too from Fabian's own note thrust under Hammersley's door, fitted in perfectly with the abandoned decoy and empty "hide." More still, it fitted in with and explained the imperative summons of the solicitor. The Major might well have felt that he could not wait before altering his will, not because of striking out a legacy to Edna Upjohn—which would be a mere detail—but in order to delete Fabian from the line of possible successors to his money. It fitted in also with his striding hot-foot, after sending the message to Mason, back to the Cottage, probably to wait there for Fabian's return.

And the poison used in Lionel's death fitted in with Fabian Cautley of the Indian Woods and Forests. The man had no alibi for either death. None the less, Pointer felt as though he held the dead-end of a telephone in his hand. He missed the stir and vibrations of a case in which he had been from the beginning. Yet it was an interesting conundrum. Very.

As for Jack's confession that the alibi which he and
Lionel had given each other was not genuine, this made
little difference to the problem. Any alibi which two
members of the circle had given each other would have
been suspected, though each had sworn to the end that it
was true. As far as Pointer was concerned, the position in
respect to Jack Cautley was just where it had been—Jack
Cautley, who stood to benefit enormously by the two
deaths, but who did not seem connected with the pearls.

Jack Cautley turned in at the Cottage, and Pointer,
after watching him from a discreet distance settle himself
down at his writing table without making any effort to
get in touch with Fabian or any one else, went on to the
police station. There, after some talk over the telephone
with his own men in town, he decided to run up himself
and see whether he could find out how much truth there
was in Daphne Upjohn's assertion that Mrs. Diamond
was keeping the necklace for her and had lent her three
hundred on it. Daphne maintained that she could not find
the papers connected with the pearls, but that she had
put them all together among her letters, though for the
moment she could not lay hands on them. A mere
detective sergeant and even a detective inspector had not
been able to frighten Mrs. Diamond into acknowledging
any such transaction. Diamond himself had indignantly
produced his books in which there was no such entry.
Pointer thought that it might well have been a private
"spec" on the part of Mrs. Diamond, and decided to
assume that Daphne had told only the exact truth.

There is a lull in the center of a storm area. That
afternoon, around cocktail time, a glance into the lounge
of Fairlawn would have suggested the most everyday
calm. Only the looks of the two girls had changed. Edna
was very wan, and Daphne had circles around her eyes
which for once were not artificial. Edna was embroidering
some knots on a new brown felt hat of Daphne's.

"I can't think why you didn't do it for me last week," Daphne was saying, looking at her reproachfully. "It makes all the difference."

No one had worn any mourning for Major Cautley, nor would wear any for Lionel. All the Cautleys felt strongly against it. Jack had not even altered his tie that morning.

"I didn't have the wool last week," Edna replied in the tone of one whose thoughts are far away, and not in any pleasant place either. "At least, I don't think I had."

"Where did you turn it up? It's exactly the right shade." Daphne spoke easily and stretched out what looked like an idle hand towards the ball of wool. "Where did you get it, Edna?"

"I found it in the pocket of this coat," Edna patted the loose tweed that she had on. "I haven't worn it for days. As for the ball, I can't think where it came from. It bulged out the whole side of the jacket or I mightn't have noticed it."

"It looks to me like the jumper that Smith person is knitting for herself," Daphne said suddenly. "If so, don't use it! I loathe the girl. Mrs. Amplett's a silly idiot not to see what is hatching under her iron eye."

"Iron eye?" Edna managed to smile. "Sounds odd. But this isn't knitting wool. It must belong to Mrs. Amplett. Fortunately I only want one needleful."

Talk flagged. Amplett came in with the evening paper and the look of harassed worry characteristic of his face nowadays.

"Miss Smith not here?" he asked, pulling out his watch. "These trains!" He shook his head.

"Those girls!" Daphne put in. "You don't suppose Miss Smith ever tried to catch a train in all her fat little life, do you, Mr. Amplett?"

"I consider Miss Smith has a charming figure," he replied to that bit of spitefulness. "Rounded and feminine. Not a boy's lanky growth coupled with a girls feebleness."

Daphne made the gesture of ducking from a blow. "Be careful of her, Mr. Amplett, she's an eater of men." Daphne began to play with the ball of wool. "I saw her making eyes at Jack only the other day."

Jack was shown in at that moment, together with Fabian. Fabian looked excited, Edna thought, but Jack, judging by appearances, had spent such a night as she herself had. She noticed, too, that the cousins were not speaking to each other, that Jack put the distance of the room between himself and Fabian as soon as possible.

"Are you feeling better now?" he asked Daphne in a kindly tone.

Daphne's eyes flashed, but she smiled at him. "Just the same," she replied. Daphne could be trusted not to let all the world know of the talk with the police just now.

"And you, what brings you here, Father Fabian?" she asked next, with an ironic stress on the title.

"I don't know," he replied vaguely, but his eyes were very bright, and restless.

"Cocktails, I hope," Amplett said hospitably, as the tray came in.

Fabian shook his head. He shook it when offered lemonade, and finally a glass of water.

"This is one of my dry days," was his excuse for refusing.

They all knew that there were days when Fabian maintained that no drop of liquid of any kind touched his lips, just as there were days when he said that he fasted from all food, and days when he maintained that he neither ate nor drank.

"Have you started altering Dunnottar yet?" Amplett asked with the look of a man hoping that his little throw will catch some passing fish. "The Colonel's love of extraordinary gadgets wouldn't be to every one's liking."

"Not yet," was Fabian's reply, "but do you mind if I sit out in the gardens a while. I have a feeling that a message is trying to rise from my subconscious?"

"Does it rise better here than at Dunnottar?" Daphne asked.

"My *daimon* told me to come here. I take it that the message will be for some one here," and Fabian passed on out through the window.

"For once he didn't say 'peace be with you,'" murmured Edna, who thought that Fabian's way of assuming a squatter's right everywhere he went really ought to be checked. Even Amplett looked as though, if he were not the host, he would say something rude. Daphne yawned and fidgeted with the ball of wool she held.

"What's inside it?" Her slender, tangerine-tipped fingers were pulling at something.

"Just the usual paper core. Don't get it out, Daphne, or the ball will all fall in. Bother!"

This last came from Edna because, as she made to take the wool away from Daphne, the ball bounded away and the paper inside, round which the wool was presumably wound, popped out, thanks to Daphne's efforts to find out what was within. It was a crumpled ball of thickish paper. Edna stooped for it. At any other time she might have noticed the size of the wad used, but her mind was intent on quite another matter, on a very dreadful and difficult matter. As she stooped for the wool, some one forestalled her and handed it to her. To her surprise it was Harbord. He had stepped in through the French window.

"Excuse my way of coming in," he said to Mr. Amplett, "but I caught sight of Fabian outside and wanted a word with him. From him to in here was but a step—"

Amplett said something civil, but Harbord declined a drink or a chair. He had come to say good-by, he explained, as he was leaving in an hour for the north.

Neither he, nor any of the four in the room, seemed grieved to part, and after, a perfunctory holding out of his hand to Daphne, which she was unable to take owing to something intricate which she was doing with a lemon at the moment, he left by the more usual entrance.

Edna had laid paper and ball down beside her without glancing at them. A moment more and she had finished. Daphne went on talking to Jack. Edna picked up the hat and the paper and went off to her own room, almost colliding with Miss Smith in the hall—Miss Smith of the red, red lips, the big black eyes, and the by no means pencil type of figure. Edna, even in her preoccupation, thought that she had been listening, but then a secretary might well listen for the moment when her employer would be free. In fact, seeing Edna's eye on her, Miss Smith now went on into the lounge.

"I'm sorry I was detained, Mr. Amplett," she said sweetly. "it was the bus to the station. I can't afford taxis, of course, and the bus had something the matter with its engine."

Mr. Amplett assured her that he knew how awkward such happenings were, when one was straining every, nerve to be on time—here he cast a glance at Daphne's sceptical face, and followed his secretary out of the room.

Daphne rose to go too, but Jack stepped in front of her.

"I want a word with you, Daphne," he began very gently.

"I don't want one with you," was the reply, as she made to pass him.

"Look here," he said in his impulsive way, "forgive my speaking as I did just now. I had to! You oughtn't to've brought Fabian's name into this awful mess, Daphne. It was the last thing that Lionel wanted, or he would have done it himself. At all costs we must keep Fabian out of things. I'll find a way to make him pay in full for what he's done, but he must be allowed to punish himself."

She eyed him scornfully. "I don't believe a word you say. Why should I? You gave me the lie direct just now. Why should I ever believe you again?"

"I had to deny what you were telling the police," he repeated doggedly. "Poor old Lionel! It could do him no good, and he would have died twice over rather than have

Fabian's dreadful secret broadcast. The man's mad, Daphne. Quite mad. You gave Lionel a dreadful half-hour or so about that necklace. I can guess how the complication began. You owe it to him now he's dead not to do the thing, of all others, which he would most abhor. Stand aside and let things take their course."

For a second she wavered. "You mean that Fabian shot the Major and killed Lionel?" she asked under: her breath, turning white, and yet with a deep breath of relief. It was one thing to say she felt sure that Lionel had not taken his own life, another to be told that it was so.

He nodded. "I do."

"But I don't think Lionel thought it was Fabian," she suddenly broke out, "nothing he ever said made me think he suspected him."

"But he did," Jack said firmly. "Of course he knew that Fabian was mad and had shot poor Howard in some fit of fury. Fabian always did go quite off his head when enraged. Fabian waited around that last day until he could have a word with Lionel alone, and that word led to another scene and another murder." Jack looked suddenly old and haggard. "He was in the garden. He had plenty of time to whittle off some pellets of monkshood root. He would know the right kind and how deadly they are. He would only have to lay them out on the mantel-shelf."

"There were some lying out," Daphne suddenly said. "I remember there were three pellets lying there. But I thought Edna had put them there; she's using pellets for plants you know—some new fertilizer she's been asked to try."

"Good God, Daphne, don't bring Edna into this!" Jack cried angrily. "Of course those pellets you saw were put there by Fabian! Which shows that he must have made up his mind in the morning early to do away with Lionel. Lionel probably threatened to have him detained in a lunatic asylum."

"Where he belongs," Daphne retorted.

Jack shook his head. "No, Daphne, not that! Fabian must go, of course, that's understood, but not to that living death. I pledge you my word that he will be called to account. Will you stand aside for the time being?"

Daphne looked mulish.

"In return, I'll see about the necklace tangle," he said pleasantly. "I mean, wipe it completely off the slate."

"And let me have a line to say it's all settled absolutely—definitely?" she asked.

"If you don't interfere any more in our family tragedy," he said with a nod.

Daphne, chilled by something in the young man's manner as much as by his words, said that she only wanted to get away and forget all this dreadful experience.

"You once loved me—" she began almost brokenly.

"But the trouble was you never loved me," he finished with a smile that showed how past the past was with him. Daphne bit her lip, and this time he made no objections to her going up to her room. As she went, she thought over the mess she had made of things—her own phrase. Jack was now the owner of the great Cautley wealth, and she had turned him down because of his poverty. And Lionel was dead. And before he died he had reviled her—had died with loathing of her in his heart. And Frank Harbord whom she had thought her slave, despised her...

Edna was some minutes in her room. When she came down, Jack was alone in the lounge.

"Didn't you say the other day that you knew Mr. Bennett Bowman?" she asked eagerly. She had wanted a word with him all day long about this man.

"You mean the Home Office graphology expert? The chap who can say positively who wrote this in that year, and who didn't write t'other in no year? They say you show him a speck of dust and he knows all about the

building it came from. Knows the place where a pearl was
fished and its sex. He's world-famous."

"Yes, yes," Edna agreed impatiently. "You sound like
the wrapper around a patent medicine, Jack. But do you
know him personally?"

"Slightly," he replied, giving her a quick glance, from
behind his smile as it were. "Very slightly though. Why?"

"He's not in the telephone book. What's his address?"

Jack looked down as though meditating. "Can't tell
you off-hand. I can give you one of his clubs and his
institutes."

She shook her head. "I want his own address—the
address where he works, where his laboratory is," she
said. Throughout, she spoke in a low tense voice, and
even glanced over her shoulder to see that they were
alone. "Who's there?" she now called clearly, as a door
handle turned.

Fabian Cautley came out. He blinked as though he
had been fast asleep.

"The message is *Danger*," he said as though
announcing the next item on a program, and passed out
of the house.

Edna again caught sight of some submerged part of
Jack Cautley which made her almost draw away from
him. A killer looked from those merry eyes for one swift
part of a second as he gazed after his kinsman's
retreating back.

"I can find out Bennett Bowman's private address for
you," he said, as though glad to do her a service. "I'll
telephone you it, shall I?"

"Yes. But—" then she seemed to change her mind. "It
sounds silly, but I have a reason for my asking it. Don't
telephone me. There are two extensions to the telephone
here. Send me a note with the address as soon as you can
get it. That way it'll be quite private."

Again he shot her one swift speculating look. Then he
came closer still. "Edna, what are you about to do?"

She made no reply.

"Look here, my dear girl. Let me in on this. There have been two murders down here. No game for a girl to take a hand in. Tell me what you want done, and I'll see to it for you."

She shook her head with a very decided shake. "It's nothing to do with these awful things," she replied, but there was a quiver in her voice, a quiver to her eye too. "At least, oh I hope not, but anyway it only concerns me. No one else," and she turned away almost as though she might break down if she said more. "Write me as soon as you can," she whispered.

"Suppose we go for a walk and put our heads together," he suggested coaxingly.

"I'll walk with you to the gate, but I don't feel like going further. My heart is too heavy," she said with a half rueful smile, "it weighs a ton."

He gave her arm a sympathetic squeeze. "It'll all be cleared up—some day. At least..."

Again, looking at him, something sent a chill through. her. Again something determined and ruthless showed up beneath the surface of that smiling face.

There was a short silence.

"Is one ever justified in taking the law into one's own hands?" he said as though far away in thought.

"I think what Father Fabian says is true," she said finally.

"Don't call him that! Don't call him Father! He's no father to you!" Jack said fiercely.

"Whoever harms another, harms himself far more."

She stopped. Such an expression of fury had crossed her companion's face that she suddenly wished she had not come out with him.

At the same moment, Fabian Cautley was talking to Superintendent Wanklyn. He had walked into the station with a brisk step and no trace of Oriental languor about him.

"Superintendent, are any of us allowed to leave England without letting you know?"

"Certainly not, sir," the superintendent said shortly.

His gorge rose at the sight of the man's lean, wicked face, so Wanklyn called it to himself. He tried to be unbiased, to remember that he had only been told a tale, perhaps by an idiot, which might truly signify nothing, but somehow Wanklyn thought the idea that Fabian had something to do with those horrible fights fitted. They had grown more frequent. More wretched dogs had been starved and goaded to frenzy. Some one must be paying for the dogs and the prizes. He had heard Hammersley once, apparently parting from some person, and though the man had explained that he was merely calling out to a pal in a field, Wanklyn now recalled that he had overtaken Fabian Cautley not two minutes later in the same lane. And the Major—if the story were true as he believed it to be—Wanklyn pitied that very fine character. To know that your own blood, blood of which you were proud, was spreading a plague... With an effort Wanklyn now repeated gruffly, "Certainly not, sir."

"Then I think you should be told that some one from Fairlawn is planning to go abroad—on the quiet."

"Quite impossible, Mr. Cautley," But Wanklyn was uneasy.

"Quite possible, my dear superintendent," was the dry reply. "A jaunt up to town, a little dodging in and out and roundabout, a coach trip to Brighton, a weekend excursion to Ostend, and the thing is done." He raised a thin hand. "I heard the plans being made, Mr. Wanklyn. One was an outsider, who can go or come as he or she pleases, but one was Miss Edna Upjohn."

"Miss Edna Upjohn?" Wanklyn could hardly believe his ears.

"She was making just that plan which I have sketched. Now in all our interests, she should-not be allowed to go away until you have cleared up these double tragedies."

Wanklyn made no reply, and Fabian, with a "Peace be with you," paced gently out again.

Wanklyn watched him, and smacked his fist on the table top. "He's playing some damned game of his own. I don't believe him! Why should Miss Edna want to go away? Why should Mr. Fabian tell us of it, if it were true? He hasn't told us anything helpful so far. That's where knowing the people helps," Wanklyn went on to Todd, "knowing that Father Fabian for a brute as a boy, believing him at the root of the dog-fights and probably of those two murders—I don't give that for his pretended information!" and he snapped his strong fingers in the air.

Chief Inspector Pointer returned from town at this juncture.

"What about the necklace?" Wanklyn asked him eagerly.

"Miss Daphne told us the truth. I—er—let Mrs. Diamond think we had the receipts for the pearls, and she finally confessed—though that word suggests penitence and an acknowledgment of guilt and Mrs. Diamond considers the whole transaction a mere commercial affair, of perhaps a more confidential kind than some others, but merely commercial. She has the pearls and has lodged them temporarily in her brother-in-law's safe in Hatton Garden. He's a man called Baruch, a most respectable jewel merchant. Both she and he quite understand that the pearls are to be held merely in custody, but she, rather acutely, feels sure that Mr. Jack Cautley won't let the story of the loan on them—all in his dead cousin's name get about. He couldn't prove Lionel Cautley was innocent. Altogether Mrs. Diamond is thinking of adding another hundred pounds for the anxiety she has suffered and the trouble to which she has been put."

There was a short silence.

"The pearls may not be the real motive after all," Wanklyn mused aloud. "This second Cautley murder suggests the Cautley property quite as much as those pearls. Both times it's the owner of the property who is done in."

"I wonder what was in that ball of wool," Pointer said suddenly. "A man who knows he's been poisoned, as I think Lionel Cautley must have known it, might have tried to leave a message behind—where the murderer might not see it, and we would. We know now that the pearls weren't in that ball. Where is it?"

"Perhaps it's been put back without being noticed," hazarded Wanklyn.

"Mrs. Amplett has used the same kind and color of wool here and there in some cross-stitch embroidery she's doing, but though she's worked quite an inch lower down, she hasn't used any of that brown since."

Pointer took a turn through the room.

"Find the contents of that ball, Wanklyn, and you may possibly find the solution to the Cautley mystery," he said again.

There was a short silence, then Pointer again had to put the intriguing question of the contents and the whereabouts of that ball out of his mind.

"Going back to Fabian Cautley," he went on instead, "did you tax him with the dog-fights?"

"No. I would like to have, but I thought two pairs of eyes watching his reactions might be better than one pair."

"We might as well do so now, then," Pointer suggested.

"He'll deny it all, of course," Wanklyn said gloomily, "and it won't be easy to prove. Hammersley and his men will all deny everything."

"I shouldn't be too sure that he'll deny the charge," Pointer said, to Wanklyn's surprise. "Mr. Fabian strikes me as being a very strange nature. Half mad, but of the kind that enjoys public penitence."

"He doesn't know the meaning of the word—any more than you say Mrs. Diamond does," Wanklyn said grimly.

Pointer laughed. "Possibly. But I think he's the kind to enjoy a dramatic confession and a white sheet and a candle, for all that. But we shall soon see. Where is he?"

"He's gone back to the Cottage to pack up some Oriental hangings of his."

Pointer, remembering that ghastly sight of the dripping rope-ends, wondered if the "discipline" went too.

At the Cottage their knocking produced no results, but, at a call up the stairs, Fabian opened his bedroom door and came down to meet them. He had a curiously dreamy, faraway, look in his eyes.

"Mr. Fabian," Wanklyn began, throwing back his shoulders and drawing himself up very stiffly, "we have had information connecting you with the dog-fights which have been disgracing this neighborhood recently. Such fights are illegal and punishable under The Protection of Animals Act of 1911 and '12."

Fabian Cautley stood with bowed head, one thin hand resting on the table near him. His head sank lower still.

"It is true. It is true!" he said at last in a low whisper. "*Mea culpa. Mea culpa! Mea maxima culpa!*" and he touched his breast as might a Roman Catholic. "I vowed to myself when Howard was shot that my penance should be to speak the truth if questioned. You can ask me what you will on that point and you will hear the truth." He looked steadily at them now. Fabian Cautley had queer eyes. At times as black and bright as anthracite, at times, when his pupils were contracted, as pale as silvery metal, but now they showed as dull as wool. "Yes," he motioned the other two to sit down, but remained standing. They preferred to stand too. Somehow Fabian looked very tall in that little room. Tall and formidable and powerful.

"Do I understand that you are willing to sign a statement to that effect?" Wanklyn asked. He felt oddly uneasy, out of his element. He had to blow, as it were, on the coals of his hot feelings against this man, not to have them turn to ashes.

"No," Fabian said to that. "I will not sign any statement. Major Cautley very strongly hoped that the truth would never come out. He held it would be an indelible disgrace to the family if it were to be known. And I agree."

He was speaking slowly in a low voice. Suddenly he lifted his head.

"I will not sign any statement, but I will tell you the whole truth, as completely as mortal man can speak truth—that of which he knows nothing."

There was a pause.

"My great grandfather was a famous 'blood' of the Regency Period. A true sportsman of his time, and as cruel as only such a man could be. There are family records—accounts of sums paid to hush things up which would seem incredible to any one living nowadays. Well, I don't know how you two look on life. You"—he stared straight at Pointer for a second, and the chief inspector felt as though he had inadvertently touched a high power wire—"you are a man who serves one god—the God of Truth. You"—he glanced at Wanklyn—"serve something vaguer you call Duty. Both of you are single-minded men. Be thankful. But the point I am trying to explain is this. That great grandfather of mine lives, and uses my body still at times. He only lives in so far as he can use it. If I can resist him, and prevent his using my body, then he dies slowly. Starved. Smothered. And he ends forever. In other words, I am a battle-field in which very warring spirits fight for their existence. At times my great grandfather wins. But I think he has had his last say. There is and always has been a side to me which loves cruelty. Not sadism as people nowadays love to call it. Sadism is complex and perverted. Love of cruelty is simple, and only too natural. That side of me broke out in India. I resigned. That side of me drew me to a part of the country where I learned that fights of great ferocity were being held. I enjoyed them." Fabian ran a thin red tongue, bright scarlet, around his thin, pale lips. The effect was ferocious. "'*Erblich belastet*' the Germans call it rightly—'Weighed down with one's hereditary taint,'" Fabian went on quietly. "Well, the Major learned something that suggested I had a hand in providing money and dogs for the fights around here. I denied it when he taxed me with it. He came upon me by chance after finding a note I had written. He showed me the note, but with it he spoke words of sympathy."

"The Major!" came in an incredulous, indignant, gasp from Wanklyn.

"Oh, not of sympathy with the fights, but with me, the man who has to pay the old scores. Yes, he knew in himself something of what my struggles were, though in a far lesser degree. He told me to fight harder, not to let the old devil, our great grandfather, win. And I—I went on, with his words still in my ears, in spite of my promise to him I went on to a dog-fight. But after it was over, after I had held the winner up for his prize"—again that red tongue shot out and licked the thin lips, and Wanklyn looking at him in horror knew where the blood had come from that had stained the man's hands; not from his bleeding feet, but from the wretched dogs—"something went out in me. I—I—I left the others to watch the next fight and went out, and—and—I loathed myself.

"Then I heard that Howard was dead. I vowed then that I would beat that cruel strain in me—drive it out of this body. By every means in my power I have striven. I am still striving. I know now that I shall conquer. Of late I have been able to penetrate further in my trances and understand—dimly—more of the meaning of this swift, narrow tunnel that we call life."

"And did your great grandfather impel you to kill Mr. Lionel?" Pointer asked suddenly.

"He drew me to the place of violence, and the sight of a quarrel when Lionel all but put a hand on the throat of a girl made him glad," Fabian said, pulling his lips back in a dreadful smile. "Oh yes, Lionel had the same great grandfather, and Daphne Upjohn little knew how near to death she was for one second. I looked into his eyes and saw my double—just for one second—and I smiled at him. The girl saw me smile and screamed. I think that scream saved her. Though she will never guess that she was in any danger. Lionel flung away from her and she, I suppose, left him. I walked on. That in me which loves violence knew it was balked."

"And that is all you can tell us?" Wanklyn asked in a stifled voice.

"All?"—and somehow the figure in the thick white robe seemed to tower up in the room—"I could tell you things, my dear superintendent, which would make your eyes drop from your head. I could have traveled but for my great grandfather far along some of the lines—" he stopped, he seemed to dwindle. "I am going down to the house the Major left me, and there I shall be quiet. One more trance, and I shall touch the Things that are Real, and be safe. Free. Released."

Pointer felt as though not two men stood in that room watching a third, but three men watching a fourth—as though Fabian Cautley stood beside himself. The chief inspector disliked odd, inexplicable things, especially if they were psychic. He disliked this feeling intensely, this dim appreciation of the possibility that something not a tiger might inhabit a tiger's body, something that hated tigers.

"One moment," Wanklyn said. "About the dog-fights— was Hammersley the man who was staging them?"

Fabian held up a long hand with cruel, talon fingers. "That is for you to find out, not for me to tell you, superintendent. But with my money withdrawn, and it was withdrawn as soon as the Major died, the fights will cease. Once they knew that you were on the watch, it was only by offering big prizes that the men were willing to train their dogs."

"Ugh!" said Wanklyn loudly and clearly. "Ugh! And you wish us to believe that the Major—the Major of all men—when he learned of your share in the fights, was going to overlook it, do nothing, not give you up to the police?" He spoke contemptuously.

"Not after he had had a talk with me and learned how—how I had struggled, how I struggled on even though I was constantly being beaten"

"Wasn't he the cause of the young lady to whom you were engaged being about to break the engagement? Forgive me—alluding to that must be a very painful memory," Pointer said gravely.

"He was." For a second Fabian's face grew set. For a second he stood quite still. Then he turned his back on the two officers and stared out of the window.

"And you bore him no grudge?" Wanklyn pressed the question home.

"Why should I? It was the greatest help towards freedom that I ever had. And what else do we live for— strive for—suffer for—but for freedom?" Fabian spoke passionately.

Wanklyn looked his disgust at this sort of talk. "Anything else to tell us, sir?" he asked gruffly, and Fabian Cautley shook his head.

"Nothing that your ears are prepared to hear." Then, as Fabian's eyes met the level gaze of the chief inspector he added, "Or are willing to hear," and with that he glided from the room.

CHAPTER SIXTEEN

IT was after dinner that Mrs. Amplett discovered that a ball of brown wool was missing. The three women were alone in the drawing-room and she was working on her *petit point* embroidery.

"I only had one pound of it all told, and I was winding the last skein off when poor Lionel Cautley mistook something for an aspirin and swallowed the wrong thing. For of course that was how his death happened, as I shall explain to the coroner at the inquest. Edna, you're looking better, but still frightfully under the weather. Why not see a doctor?"

"There's a ball of brown wool just that color on the mantel in the workroom," Edna said, as she went to fetch it. She felt all nerves tonight. When would Jack send her the address of the great analyst, so that she could-know for certain. Be sure.

Mrs. Amplett took the wool and gave an exclamation of annoyance.

"What has happened to it? It's all soft. There's no core to it. I always wrap mine around a thick ball of paper."

"Perhaps the cat has been playing with it," Daphne threw in.

Mrs. Amplett thought this highly probable, and went on to speak of the advantages and disadvantages of domestic pets. She was summing up, quite like a judge, when Edna went upstairs. She could not stay long in one place. She hoped that everything would turn out all right, that her first awful fear was unnecessary, but she must know. She got out a little box done up in brown paper and carefully sealed which she had carried around with her all day. It had Mr. Bennett Bowman's name carefully printed on it, but it had no address.

It was quite an hour later when a knock came on the door of her room. A letter was handed her which

evidently had been delivered by hand, for there was no
stamp on it. It was in Jack's writing. Edna jumped at it.
At last!

"Did Mr. Jack Cautley leave this himself?" she asked.
The maid said that it was lying in the letter-box with one
for Mr. Amplett. Edna tore it open. Instead of the address
which she so impatiently wanted to learn, there was
something penciled inside which ran:

> *"Get Mr. Amplett to bring you to Dunnottar at once.
> This is most important and confidential. Don't come
> alone. Excuse scrawl.—Jack Cautley."*

She stared at it, dropped the little parcel back into her
wrist-bag—she might yet be able to post it tonight—it
was only a little past nine, and put a cloak round her.

Down in his study she found Mr. Amplett just staring
at a similar scribble.

"What on earth does this mean?" he asked, as she
came in. "This your doing, Edna?"

She shook her head and looked at his. It ran:

> *"Please bring Edna at once to Dunnottar. This is most
> important and confidential.—J. C."*

"Here is what I've had." She held out her own slip. He
read it through and compared the two.

"Practically the same 'confidential' and 'important',"
he murmured.

"Well, guardie, what about getting a move on?" Edna
asked briskly. "The sooner we get there, the sooner we
shall understand it."

"I can't possibly take you to Dunnottar at this time of
the evening," Mr. Amplett pointed out, "Mrs. Amplett
would consider that she should be consulted, and as Jack
says confidential, I hardly like to do that—"

"Of course you mustn't. It's only ten minutes' run from here. Come along, I'll spin you down in my Hornet in no time."

"It's a bit awkward," Mr. Amplett murmured, his head drooping to one side. "But if we're back in half an hour—"

"Easily. If we hurry." And they hurried.

"I can't think why he's sent for us," she said as they settled themselves in the little car. "However, as I'm frightfully keen on having a word with him anyway—I want an address in town—it fits in all right."

Mr. Amplett coughed meekly. "Not with my work, my dear, at all. Nor, I'm afraid, with Mrs. Amplett's plans for later on this evening. We're due at Barsont Towers for—"

"Oh, that's not till ten, guardie. Years and years off!" And Edna made the little Hornet go like a Bentley.

She stopped before she got to the gate.

"The drive inside is rather tricky. The late Colonel Barstairs was plainly thinking of a corkscrew when he had it altered."

Mr. Amplett got out too, and they walked side by side up to the big house set in its five-acre garden. Amplett had a torch from the car, otherwise they were in darkness, for the drive was rather shaded by trees, which kept the moonlight from being of much use. Edna felt glad that he was there. She had an absurd feeling that she did not want to go to the house at all. They came in sight of it. No lights showed. Amplett stopped. So did she. Both looked at the windows of the front upper room— Colonel and Mrs. Barstairs' bedroom it had been. Both stared. Fabian Cautley was sitting in the window now. They could see his white face above his whiter robe, with the eyes shut, and a faint smile on the thin, cruel lips. Suddenly Edna felt a horror of him. But she was a sensible girl. She had a tremendous amount of self-control. She had come here in answer to Jack's message, and she certainly did not intend to run away because she saw Fabian sitting meditating in the moonlight. But she did not hail him. For some reason which she could not name, she felt disinclined to do that.

Amplett also stared at that sitting figure; he, too, seemed to feel the same reluctance.

"He's in one of his trances," he murmured, as he rang the bell. There was no answer.

"Jack must have stepped out to meet us," he murmured. "There don't seem to be any servants—" He tried the door. It gave.

"Ah, then, he has just stepped out." Amplett looked relieved. "Shall we wait in here?" He switched on the light, then he opened a door into a room that had been Colonel Barstairs' own particular little den. "Not much changed," he said, looking around it. "Ah well! Shall we make ourselves comfortable? Jack won't be a second, I feel sure. He's bound to see our car and know you're here."

"I suppose nothing—nothing—could have happened to him?" Edna asked suddenly. It was a question so totally unexpected—from her—that Amplett rubbed his glasses and then looked at her afresh.

"Would you like me to have a look round for him?" he asked briskly. "Or would you rather I stayed and waited here with you?"

"Oh, stay!" she said at once, and then flushed at herself. "I don't mean that. He may need help—some accident—please see where he is and tell him to hurry up."

Amplett looked as if he had a bright idea. "I'll put my head out of the window and give the whistle that he knows. Our dog signal. He'll hear it and answer."

Edna's face showed relief and approval. He went to the window and tried to raise it. Then he fumbled with the catch. Then he heaved again. The window stayed shut, and what was more, on drawing aside the thick velvet curtains they saw that the outside shutters were closed too.

"No wonder it seemed a bit stuffy in here." Amplett dusted his fingers. "There was some way of locking those shutters from the inside, I remember, and taking the handle—or key—off with you. One of poor Barstairs' gadgets. Suppose we go into the next room?" He turned the knob of the door to open it for her. With an exclamation he tried it again. The handle turned, but the door did not open.

"Another of old Barstairs' dodges probably gone wrong," he said, with what looked like rather a forced smile. "Fortunately, Jack will be back any moment, even without my whistle. Tell me, Edna, why did you decide to change the bed of phlox—Riverton Gem, I think you call it—for a shorter kind? I thought those tall, upstanding chaps awfully fine."

Now Edna had not noticed the trouble over the lock, she had been endeavoring to find out the secret of the shutters, and had her back to her guardian during the little contest between himself and a locked door. For there was no gadget whatever about the lock. A key had been turned since they came in. Edna realized that he was merely making conversation, but she did her part too. They talked flowers patiently for a couple of minutes. Then she sprang up. Something seemed to be calling to her.

"I think we will go and hunt Jack up," she said, with a half apologetic smile. "I begin to think something's happened to him. After those notes to me and to you—"

"He can't be far," Amplett said reassuringly, "for I'd stake my oath I saw him slip around the corner just as we stood watching Fabian. He had his back to us. If Fabian hadn't rather—well—surprised me, I should have hailed Jack."

"Oh, I wish you had! Are you sure it was Jack?"

And with that assurance her greatest fear left her. If Jack had been all right when they arrived, nothing much could have, happened to him since. They had heard no sound except such as they made themselves.

Do you think Fabian's in a real trance?" she asked
after a moment's pause. After all, it might be a bit hard
on Mr. Amplett to ask him to go walking about after
dark. The country roads were dangerous enough with
cars nowadays. Mr. Amplett was a nervous man, as she
knew. She sat down again and tried to speak brightly of
something that would presumably, interest her
companion.

"I'm not sure," he replied cautiously.

"Well, suppose we both go and see," she suggested,
and then she laid her hand on the door knob in her turn.
Again he said his little sentence about one of the late
Colonel's gadgets having gone wrong. She glanced at him
over her shoulder.

"It's a bit awkward," he murmured, with his head a
little on one side.

She gave his arm a sudden squeeze, then she clung to
it. "We're locked in." She spoke under her breath. "Why,
guardie? What is happening to Jack outside?"

Her eyes were enormous in her little pointed face. He
patted her hand.

"Now, my dear, don't get the wind up. Remember
Colonel Barstairs' passion for mechanical aids and how
he was forever being shut in his garage or locked out of
his house. Just like the shutters, I think there's some
trick about the lock—"

She stepped back, relief for a second in her eyes. "I do
remember his telling us about this very room." She
groped back to a half-heard sentence spoken some three
or four years ago. "Something about no drafts, and yet
air." She eyed the door doubtfully, but her first, wild
terror for Jack had died down.

"Here's Jack's pipe on the mantel!" she exclaimed, "he
must have dashed out in a hurry."

Somehow that warm pipe comforted her.

Mr. Amplett began to make conversation. After a few
sentences, Edna's attention wandered. Once again she
was seized with vivid fear that something had happened

to Jack, or was about to happen to him. Why was he so long? He must see their car, and would know that she had arrived. What was the important—and confidential— something for which he had asked them both to hurry down here? Here where sat that immobile figure upstairs in the moonlight.

"What a strong smell of gas!" Mr. Amplett suddenly exclaimed. Edna had been too engrossed to notice it. "One of the taps of the gas stove—" he murmured, going over to it. "Mrs. Barstairs liked a room nearly ninety in the shade. I used to wonder how he stood it. But there's certainly some escape, though both these taps are off."

There certainly was. A few minutes more and Mr. Amplett broke the window panes, but the iron shutters outside prevented any escape of the gas now slowly filling the room.

"Lie down by the door," he told Edna. They both lay down, mouths to the crack, but a draft excluder had been nailed around the door. Even the keyhole was no help. Amplett pushed the scutcheon up on its side, only to see it down on the other side.

"Jack will be back any moment now. Call, Edna!" Nothing answered.

"Lie down and keep very still," Mr. Amplett said then. "Don't move or call any more. Try to breathe as lightly as possible " He himself sank into an armchair by the writing-desk and soon Edna could hear short, stertorous gasps coming from him. The gas was horrible. She felt herself going. Then came a terror that Jack would come in and strike a match. Mr. Amplett and she would both be dead, but he need not be sacrificed. Mr. Amplett had switched off the light, saying that it, too, used up oxygen. Perhaps it did, but Edna tried to get to the switch. If Jack should come in and strike a match... she could not find the switch... she could no longer find the wall sickening, suffocating gas seemed to fill the world.

Superintendent Wanklyn was at once informed that Miss Edna Upjohn and Mr. Amplett had driven off in her little Hornet together. There was only enough petrol to run her for half an hour or so. He fancied that she had gone for some fresh air, and that Mr. Amplett had decided she ought not to go alone. Jack Cautley had dropped something into the letter-box at Fairlawn, but more than that the superintendent did not know. His interest lay in Fabian Cautley. Fabian at Dunnottar was being watched, but by a constable whose own little home overlooked the window of the room which Fabian used exclusively. As long as Fabian was visible the policeman could keep an eye on him in comparative comfort. By day, a fresh watcher relieved him.

But there are other people in the world besides the Cautleys, and the superintendent got an urgent message from a house where a servant had taken a fancy to some of the guests' jewelry. Armed with his notebook he drove there to conduct a long inquiry into the past as well as the present.

Pointer had had to go up to see the A. C. at the Yard. He came down by a late train and decided to walk to Fairlawn. He carried about with him in his letter-case a little fragment of brown wool off a winder, and he hoped yet to come upon the ball.

As he was shown into the lounge drawing-room he saw that Mrs. Amplett at last was working on her wool embroidery. Even he could hardly refrain from giving a little start as he saw the lady threading a needle with some of the identical wool, snipping it off a large but rather shapeless brown ball—a ball he had not seen before, but of the same wool.

"Allow me," Pointer said officiously, picking it up and holding it out. There was nothing inside it—not even tissue paper. Mrs. Amplett looked bewildered.

"I beg your pardon," he apologized nicely, "I thought you were going to wind it, or something. I'm afraid I'm not much used to embroidery frames."

"It ought to be rewound," she said, putting it back on the table from which he had taken it, "the paper inside it has got lost. But about Mr. Lionel Cautley, chief inspector, I feel more than ever certain—" and she developed her theory of a mistaken pellet.

So she knew nothing about the contents of that ball. Who did? A word of hers gave him his chance—a word of praise about Scotland Yard.

"Oh, we're often quite blind," he said pleasantly. "For instance, just as the merest illustration of what I mean, of course—I missed that ball of wool from among your embroidery things—there was some wool on the winder, but no ball to match it, and I've kept my eyes open for it since. Yet this is the first time I've found it."

Daphne had strolled in. Something about her made Pointer give her a thoughtful look. She had had some sort of a jolt. Recently, he fancied.

Mrs. Amplett said some well-deserved things about how thorough-going our detectives were, and then mentioned that she thought one of the "girls" must have borrowed it for a while.

"They are always pilfering my wools and silks," she said good-humoredly, but with a gleam in her eye. "I scarcely know what to do about it. One can hardly lock one's work-bag up in a safe "

"I'll tell you what happened," Daphne put in, her voice excited and hurried, "I nearly stepped on it one day, picked it up, quite by chance, and stuffed it—without thinking—into the woolen coat I was wearing. It happened to be one of Edna's. I always borrow hers. She found the wool just now, and put it on the mantel in her workroom, where she's got it for you." There was a shade of defiance in the manner and the tone, a watchful look in the eye. Yet, hitherto, any talk of wools and balls of wool—and Pointer had managed to throw in a good many such remarks—had met with no reactions of any kind whatever.

Pointer rose on the instant. Could he have, a word with Miss Edna Upjohn? He conveyed the impression that he had only come to Fairlawn for this purpose.

"She's probably in her workroom, as she calls it," Mrs. Amplett said. "If you will be good enough to ring—"

But Pointer suggested that perhaps Miss Daphne would show him the way, as he wanted a word with both young ladies about their future plans.

The workroom was empty. A passing maid told them that Miss Edna had gone out in her Hornet with Mr. Amplett a few minutes ago.

Pointer closed the door behind the maid and turned to her. The question was, had Edna taken the contents of the ball with her? It looked like it, and the presence of Mr. Amplett—did she know that there was danger? How much would he be able to bluff out of Daphne?

"Miss Upjohn, I want the paper that was inside that ball of wool. And anything else it may have held."

She acted bewilderment, but her pupils betrayed her.

"You say you had no hand in the Major's death, nor in that of Lionel Cautley. If that is true, why do you hesitate? We know now that the pearls were not put in the ball, as was at first believed. But something infinitely more important was, for I believe that, dying, Lionel Cautley wrote some lines which would tell us who murdered first Major Cautley and then himself."

She hesitated. She was not to be easily swept off her feet by any appeal to altruism. Self-protection was the law of her being.

"As you hesitate, I think I can assume that he wrote the lines in cipher. Ciphers were his chief work down at his aeroplane works."

"I don't see why you guess that," she said hastily.

"Because if you could read what he wrote, I don't for a moment believe that you would hesitate to let me have it." Pointer spoke with a great deal more certainty than he felt. Why had Edna gone out just after that ball had been rifled? Why had she taken what looked like a protector with her?

"You can't deny," he went on gently, "that you picked it up off the floor, not far from Lionel Cautley's body, when you first went in and found him—dead."

To his surprise he saw that he had startled her and shocked her.

"So that was when it was! Oh, yes, yes! I do remember now! I got my foot tangled in the wool and jerked the ball free, and I must have stuffed it, without knowing what I was doing, into the jacket I had on. I had put on one of Edna's to go into the garden just a moment before. So that was how it got into her pocket!"

"And being in cipher," Pointer went on, "you are afraid, I think, lest he may have written down something about your share in the pearl necklace transaction? However, I don't think that he did. Will you chance it?"

Still she stood uncertain. Had Edna taken the paper, or had she got it? he wondered.

"Come," he urged, and Pointer could be most persuasive. He had a great store of personal magnetism when he cared to use it. "Come, you insist that Mr. Lionel Cautley didn't kill himself. Give me that paper, and I think we can prove it."

That did it. In a flash she opened her wrist-bag, took out a crumpled paper and handed it to him. He saw lines of meaningless words in Lionel's hand-writing, but as though written in a swaying car, large—slanting—sprawling. It was written on the back of a bill.

"Edna picked it up when it jumped out of the ball and left it on her dressing-table. Of course I had recognized Lionel's writing on it at once, so I came upstairs and found it just a scrawl of words."

"Why did you keep it?" Pointer asked. His mind was on Edna, the finder of the paper, the girl who had left it lying out—for how long?

"I thought it might be useful," she said to that. "As I only told you the truth, I thought it might confirm it. It couldn't contradict it. But I never thought about it having to do with the Major's death."

That was characteristic of Daphne Upjohn, Pointer thought. Without enjoying a long acquaintance with her, he would expect anything that touched her herself to drive all other ideas off the board.

"How long was it after the paper dropped out that you took charge of it?" he asked.

"Edna left it lying beside her for a few minutes. Until she had finished some work she was doing. Then she went upstairs and was some time in her room. I waited about, and as soon as she left it, I popped in, saw this and took it."

Pointer walked down to the gate feeling uneasy. Daphne had taken the paper off with her. But suppose some one who had also watched Edna find it, also recognized the writing, guessed what it might contain, had seen her, take it to her bedroom, had gone in, but too late to find it—might not such a person—the murderer probably—assume that she had it with her? That she knew of its importance?

Pointer, was deeply uneasy. He did not share in the least the superintendent's certainty as to Jack Cautley's innocence. He never had. Nor could Fabian be left out of the count by any means. A question up at Fairlawn had shown that no one knew where Edna had gone, except that the chauffeur was certain she only had enough petrol for a short run. Nor would Mr. Amplett be likely to absent himself for long.

A shabby little figure fell in beside the chief inspector. It was the rector coming back from one of his many errands of mercy. The two talked of the Cautleys, especially of the elder cousin. Mr. Tunbridge mentioned the odd question put him by the Major, about whether the rector had seen any one resembling him about the place, and then had to repeat all that was said on both sides.

Just for one second Pointer stood so still that the rector thought that he had dropped something and was looking for it. The good man never knew that by repeating that question of Major Cautley's to the astute Scotland Yard man, he had as clearly indicated the criminal as though he had pulled a screen away from around him. The difference between a really good and a fairly good detective is as much in the speed as in the quality of his brainwork. Chief Inspector Pointer was as instantly certain of where that Hornet had gone—must go—as though he had watched it.

Fortunately, he was near the police station and he made the distance there on the run. On to a motor bicycle he leaped, and off he went, roaring down the road. Jumping off at the gates of Dunnottar, he almost stepped on a man who came out of a little lane close to them. Pointer's torch was strapped to his left arm. One touch, and he saw Jack Cautley's strained face staring intently at him.

"What's wrong?" Jack asked breathlessly.

Pointer was sprinting up to the house. "This way, Mr. Cautley," Pointer called loudly, "the superintendent's behind!"

Jack Cautley might look dull, but he jumped to the right conclusion on the instant. The chief inspector wanted a noise to be made, wanted those in the house to know that the police were rushing up.

"House ringed round, eh?" he shouted back. "Come on, Harbord!"

Then both stopped dead. Just as Edna and Mr. Amplett had stopped a quarter of an hour before.

The figure in white sitting by that upper window did not stir, nor turn that white face on which the moonlight still shone. Pointer, calling to his companion, ran without stopping again once around the house, then he tried the front door. It was locked and bolted inside at the bottom. The first he could have dealt with in a moment, but not the bolt. Without pausing for more than that one swift trial of the door he was round to the side and shouting to Jack to follow, swarmed up a stack pipe to a lead roof, through a window which gave on it, and down the stairs, Jack some seconds behind him. The noisy chief inspector seemed to have second sight as to which room to make for. In reality, he had noticed those closed stout shutters, the only closed ones to be seen. He expected the door to be locked, and was ready with his little wonder-tool, a souvenir of a visit to Vienna. A shout, a swift turn, a sharp creak, and he flung the door open, to be met by what seemed a tangible wall of gas—so thick was it.

"Where's the wall switch, do you know?" Pointer asked, but already his long arm and groping fingers had found it. Drawing each a deep breath they rushed in. Another moment and the two motionless figures were dragged out to the front step. One had collapsed close to the switch, one by the desk. They were in time. Both were breathing, though Mr. Amplett's face was gray-white and livid, whereas Edna's was flushed a rosy pink. Jack knew where the telephone was, and was calling up the nearby hospital in another moment. "Case of gas poisoning at Dunnottar. Could they send a doctor?"

"And a couple of cylinders of oxygen," Pointer suggested. The idea was approved at the hospital. Dr. Broadmore and two nurses and two cylinders would be round in a moment. Meanwhile, if the gassed person was cold, dash warm water over the head and down the spine; if warm, do the same with cold water.

"What brought you so opportunely to this spot?" Pointer asked, as they carried out instructions.

"Had a note, ostensibly from Miss Edna Upjohn, telling me to hang round, something about the pearls changing hands here tonight, outside the gate probably. But what about that mad devil upstairs? Sure he can't escape? I—I hand him over to you. Lock him up. Take him away. He was in it all—the dog-fights—both murders."

Pointer gave him rather an odd look, but said that no one could escape. They heard the hospital car honking from the gate. A moment later a very efficient-looking trio stepped, out, lugging two long cylinders with them. Pointer lingered just long enough to hear that both patients ought to come round soon, then he ran lightly up the stairs. Jack Cautley had to be asked to follow him, but when he grasped the idea, he too rushed for that room where sat his kinsman in the moonlight.

Pointer was bending over Fabian. Jack, with an exclamation, tried to lift one of the hands placed, forefingers and thumbs forming each a ring, on the figure's knees. He could not shift them. Fabian Cautley was stiff and cold, dead some hours, with that curious half smile on his thin, cruel lips.

"He's killed himself! He's escaped!" Jack Cautley was fairly trembling. For a moment it looked as though he would have shaken that rigid form, struck that blandly smiling face, set as though carved in stone.

"We'll get the doctor to have a look at him," Pointer said quietly, as he left the room, after one keen glance round.

Tibetan prayer rugs hung from the corners, a curious drawing on the parquet floor surrounded the dead man himself. There was the smell of strange incense in the air still, faint but quite noticeable.

Pointer noted all these things in his remarkable memory. He would have liked to go at once to the room still reeking of gas below, but he did not wish to leave the dead body with only Jack Cautley. His dilemma was over even as it arose, for the quick whirr of a couple of motor cycles outside announced that the two police whom he had told to follow had arrived. To one of them was given the task of watching over Fabian Cautley's "remains"—a good name Fabian always considered that rather old-fashioned word—and he himself went downstairs. The doctor nodded briefly when told that there was a dead man upstairs.

"These were lucky in being saved early." He was very young, and trying to be impressive on this, his first encounter with the police. He evidently assumed that the third person had died from the same cause—a gas escape. Pointer said he would take him up as soon as he thought that the two over whom he was now working could be left to the nurses. A glance from the elder of the women suggested that in her opinion nothing was, or had been, gained by the presence of young Dr. Broadmore.

Pointer found the room still not safe to go into, and after a few minutes' waiting, the medical man came out of the dining-room into which Edna had been carried and nodded. "She'll do now. So will he. Both are on the right road, though he's still unconscious. Harder to rouse than the girl—as one would expect, seeing the difference in ages."

"This way," Pointer said, and led the other to where Jack Cautley stood, hands in pockets, and with a grim look on his face, staring down at Fabian as though mutely asking several questions. The policeman on duty in the doorway watched both the living and the dead Cautley.

"How is she getting on?" Jack whirled around on the doctor's entrance.

"Quite safe, now," was the comforting assurance,, and Jack's set face relaxed into what looked like heartfelt relief. He went below, and the doctor bent over Fabian. Then he stared with wide-open eyes at Inspector Pointer.

"He hasn't been gassed!"

"Indeed?" Pointer looked quite surprised. "Then, in your opinion, how did he die, doctor?"

"He looks positively uncanny!" Dr. Broadmore murmured under his breath, as they tried to lay him down. It was as though they had hold of a statue of Buddha. Fabian had stiffened in the cross-legged, hands-in-lap position in which he had evidently died.

They undressed him with difficulty. There were no marks on him, except on the back, which was deeply lacerated, scarred and bruised.

"Looks as if he had been in the hands of the Cheka," the young medical man murmured, catching his lip between his teeth. "Fabian Cautley told me himself that he had traveled a lot in the East. But these cuts on the back, marks of floggings evidently, look to me quite recent."

Pointer could have told him how very recent some of them were—how Fabian Cautley had tried to drive out that horrible strain which at times swamped everything else in him.

"And the cause of death?" he asked instead.

"No symptom of gas poisoning. Nor any other poison. Looks like plain heart failure. But the autopsy will make it clearer."

It did not. Heart failure was the nearest they ever got to knowing just how Fabian had died. A "fellow climber," as he called himself, told Pointer long after that Fabian had once said that, should he ever find his strain of cruelty in him growing too strong to conquer, he would leave his body, as a Malay can, by willing to die. And he added that Fabian had been for three years the pupil of a man at Benares who taught that method of liberation from the body's chains.

Pointer followed the young doctor downstairs again, and this time he was able to get into the room which, but for him, would have been a death-trap.

CHAPTER 17

POINTER spent only a few minutes in the room. The brass gas pipe had been detached from the stove, corked and bent forward against the metal curb in such a way that if the curb were shifted ever so slightly and the cork taken out, the gas would pour out unimpeded. Yet, bent back against the curb, it was not at all easy to see that anything was wrong. From the freedom from dust it looked as though the job were a very recent one.

He went back into the hall. Edna had been carried by the nurses into the drawing-room and made comfortable there. Mr. Amplett had been taken into the library and stretched out by the window. A nurse was just feeding him with brandy as Pointer came in. The doctor said that Mr. Amplett seemed to be going on all right now. Pointer thanked him for the speed with which he had rushed over, and assured him that the police could now manage quite well. If they left one nurse for Miss Upjohn, that should be ample, and she too would probably soon be released. The doctor and the other nurse were only too glad to get back to the hospital. Pointer went in for a word with Edna. He found Jack Cautley in the corridor outside and took him in with him. Edna was to talk as much as possible, the doctor had said. Using her lungs would help to work out the gas.

She looked up with big eyes as they entered, eyes that had not expected to open again, ever.

"Are they poisonous? she asked tensely, in a tone of agonized interest "Was there aconitum in them? Oh, don't you know yet—" Her voice grew resigned.

"Didn't I send them off?" she asked next. Her gaze was on Jack, and her expression grew more like itself. "I remember now. You didn't give me his address."

"Whose?" Jack's voice was that of a man completely bewildered.

"Mr. Bennett Bowman's address. I wanted to get him to analyze for me some plant food pellets which I had left on the mantel. They looked rather like big round aspirin tablets, and I've been so horribly afraid they might have been what killed Lionel. I put some out in front of the mirror to use for the plants. I hoped I had only put three out, and if so, no one had touched them, for I found all three there, after his death, but I couldn't be sure. I might have put out five, or six, and Lionel—" Her voice grew tired. She closed her eyes for a second. "I ought to have told you, I know." She fixed her eyes on Pointer when she opened them again, "but I couldn't! If it had been my fault, it would have ruined Daphne's life. And Jack would never have forgiven me... it would have broken his heart too..." She held out a shaky hand, which Jack clasped.

He looked interrogatively at the chief inspector. "Is she wandering?" his eyes said.

Pointer bent down. "I can set your mind at rest, Miss Upjohn, about those pellets. I take it they're the same as the ones in your desk. The ones labeled '*Plant Food Drops*'?"

"Yes, yes!" Edna said eagerly.

"We had them analyzed at once. They're potash. I don't say they would do a person any good, but the analyst told us that there's not a touch of aconitum in them."

"You're sure?" she asked. "I thought Mr. Bennett Bowman would be the very best man to send them to?"

"He's a wonderful expert certainly," Pointer agreed, "though best known for his cipher work and as a handwriting expert, but you may be quite sure there's no mistake," and he patted the little brown hand clutching nervously at the quilt thrown over her.

"Thank God!" Edna said and closed her eyes again.

Three pellets... Pointer thought of the three marks in the dust which Wanklyn thought might have been made by the Cautley pearls.

"And when did you send them off to be analyzed?" he asked.

"I haven't sent them at all." Her voice was growing more flexible again. "At first—just now—I fancied I had done as I meant to do. I got them all ready and asked Jack to let me have the address without fail. I didn't want any local man to have them, or any one in the house to know what I was doing."

"One moment, Miss Upjohn, did any one hear you ask Mr. Cautley for the address?"

"Miss Smith might have heard, but I don't think so, and, as far as I knew, no one else was anywhere near."

Pointer was quite certain that some one had heard and had thought that what Edna intended to send off was the paper which she had taken from the ball of wool, the paper whose existence the murderer had at first suspected, and then decided against, believing that Lionel Cautley had not been able to use his pen during the dreadful agony of his last moments. It was the popping out of that paper core with Lionel Cautley's writing on it, the words of Edna's about wanting the address of a man famous as a cipher-expert, which, Pointer thought, had been the cause of that gas-filled room.

"And now that that is settled, and forever, suppose you tell us why you and Mr. Amplett came down here," he went on.

"Because Jack asked us to come, and at once!" She went on to tell of the two notes. Jack Cautley would have interrupted, but a look from the chief inspector made him close his mouth with the words unsaid. Pointer made light of the whole affair. Edna had had a very close shave, but not until tomorrow would she know that the peril had been intentional. Had she got the note with her? She thought it might be in the pocket of her cloak. There was nothing there but the counterfoil for a stall ticket forgotten from weeks ago.

He listened very carefully to her account of the dreadful moments in the room downstairs. Then he and Jack left her.

"Well, Mr. Cautley?" Pointer asked when they were out of hearing.

"She was got down here, just as I was, by a forgery. I sent her, as I promised, Bowman's address—dropped it in their letter-box. I never wrote to Amplett at all. I got a line from her myself after dinner saying that I was to hang around the farther end of the lane that starts here at the house, as she had learned that something was to take place there tonight connected with those damned pearls. It was a most mysterious line, but *'confidential'* and *'urgent'* were underscored. The scrawl looked like hers and was on the rather peculiar paper she uses. Of course that mad brute up there, Fabian, meant to get all three of us. Just me alone would be too obvious."

"Have you the note?" Pointer asked.

Jack Cautley said that he had been asked in it to destroy it, and had done so immediately. "'Burn this as soon as you have read it' were the directions."

"Suppose we hear what Mr. Amplett has to tell us," Pointer said next.

They found him looking far less well than Edna, and with a voice that was but a choking whisper. He added nothing to what Edna had told them, and when asked for his note, thought they would find it in his coat pocket. It was not there however.

Jack told him of the summons which he himself had received.

"And your pipe?" croaked Amplett, "it was your pipe on the mantel."

Jack could only say that obviously it was not difficult to get hold of one of his six or seven pipes and put it wherever it would look most effective.

"Lucky you didn't come in," Amplett said. "We first, and then you, was the menu, I suppose? The gas must have been turned on just as the two of us got to the house."

Jack agreed with set jaw. "I wasn't far from the house at any time—yet far enough for her to have been murdered. For, of course, that gas wasn't accidental, was it, chief inspector?"

"No," Pointer said gravely. "It was a planned, attempt at murder, Mr. Cautley."

"And the man who planned it has escaped us," Jack finished.

Wanklyn now arrived unannounced.

"The unmitigated fiend is in hell at this moment, I hope," Jack went on passionately.

"Suppose you go back to Miss Upjohn and get her to talk some more," Pointer interposed. Jack Cautley was out of the room in a moment, his further wishes for his cousin left unheard for the moment.

Wanklyn would have spoken, but Pointer made him a sign to keep silent. Amplett suddenly began to toss on the chaise longue.

"He's been twitchy, sir, at intervals," the constable beside him said. "The doctor was a bit worried, but he thought the intervals would grow further apart."

"Fabian!" came from Amplett now, "I hear you walking to and fro outside the door. Open it! Break it down! Help! Gas! Help!" The last was a strangled half-cry.

The constable, in obedience to Pointer's glance, went outside.

"We shall be able to manage him quite easily," said the chief inspector, as he laid a hand on the twitching man's shoulder.

"Don't trouble to act any more, Amplett. I arrest you for the murder of Major Cautley, for the murder of Lionel Cautley, and the attempted murder of Miss Edna Upjohn here tonight. I warn you that any statement—" He proceeded to do so, with both hands holding Amplett down by main force. And to Wanklyn's horrified eyes it was as though Amplett was changing by some incantation into a sort of werewolf with horrible, murderous eyes and slavering jaws.

"We had better fasten your hands together," Pointer snapped the handcuffs on as he spoke. A tap on the window pane and two constables came in. To them Amplett was given in charge. They were to take him to jail, lock him, handcuffed, into a cell and wait for further orders.

Wanklyn frankly wiped his forehead when the police car had driven off.

"Are you sure he's not really ill?" Wanklyn asked. "He looked like a madman and—I suppose he must really have been gassed—" Wanklyn was all at sea. The report he had received on arriving did not fit in at all with these developments.

"Come into the room where the gas was turned on—by him," Pointer said to that. "See this old painted tile on the wall, one of a pair on both sides of the bureau? Lift it off its nail and you'll find—" He showed the other end of what looked like a speaking tube. "It's an air tube, merely leading into the fresh air outside. Mrs. Barstairs was fond of stiflingly hot rooms; her husband had this tube put in here when the gas stove was put in. The idea was that it could lie on his desk or on the top of his armchair here beside it, and he could get a breath of fresh air while his wife baked by the fire. Ingenious, eh? See these keys in this drawer,"—Pointer pulled one open to show the usual huddle of unwanted spare keys—"one of them will be the key to this room or I shall be much surprised. This one for choice." And picking it up with his handkerchief—it was a bright-looking key—the chief inspector tried it and showed Wanklyn how it fitted.

"But—but—when? Immediately on entering, of course—" Wanklyn answered his own question.

Pointer nodded. "The lock was oiled. Probably Miss Edna would wrestle with those shutters and wouldn't hear anything that he did. Just as he must have shot that bolt home on the front door, when closing it behind them both. Shot it home with his foot while feeling for the wall switch in the darkness, we may be sure. Here's a key that probably would unlock those shutters—" Pointer picked another out.

"But who closed them?" Wanklyn asked.

"Oh, Amplett, of course. When he ran down here in his own little car and set this stage."

"And when was that?" Wanklyn could not sort things out yet.

"As soon as he could slip away after hearing Miss Edna ask Mr. Jack for the address of a handwriting and cipher expert. She wanted him only as an analyst, but Amplett didn't know that, and he had just seen her pick up a paper written by Lionel Cautley in cipher. His keen little eyes would have seen the lines of words. It's but a few minutes in a car, and Amplett's little Sunbeam could do it nicely. I feel sure that the chauffeur will tell us— when we ask him—that Amplett drove off to the station, or the post, or some such innocent little errand this evening before he accompanied Miss Edna. Then when he got back, he found the note Mr. Jack Cautley had dropped in the letterbox giving the expert's address. He slipped in quite another note and put it along with one to himself, written in the same strain."

"Meanwhile he had come down here, locked those shutters, bent and corked that gas-pipe, oiled that lock—" Wanklyn stared about him. "He knew this house well," he said finally. "He and old Colonel Barstairs were great friends.

"Then when that Mr. Fabian wanted me to lock her up, or keep an eye on her—was it for her own sake? Did he know she was in danger?" Wanklyn was struck by this new idea.

This was the first that Pointer had heard of the warning. He listened to it now and nodded.

"It looks like it. Whether finally, or from the first, he seems to have suspected Amplett. Those meditations of

his were never far from him, if you remember. He may
have been more psychic than we know."

"Well, he tried to do one good turn to some one,
anyway," Wanklyn said half-grudgingly. "Little Miss
Edna has a great look of the girl who died, to whom
Fabian Cautley was once engaged. Was it he who
knocked out Todd that first night of the Major's death, do
you think?"

Pointer did not. He suggested that a question to Jack
Cautley would show that Lionel and he had hoped to
have a quiet inspection of the stile, that Lionel had been
pounced on by the watching constable, and that he, Jack,
had laid Todd out with a neat uppercut. A later question
established this guess as the truth.

"But, look here, Pointer," Wanklyn now said almost in
a tone of pain, "Why Mr. Amplett? Mr. Amplett, who
always found things rather awkward? What in God's
name had he to gain by the Major's death, and by the
poisoning of Lionel Cautley? Obviously it's not for the
sake of the Cautley fortune that he killed them both.
What had he to do with the pearls?"

"Ah!" Pointer gave a faint smile, "as regards the
Cautley pearls, I fancy that Amplett acted the part of
justice, retribution, and so on. Miss Daphne is about as
careless a damsel as exists about letters and personal
memoranda. I fancy we shall find that Amplett, having
decided to do away with Major Cautley, looked about for a
safe cover should one become necessary, and found out
from her papers that all was not as it should be with that
necklace. I think he took possession of the papers that
she has missed and decided to stampede whoever was
concerned, Daphne Upjohn alone, or Lionel Cautley with
her, into some foolish action or actions—as he did, with
his talk of Major Cautley asking for the return of the
necklace when he should come down to Fairlawn. All
along that struck me as a trifle quaint; but not at all if
Amplett had suggested to the Major that Lionel had the
pearls with him and intended to return them then."

"And the real motive was?" Wanklyn asked, after rubbing his chin hard.

"I don't know yet. Not until these lines of Lionel Cautley's are deciphered." He showed him the paper and told its history.

"And you think we shall find—what?—written down here," Wanklyn scanned the meaningless words rather hopelessly.

"I think we shall find the whereabouts of a paper to which—as I think—Amplett had forged the Major's name. If I'm right, Amplett couldn't destroy it, any more than would the Major."

"What paper?" demanded Wanklyn.

"Some paper authorizing the sale of some of Miss Edna Upjohn's property," was the reply.

Wanklyn stared.

"I should expect it to be a Power of Attorney," Pointer went on serenely, "as the simplest and most comprehensive. At any rate, I think we shall find that Amplett forged the Major's signature to it. That in some way—perhaps through a bank manager's casual words—Lionel Cautley came to hear of it."

"Ah!" breathed Wanklyn. "I heard him turning over some papers when I left him after seeing him at his club. They might have been notes of his about what he knew or had been told." They were. "When we first learned about a C.A. having been asked to go through his books, I thought they had to do with some defalcations. But we've just learned, or I have—I haven't had time to tell you yet—that all his books are in perfect order, only vilely kept. So when he broke into the Major's flat, and was nearly caught by the porter, it would have been for some letters or statement received by, or written to, the Major? Pity he didn't find any."

"I think he found it all right, Wanklyn," Pointer said. "I think the crackle you heard when he was looking through the Major's papers with you and Mr. Mason was made by one he slipped up his sleeve, much more likely than by one he dropped. If I'm right, the cipher message he left may refer to it." They were very shortly to find that it did.

"It's just the sort of way Mr. Lionel would have acted under those circumstances," Wanklyn went on half to himself, "that's where knowing a man beforehand helps. Yes, Mr. Lionel Cautley would want to convict Amplett himself if he thought he had murdered his cousin. A Cautley killed would demand a Cautley avenger to his way of thinking."

Then Wanklyn left the Cautleys on one side for the moment, and came back with a jerk to the present, as Pointer went on:

"Be that as it may. I think Amplett, when questioned by the Major, maintained that some one had impersonated the Major, and that he, Amplett, had been completely hoodwinked on a foggy day."

"But when did you learn of all this? Why didn't you tell me?" Wanklyn was deeply hurt and surprised. This didn't seem like Chief Inspector Pointer at all.

"I only tumbled to it myself an hour or so ago. You were away, or, of course, I should have told you at once. The parson met me and said that the Major had asked him if he had ever met any one resembling him on his walks around Woodhampton. Well, that pointed straight to the truth—to the real criminal."

"I'm glad you call that straight. How did it point to Amplett?" Wanklyn demanded almost indignantly.

"The Major had not asked any such question down at his works, only here at Woodhampton, and Mr. Amplett had not mentioned it to us. Yet was it likely that he would ask the parson, and not Amplett? Then why had Amplett kept it back? It was not the kind of question he would have forgotten, he who remembered so carefully so much about the Major's alleged absent-mindedness, and odd interest in that gap by the stile. Then why had he not spoken of it to us? The question could have but one answer. Because it was he who had spoken to the Major about mistaking some one else for him, and did not want us to know about it—because it was a lie. The only connection in which such a lie that the Major had an impersonator—would be of any use to Amplett must be in reference to Miss Edna Upjohn. For a trustee can't delegate his authority, he must sign in person, as you know. Suppose Amplett to have been tampering with Miss Edna's property—he might even have chosen the Major as his co-trustee on General Vesey's death because he thought him not overquick at noticing—"

"He looked dull," Wanklyn threw in, "but was as keen as a hawk."

"So I think Amplett found. By the way, the lens Lionel Cautley was to fetch now fits in, eh?"

"By jove!" agreed Wanklyn fervently "Of course! To examine that alleged signature."

"And that about Mr. Lionel having wanted to write a letter!" Wanklyn's tone of disgust drew a nod from Pointer.

"Just so. The pellets were where Mr. Lionel would be sure to take them before the interview for which he had asked Amplett. If, indeed, they weren't swallowed immediately after his talk with Miss Upjohn."

"Supposing Mr. Lionel hadn't taken them at all?"

"We may be sure, at least I am, that Amplett would have resorted to other, but equally efficacious methods. Of one thing I feel certain, Mr. Cautley would not have left that interview alive."

"I suppose Amplett found him dead when he went in..." and Wanklyn began putting together his notes of what had just happened at Dunnottar.

At the trial it was found that Edna had owned a row of small houses near Smithfield Markets. An offer had been made for these by a big meat importing firm. Amplett had discussed the matter with the Major, who made some inquiries, and thought that a far better price could be obtained in another ten years. Amplett, a tobacco broker, got into difficulties over some speculations he made and was only able to save himself by bolstering up his bank account with a couple of thousands obtained by an immediate sale of the houses in question. A worse moment could not have been found than the actual one for a discovery that the property no longer belonged to Edna, and that the money obtained for it must be accounted for. Confronted with the Major's utterly unexpected questions about it, Amplett, unable to deny the sale, alleged that he had had a telephone message purporting to come from Major Cautley, and that he thought it was the Major who, in the Major's car, had stopped for a moment at Fairlawn, refused to come into the house, signed the Power of Attorney on his knee and driven off, in what he claimed was a most tremendous hurry.

It was not a story that would hold water, but Amplett was taken absolutely unprepared, and there were not many stories he could have told that would fit the facts.

"I have an idea that Amplett did all he could to throw suspicion on Lionel Cautley. The Major, who seems to've been alert enough with things that he could see, but not particularly quick where people were concerned, seems to've been half inclined to believe Amplett's story— indignation—amazement. But Lionel apparently came down from town with some letter, or new fact, that he had hunted out which the Major at first refused to believe and then, after telling Lionel to do his damnedest, began to think it over, and it looks as though the more Major Cautley thought it over, the less sure did he feel of Amplett's good faith. At any rate, he decided to send a telephone message summoning Mr. Mason hotfoot, to put on record his repudiation of the signature in question, we may be sure."

"And, of course, he would send it from the post-office telephone," Wanklyn struck in.

"He would. And very possibly he wanted to delete Mr. Amplett's name as a possible co-executor to his own will. At any rate, after the last high words with Mr. Lionel, I think he intended to go straight back to Fairlawn and have it out with Amplett at once—who forestalled him."

"Having overheard the meeting between the two cousins and guessed the reason for the telephoning, Wanklyn finished, "and after the Major's murder, Mr. Lionel would have gone for Amplett," Wanklyn went on. "He loved to play a bold game always. I shouldn't wonder if he taxed him to his face with the double crime. Theft, and murder to cover up theft."

"After apparently waiting to receive some paper," Pointer thought. "Or why the delay?"

They learned at the trial that it was a letter from another solicitor referring to previous sales of property which Lionel needed. As for Edna Upjohn herself, by her father's will she had no power of interference of any kind in her inheritance until she should be thirty years old.

"Anyway, Amplett had plenty of time to prepare his pellets, should they be needed. I believe that fortunately for us, while dying, Lionel Cautley wrote down all the facts the prosecution must know in order to trace what Amplett had done. That Power of Attorney, too, which I think will be at the heart of all this, luckily can't be injured in any way, for it's Amplett's authority. He must always be able to produce it."

"Clever hiding-place Mr. Lionel found. But then he was clever. And it was like him, too, to put Mr. Amplett off with fingering those plants. I suppose Amplett got in in some way before any one else and had a look-see?"

Pointer thought so. He believed that Amplett had locked Lionel Cautley in just as he had locked Edna Upjohn in. But in the former case, when he was quite sure that life was extinct, Amplett would have gone back to make certain that there was no incriminating paper on him, and to put the door-key in the dead man's pocket to stage suicide. That was when that hasty lifting up and repotting of the plants in front of the mirror had taken place. Fortunately for justice, the murderer had not thought of the brown ball of wool which, with his last effort, the dying man had rolled far away from himself so that only a loop of brown wool remained on the floor, the loop which had caught in Daphne's shoes.

"As for Miss Edna," Wanklyn said, coming out of deep thought once again, "I don't doubt but that Amplett would think it high time she was got rid of. His stewardship wouldn't have to be accounted for then, as her money goes to Miss Daphne, and he would have been her trustee, too. Yes, but for you, Pointer, Miss Edna was certainly for it. But what about her marrying Mr. Jack? By jove, Mr. Amplett must have raged inwardly when he had to clear away Mr. Lionel, which would give Jack Cautley the Major's fortune, and so let him marry Miss Edna. For Mr. Jack would want a very strict account of Mr. Amplett's guardianship."

Pointer agreed that the attachment between his ward and the man whom his two murders made owner of a big fortune must have been very galling to Mr. Amplett. He had not in the least objected to their attachment so long as it looked quite hopeless for Jack to marry for years, but it was precisely because he became wealthy that Mr. Amplett decided that he must be implicated in Edna's death, and so by inference in those of his cousins. It would have been very hard for Jack to prove his innocence once Mr. Amplett finally got his plans well going, Pointer thought, and as Jack suspected Fabian, the real criminal would have been able to hatch quite a successful egg.

"But what made you guess Amplett would make for Dunnottar?" Wanklyn asked after they had discussed the probable fate intended for Jack. "I heard from two constables that you sped off as straight as an arrow and nearly as fast."

"There wasn't any other place for him to take her," Pointer said serenely. Then in answer to Wanklyn's stare, he explained: "It wouldn't do to have a third death anywhere near Fairlawn. Fabian Cautley really did lose all consciousness in his trances at times. He had told the circle at Fairlawn that he was here in solitude to practise losing himself. He had no servant, for as he was fasting except for a little fruit, he needed none, he said. Fabian Cautley was an ideal man for the murderer to pick on as his dummy."

"But how did he put it past the doctor?" Wanklyn suddenly broke out. "Gas-poisoning—how did he do it?"

Pointer was inwardly amused at the question.

"My dear Wanklyn! Think of the scene. Two bodies dragged out of a gas-filled room—one half-dead, one appearing to be unconscious—both reeking of gas, for Mr. Amplett's hair and clothes were saturated with it. You can't prove gas poisoning except by blood tests and an autopsy. Of course, the doctor—a young 'un too—was taken in! Any doctor would have been. Amplett looked ghastly. It's not a light matter to murder a girl you don't dislike. And Amplett didn't dislike Miss Edna we may be sure. Also, he must have trembled for fear he had made some slip. For, until the detective makes one, the criminal can't be sure he himself hasn't!"

"Thorough-going actor," Wanklyn said slowly, "Miss Edna seems to've had no idea—I mean he evidently kept it up to the end—" Wanklyn's tone was a question.

Pointer almost laughed. "Remember Fabian Cautley up above unexpectedly up above as far as Amplett was concerned. He must have had a fearful shock when he first caught sight of him at the window, but, without knowing he was dead, he knew those trances of his. But there was just a chance that he might come downstairs and spoil things—which was why he took no risks and, as you say, played the game in front of Miss Edna to the end. Though I doubt if he wouldn't have done so anyway. He wouldn't have wanted a scene anything awkward."

"Thorough-going actor," Wanklyn repeated, who could not see Mr. Amplett in that part at all, not even yet, "to have locked himself in with Miss Edna and the gas. He might have locked her in, and slipped away out of the house?"

"And be known to have driven her here? Couldn't be done, Wanklyn. Also there was Fabian Cautley sitting up aloft. But put yourself in Amplett's place, and remember that you are a cold-blooded, utterly selfish, nervous little man. Major Cautley is killed near your house while staying with you. Lionel Cautley is poisoned in your house. Your ward is to be found gassed not far away... Each one linked with Amplett and Fairlawn. No, his only chance was to do what he did—appear to be a victim too, and appear to be saved only with the greatest difficulty."

"That was why he was so hard to bring round," Wanklyn began to get Amplett in the right focus.

"That and genuine shock and exhaustion. His third murder, Wanklyn, and Jack Cautley marked down as still one more."

"Good brainwork, Pointer," the assistant commissioner said, when it was all over, and Amplett, duly hanged, after writing a full confession, which showed how correct had been Pointer's reasoning. "Good brainwork to have seen the light from that one question about a man resembling the Major."

"Not so quick as it sounds, sir." Pointer always tried to whittle away a compliment. "We had been trying all other possibilities. A shame Major wouldn't fit in with the dog-fights. No one had tried to pretend that he had been present at any, or had anything to do with them beyond trying to stop them, and it wouldn't fit the Cautley pearls, about which we knew everything. Those had been our two strings up till then. But it must fit something. He was Amplett's co-trustee. In a flash the light fell where it belonged," Pointer finished vaguely with a smile.

"That pearl necklace, of course, was a godsend to Amplett." Major Pelham lit a cigar.

"I rather fancy he finally thought that the idea of using it was sent him straight from the devil, sir. Of course, he had not intended to let out a word about its being missing to us, as long as the Major's death passed for an accident. But Mrs. Amplett barged in and forced it immediately into the front rank. Supplied a motive just when Wanklyn was hunting for one. Then, too, Mr. Mason came down instantly, and joined in the hunt. Of himself, Mr. Mason would never have breathed a word of its loss to the police, nor to any one but Mr. Lionel."

"I wonder what Lionel Cautley really knew about it." Pelham had speculated more than once on this.

"I think at first he was afraid that Miss Upjohn had got it—through Harbord—back at once from the Major's pocket. At any rate, he saw that as Wanklyn was making it the motive for the Major's murder, Amplett would be only too glad to bolster it up as that, and would snatch at any slip Miss Upjohn had made, or would make, either to use as a weapon against her, or to escape from him, Lionel, and he dearly wanted to catch him himself. Apart from any question of his own honor being involved in All the trickery about the duplicate, I think he was transported with fury at her for having provided Amplett with such a hold."

"And Jack Cautley, the only Cautley left now, suspected his cousin Fabian?"

"From the first. He says his original fear was lest the Major's death be foisted on to Lionel, which was why he insisted on supplying him with a false alibi. He thought then—wrongly as we know—that Lionel suspected Fabian too.. When Lionel himself was murdered, his suspicion became a certainty. He intended to draw Fabian on to try to kill him—Jack—and then get him!"

"I wonder if he would have handed him over to justice even then" mused the assistant commissioner. Pointer wondered too. He doubted it. At any rate, he felt sure that Jack Cautley would have laid a revolver down by his cousin's side and left him alone with it before telephoning to the police.

"Curious character, Fabian Cautley's. Terrible legacy his," Major Pelham said. "I met him years ago. Brilliant young fellow then."

"Poor devil!" Pointer said under his breath. "I think he had a feeling that something was wrong before the Major came down, but couldn't place it. I think at first that he believed—as we all did that the pearls were at the root of the Major's death. He watched Miss Daphne and that Harbord lad like a lynx. But in the end I fancy he guessed the real criminal and the real motive. Which was why he tried to get Miss Edna out of danger by having Wanklyn lock her up or watch her very closely. Unfortunately, anything coming from him just then was more than suspected. We had learned that very day about his connection with those dog-fights."

"Yes, that's one thing this case has accomplished besides removing Amplett—those fights have stopped entirely."

There was a short silence.

"But what was the real reason?" the assistant commissioner asked, after the whole story had been carefully unfolded step by step. We know that you were quite right about the cipher, about the forged signature to the Power of Attorney and the rest but what was the reason behind the motive? Amplett has a rich wife, a good standing in the county? What lay behind it all?"

"Miss Smith," was the unexpected reply. "Or perhaps, going further back, one should say Mrs. Amplett. At any rate, Amplett was madly in love—if one can call his infatuation by that fine name—with his secretary. The secretary wouldn't run away with him without ample funds, but would go to South America as his ostensible wife, if a certain settlement was made on her. Mrs. Amplett had the money, not Amplett, and he couldn't get hold of her funds as he could of Miss Edna Upjohn's. Incidentally, I've found that Miss Smith's father was Pinckney."

"The forger? You think she inherited his gifts?" "She may well have done, sir."

"How convenient for Amplett. But the prosecution didn't suggest it, did they?"

"No sir. Miss Smith gave them too much help. She was prepared to hand over any letters or papers in return for immunity." Pointer began putting his papers together. "Excuse me, sir, I've promised to be at Mr. Cautley's wedding, and there's not much time."

"No wonder he insisted on your being there. But for you, he would now have to be looking around for another bride."

Which might have been put differently, but Pointer only flushed and hurried away.

THE END

Other Resurrected Press Books in *The Chief Inspector Pointer Mystery* Series

Death of John Tait
Murder at the Nook
Mystery at the Rectory
Scarecrow
The Case of the Two Pearl Necklaces
The Charteris Mystery
The Eames-Erskine Case
The Footsteps that Stopped
The Clifford Affair
The Cluny Problem
The Craig Poisoning Mystery
The Net Around Joan Ingilby
The Tall House Mystery
The Wedding-Chest Mystery
The Westwood Mystery
Tragedy at Beechcroft

MYSTERIES BY ANNE AUSTIN

Murder at Bridge

When an afternoon bridge party attended by some of Hamilton's leading citizens ends with the hostess being murdered in her boudoir, Special Investigator Dundee of the District Attorney's office is called in. But one of the attendees is guilty? There are plenty of suspects: the victim's former lover, her current suitor, the retired judge who is being blackmailed, the victim's maid who had been horribly disfigured accidentally by the murdered woman, or any of the women who's husbands had flirted with the victim. Or was she murdered by an outsider whose motive had nothing to do with the town of Hamilton. Find the answer in... **Murder at Bridge**

One Drop of Blood

When Dr. Koenig, head of Mayfield Sanitarium is murdered, the District Attorney's Special Investigator, "Bonnie" Dundee must go undercover to find the killer. Were any of the inmates of the asylum insane enough to have committed the crime? Or, was it one of the staff, motivated by jealousy? And what was is the secret in the murdered man's past. Find the answer in... **One Drop of Blood**

AVAILABLE FROM RESURRECTED PRESS!

GEMS OF MYSTERY
LOST JEWELS FROM A MORE ELEGANT AGE

Three wonderful tales of mystery from some of the best known writers of the period before the First World War -

A foggy London night, a Russian princess who steals jewels, a corpse; a mysterious murder, an opera singer, and stolen pearls; two young people who crash a masked ball only to find themselves caught up in a daring theft of jewels; these are the subjects of this collection of entertaining tales of love, jewels, and mystery. This collection includes:

- **In the Fog - by Richard Harding Davis's**

- **The Affair at the Hotel Semiramis - by A.E.W. Mason**

- **Hearts and Masks - Harold MacGrath**

AVAILABLE FROM RESURRECTED PRESS!

THE EDWARDIAN DETECTIVES
LITERARY SLEUTHS OF THE EDWARDIAN ERA

The exploits of the great Victorian Detectives, Poe's C. Auguste Dupin, Gaboriau's Lecoq, and most famously, Arthur Conan Doyle's Sherlock Holmes, are well known. But what of those fictional detectives that came after, those of the Edwardian Age? The period between the death of Queen Victoria and the First World War had been called the Golden Age of the detective short story, but how familiar is the modern reader with the sleuths of this era? And such an extraordinary group they were, including in their numbers an unassuming English priest, a blind man, a master of disguises, a lecturer in medical jurisprudence, a noble woman working for Scotland Yard, and a savant so brilliant he was known as "The Thinking Machine."

To introduce readers to these detectives, Resurrected Press has assembled a collection of stories featuring these and other remarkable sleuths in The Edwardian Detectives.

- The Case of Laker, Absconded by Arthur Morrison
- The Fenchurch Street Mystery by Baroness Orczy
- The Crime of the French Café by Nick Carter
- The Man with Nailed Shoes by R Austin Freeman
- The Blue Cross by G. K. Chesterton
- The Case of the Pocket Diary Found in the Snow by Augusta Groner
- The Ninescore Mystery by Baroness Orczy
- The Riddle of the Ninth Finger by Thomas W. Hanshew
- The Knight's Cross Signal Problem by Ernest Bramah

- The Problem of Cell 13 by Jacques Futrelle
- The Conundrum of the Golf Links by Percy James Brebner
- The Silkworms of Florence by Clifford Ashdown
- The Gateway of the Monster by William Hope Hodgson
- The Affair at the Semiramis Hotel by A. E. W. Mason
- The Affair of the Avalanche Bicycle & Tyre Co., LTD by Arthur Morrison

RESURRECTED PRESS CLASSIC MYSTERY CATALOGUE

Journeys into Mystery
Travel and Mystery in a More Elegant Time

The Edwardian Detectives
Literary Sleuths of the Edwardian Era

Gems of Mystery
Lost Jewels from a More Elegant Age

E. C. Bentley
Trent's Last Case: The Woman in Black

Ernest Bramah
Max Carrados Resurrected:
The Detective Stories of Max Carrados

Agatha Christie
The Secret Adversary
The Mysterious Affair at Styles

Octavus Roy Cohen
Midnight

Freeman Wills Croft
The Ponson Case
The Pit Prop Syndicate

J. S. Fletcher
The Herapath Property
The Rayner-Slade Amalgamation
The Chestermarke Instinct
The Paradise Mystery
Dead Men's Money

The Middle of Things
Ravensdene Court
Scarhaven Keep
The Orange-Yellow Diamond
The Middle Temple Murder
The Tallyrand Maxim
The Borough Treasurer
In the Mayor's Parlour
The Saftey Pin

R. Austin Freeman
The Mystery of 31 New Inn from the Dr. Thorndyke
Series
John Thorndyke's Cases from the Dr. Thorndyke
Series
The Red Thumb Mark from The Dr. Thorndyke Series
The Eye of Osiris from The Dr. Thorndyke Series
A Silent Witness from the Dr. John Thorndyke Series
The Cat's Eye from the Dr. John Thorndyke Series
Helen Vardon's Confession: A Dr. John Thorndyke
Story
As a Thief in the Night: A Dr. John Thorndyke Story
Mr. Pottermack's Oversight: A Dr. John Thorndyke
Story
Dr. Thorndyke Intervenes: A Dr. John Thorndyke
Story
The Singing Bone: The Adventures of Dr. Thorndyke
The Stoneware Monkey: A Dr. John Thorndyke Story
The Great Portrait Mystery, and Other Stories: A
Collection of Dr. John Thorndyke and Other Stories
The Penrose Mystery: A Dr. John Thorndyke Story
The Uttermost Farthing: A Savant's Vendetta

Arthur Griffiths
The Passenger From Calais
The Rome Express

Fergus Hume
The Mystery of a Hansom Cab
The Green Mummy
The Silent House
The Secret Passage

Edgar Jepson
The Loudwater Mystery

A. E. W. Mason
At the Villa Rose

A. A. Milne
The Red House Mystery
Baroness Emma Orczy
The Old Man in the Corner

Edgar Allan Poe
The Detective Stories of Edgar Allan Poe

Arthur J. Rees
The Hampstead Mystery
The Shrieking Pit
The Hand In The Dark
The Moon Rock
The Mystery of the Downs

Mary Roberts Rinehart
Sight Unseen and The Confession

Dorothy L. Sayers
Whose Body?

Sir William Magnay
The Hunt Ball Mystery

Mabel and Paul Thorne
The Sheridan Road Mystery

Louis Tracy
The Strange Case of Mortimer Fenley
The Albert Gate Mystery
The Bartlett Mystery
The Postmaster's Daughter
The House of Peril
The Sandling Case: What Would You Have Done?
Charles Edmonds Walk
The Paternoster Ruby

John R. Watson
The Mystery of the Downs
The Hampstead Mystery

Edgar Wallace
The Daffodil Mystery
The Crimson Circle

Carolyn Wells
Vicky Van
The Man Who Fell Through the Earth
In the Onyx Lobby
Raspberry Jam
The Clue
The Room with the Tassels
The Vanishing of Betty Varian
The Mystery Girl
The White Alley
The Curved Blades
Anybody but Anne
The Bride of a Moment
Faulkner's Folly
The Diamond Pin
The Gold Bag
The Mystery of the Sycamore
The Come Backy

Raoul Whitfield
Death in a Bowl

And much more!
Visit ResurrectedPress.com
for our complete catalogue

About Resurrected Press

A division of Intrepid Ink, LLC, Resurrected Press is dedicated to bringing high quality, vintage books back into publication. See our entire catalogue and find out more at www.ResurrectedPress.com.

About Intrepid Ink, LLC

Intrepid Ink, LLC provides full publishing services to authors of fiction and non-fiction books, eBooks and websites. From editing to formatting, from publishing to marketing, Intrepid Ink gets your creative works into the hands of the people who want to read them. Find out more at www.IntrepidInk.com.

www.ingramcontent.com/pod-product-compliance
Lightning Source LLC
Chambersburg PA
CBHW072323280626
47159CB00027B/1114